PAYBACK

kristin harte

Payback: A Good Men Doing Bad Things Novel
Copyright © 2017 by Kristin Harte

EBook ISBN: 978-1-954702-71-4
Paperback ISBN: 978-1-944336-75-2
Large Print Hardcover ISBN: 978-1-954702-00-4

Edited by Silently Correcting Your Grammar, LLC

Cover by Kinship Press

For inquiries contact Kristin@KristinHarte.com

PAYBACK

kristin harte

Chapter One

ALDER

Nothing good ever came from one of my men barging into my office. Especially not when they started the conversation with the acknowledgment that we had a problem.

"We've got a problem, boss."

Nothing good. If I hadn't already been in a foul mood, those words would have gotten me there. "What is it now?"

"Motorcycle gang up on Widow's Ridge." Camden Reese—born and bred in Justice, friend of my youngest brothers, and former Marine sergeant—launched into a speech about his team running into some bikers up by the Hansen property. We'd recently signed a contract with Miss Hansen to harvest eighty acres of dead Ponderosa pine on that hill, so anything getting in our way was definitely a problem. A big one.

As Camden laid out the events of the altercation, I checked over the satellite images of the area on my desk, making notes and marking locations. A star on the house to the west where the elderly Miss Hansen still lived, another to the east on the patch of earth where a trailer sat, all alone. The only two residences up that long, rough stretch of road leading to a drop-off on the far west side.

That rocky piece of land sat just outside the city limits, so things like road maintenance were all but forgotten unless the two residents brought them to my attention. No biker would intentionally ride up such a rutted, gravel road without a reason—too hard on their bike and their face if they were trailing someone else.

"He tried to call out Finn, but I squashed that shit," Camden said, securing every bit of my attention for the moment.

"What the fuck was Finn doing on a job?" My brother didn't work for me except for the occasional project, and I knew for a fact he hadn't been assigned to the Hansen job.

"He'd driven with me to check in on Miss Hansen. We never made it out there, though, because we ran into the bikers on the way up. One guy said some shit about Finn's drug days, how they missed him over at the strip club in Rock Falls."

Jesus. "You get a name?"

"Patch on his vest said Spark."

"Spark." I sat back, balancing my chair on two legs. "As in plug?"

Camden blinked, a cocky smile breaking across his face. "Yeah, like plug. I didn't see the other guy's name."

"So Spark knows Finn from what...ten, twelve years ago?" From the time *before*, as we called it. Before prison and recovery. Before he sobered up. "He look familiar to you?"

Cam shook his head. "Never seen him."

That caught my attention. Justice was a small town planted squarely between two slightly larger towns, all in the middle of fucking nowhere. People didn't happen into Justice—they came here for a reason.

And if that *reason* was named Finn Kennard, Spark and his friend needed to be dealt with and quick. "How'd my brother handle the run-in?"

"Finn ignored the bullshit from Spark. I wasn't as restrained."

Not surprising. Cam always did have a bit of a temper. "If the sheriff gets called again on you—"

Camden waved me off. "I knocked his legs out from under him and put him on the ground. Didn't even leave a mark, I don't think. But I made my point."

"And what point was that?" Not that I needed to ask.

"That Kennard Mills would be harvesting the lumber on that side of the hill, and their club had better not have any business up there. They drove off after Spark picked himself up out of the dirt, the other guy saying something about bigger fish." Camden frowned. "I recognized the other guy."

"Local?" I couldn't think of anyone in Justice who rode with an MC, but I might have missed someone. Three hundred plus people were a lot to keep track of.

"No. He came into the truck stop one night when Leah and I were there for dinner." He blew out a breath and shifted his weight. An almost unconscious gesture, but one that stood out. Normally almost confident to a fault, Cam suddenly seemed nervous, which meant I wouldn't like what he had to say.

"Yeah?" I prodded, wondering how a night out with his wife would piss me off.

"Leah noticed something was up when she went to the restroom and came to get me. The asshole had Shye cornered in a back hallway and wasn't letting her pass."

The snap of the pencil I'd been holding breaking in two might as well have been a gunshot. "And you let him walk away?"

"I had Leah and Shye looking on. I had to."

Picturing perfect little Shye—at least ten years my junior and so damn sweet, every one of her smiles would give you a toothache—watching as I kicked the shit of some asshole was about as unappealing as a thought could get. I probably would've wanted to do the same as Camden and let the guy walk with a warning if I'd been there. I wouldn't have, but I'd have wanted to. Because I *wanted* her, and the idea of Shye being scared of me made my gut sink like a rock.

I sighed, rubbing my forehead and sitting deeper into my chair, bringing all four legs back to the floor. I needed to stop thinking about Shye Anderson. An impossibility as of late, which directly correlated to why my mood had been so foul all day.

"All right. So they rode off after you knocked Spark to the ground. Any indication they'd keep hassling you or come back for Finn?"

He shrugged. "Not really, though you never know with these types of guys."

Lawless, clan-like, arrogant. Yeah. You never knew a damn thing with them. "Did you recognize the club logo?"

"Definitely the Soul Suckers."

Of course. I'd heard they'd added a clubhouse not too far over the county line to the west. I probably wouldn't have thought twice if I'd seen their bikes on the highway through town or heading toward the new restaurant on Main Street. I would now, though.

"Might be time to set the club straight on what they can and can't do as they ride through Justice. I'll talk to Deacon, see if he knows anyone. Head back to the ridge and get the Hansen site plot worked out so we can start cruising and marking trees. This might be our last big harvest before the rains come, and I want to take advantage of the summer weather while we have it."

"We'll get it done."

"Good. And if you see Bishop on the mill floor, have him call me."

Camden nodded, then left without another word, leaving me to stew over this new mess.

Fucking messes all over the place lately, it seemed.

I looked over my satellite images again, tracing roads and logging paths I'd known my whole life. Acres of Widow's Ridge pine forest stared back at me, a mottled brown and green landscape. Half the trees stood dead or dying, a sign of the mountain beetle infestation that had nearly bankrupted my late father and destroyed Kennard Mills. But the bug that had nearly killed us failed and had instead left us flush with jobs and cash. The droughts hadn't stopped this mill, the industry collapse hadn't either, and the fucking plague of beetles killing the forests around us had actually been a boon instead of a death knell. Everyone in Justice had enjoyed the bonuses beating our sales plans every month brought, and no fucking *bikers* would make us end that streak. I had a town to employ.

But Justice, Colorado was more than a town to me—it was my responsibility. The place my ancestors had planted our family tree. Where they had tended to each and every resident over the years, giving families time to grow good, strong roots. Kennard men had run Justice like a homestead for nearly two centuries with the mill as the central business fueling everything else, and I'd live up to the legacy set before me as the oldest living Kennard. That meant making sure people had jobs, food, shelter, and that they felt safe.

Another thing bikers wouldn't be taking away from us, even though it seemed as if they were trying just that.

An annoying, robotic song interrupted my thoughts. The words

"Bishop Kennard"—name of my closest brother who also happened to be my VP of sales and marketing—flashed on the screen of my phone as it played that stupid song again. I swiped to answer and brought the device to my ear.

"Bishop."

"Camden said you wanted me," he said, not bothering with a greeting.

"We've got trouble on Widow's Ridge."

"I heard. Finn all right?" Because, as the second oldest Kennard brother, our family would be the first thing on Bishop's mind. As it should be.

"Camden thinks so. Let's run by the bar tonight and be sure, though. And I'll need you to check in on Miss Hansen—make sure she's okay out there."

"Sounds good. I'll call as soon as we hang up. Anything else?"

"Sell some fucking lumber, Bishop."

"On it, boss. I'll be ready to go at six."

I tossed the phone back onto my desk, the maps snagging my attention again. One spot in particular, actually, and not the one belonging to Miss Hansen. I ran a finger over the east side of the hill, circling the little trailer that sat on a barren, flat piece of rock. Just outside the city limits, it technically rested beyond my protective net, but Shye Anderson lived in that trailer. New girl in town at only three years since she moved to the area, waitress at the truck stop over in Rock Falls, and the only woman I'd ever met who could drive me mad with frustration and desire all at once.

I'd been ultra-aware of Shye since I first met her. Slightly obsessed, really. The girl captivated me; stole all my attention with her sweet little smile and never let me go. It didn't hurt that she looked like a damn angel —long, blond hair and big, dark eyes, a tiny little body that I wanted to get my hands on more than anything else. Sweet as honey, that one, but she lived up to her name. She blushed and stuttered around me, avoided my eyes when I tried to catch her gaze. If I pushed too much, she ran, so I held back. Made myself available but waited for her to come to me.

Which was how I ended up eating at the truck stop five nights a week —all on Shye's shifts. I'd had to up my workouts to keep from getting soft on all the grease and baked goods, but seeing that smile every night was worth it. The coffee—man, that was a harder pill to swallow. How a restaurant—especially one based out of a truck stop—could have such bad coffee was beyond me. I drank cup after cup of the foul brew so she'd come to my table more often to pour me refills. Without the coffee, I didn't get much time with Shye, so I suffered.

And when I worked? I sent my guys in there. Shye had no family in Justice, so I made sure everyone understood they were to treat her as they would a Kennard. Making my men see her as mine kept them watchful around her. Hell, I paid Bishop to eat his lunches there so he could keep an eye on her, and everyone on my team headed that way at least once a day if I had to go out of town. They mocked me relentlessly for chasing her around like a damned puppy, but I didn't give a shit. I needed to know she was happy and safe. That she had everything she needed...even if she wasn't ready to willingly take things from me yet. We'd get there. Three years I'd waited for her to come around, and she would. Eventually. I just had to figure out the right plan.

As I pondered honey-blond hair, sugary smiles, and how many times I could use the excuse of working on the ridge to stop and see her at her place, my phone rang again—Camden, this time.

I swiped to answer and hit the button for speakerphone. "If you tell me we have another problem, I'm going to toss a grenade in your truck."

"So I shouldn't tell you we've got a fire on the mountain?"

Motherfucker. The trouble with harvesting the blue-stained wood left behind by the mountain beetle infestation was the trees needed to cure standing for a number of years. But dead trees meant dry trees, and with the droughts of the past few years and the mild winters we'd had, that meant trouble. Big, dry, tinder-type trouble. A single lightning bolt could ignite an inferno, while a forest fire could destroy the whole damn town.

And apparently, we had one to deal with.

"Where?" I grabbed my keys and pressed the mill-floor alarm to get the team's attention.

"Eastern slope. Just past the Hansen property."

My steps stumbled, then sped. "That's by Shye's place."

An engine roared in the background. "I'm already on my way there. Two minutes out."

She could be hurt in two minutes. Dead. Jesus fuck, I was too far away. "Drive faster."

I hung up and stormed down onto the mill floor. My team stood at attention, looking at me expectantly, ready to fight the fires we knew could ruin everything we'd all built here.

"Fire just east of the Hansen site. Let's get two water trucks up the eastern side of the ridge and send one up to the west side to be safe." I met the eyes of Gage Shepherd, former Navy SEAL like Bishop and current heavy machinery engineer of Kennard Mills. "It's close to Shye's place."

Without another word, Gage began issuing orders to the team. He understood the severity of the situation from every angle—the loss of our product, the potential for destruction in the town, and the possibility that the woman I had my eye on could be in danger. He'd get shit done for me.

As Gage loaded the water trucks with oxygen tanks and medical equipment—something that made my gut churn—his dog Rex trotted after him, looking as if he was headed for a joyride instead of into a fire. Wouldn't be the first time he'd been on site at a fire, though. Gage never went anywhere without Rex.

While Gage made sure the team knew where to go and what to do, I raced to my truck. My heart pounded as I started the engine and peeled out of my spot, heading for the ridge where smoke was beginning to turn the sky black above the tree line. Fuck, if Shye was up there, if she was hurt—

I didn't get to finish my thought because my phone rang right as I turned onto the highway heading toward the mountain. Camden again.

"Tell me good news."

"She's not here," Camden said, sounding slightly out of breath. "It's her trailer on fire, though."

"The water trucks are on the way."

"Don't think they'll do any good for her, to be honest, but we need them for the tree line. It's so dry up here, a single spark could set the whole mountain on fire."

Confirming my earlier thoughts. *Fuck.* I yanked the wheel sideways, making a sharp turn onto the road that would take me up to Shye's place, looking over all the dead, brown pine on the hillside as I flew over the rutted, gravelly path through the woods. "Gage had the team rolling out right behind me. They're likely four minutes out, though."

"Want me to call the fire department in Rock Falls?"

Wouldn't do any good at that point, which was why Kennard Mills had as many water hauling trucks as we did. "No use, though you'd better call the sheriff."

"That useless piece of shit? What for?"

Useless wasn't the term I'd use—corrupt sounded better for the county sheriff we were forced to deal with. I didn't have time to correct Camden, though. "He'll throw a tantrum if he's not informed. Knowing him, he won't come out to investigate anyway. Just make the call."

"Yeah, got it...hang on." Voices yelled in the background, and the sound of Camden moving fast created static on the line.

"Cam?"

"We've got a problem."

That phrase spoken about my girl's place made me want to growl my frustration to the universe. "What fucking problem?"

"There are motorcycle tracks in the dirt around her property. Lots of them."

Rage unlike anything I'd felt exploded in my chest. "Call the sheriff and put the word out—anyone sees a fucking Soul Sucker in Justice, I want to know about it."

I hung up and threw my phone across the bench seat before taking the switchback turn way faster than I should have. Not that the worry burning in my gut had anything to do with me—Shye owned that ache.

Shye may not have known it, but she was mine. I'd do whatever it took to protect her.

And if this fucking motorcycle club had threatened my girl?

I'd gut them and leave their bodies for the predators.

Chapter Two

SHYE

Some days, you came home from running errands to a quiet living room, an overpriced frozen dinner, and a plan of watching bad reality television until it was time to leave for your night shift. Others, you came home to your trailer on fire. Or the charred remnants of one, really. The kind of ashy smokiness that indicated the heat had been hot enough to melt metal and destroy lives, not that mine hadn't already been through the wringer once or twice. *I'll take how can my life get any worse for $500.*

Today was supposed to be the first kind of day—a lazy, easy, and totally normal Wednesday in Justice—but had turned into the second as soon as I'd started up the mountain road home. My trailer—the cheap, single-wide I'd been renting from my stepbrother for close to three years—had burned where it stood. Though, if I was being honest, it hadn't *just* burned. That fire had devoured my crappy little place. It was a miracle the whole forest hadn't gone up with it, what with how dry the mountain was. But as I took in the scene of destruction before me, I saw how it wasn't so much a miracle as a well-trained, dedicated team of loggers watering the ground and keeping the fire from spreading.

I pulled to stop at the end of my gravel drive, hopped out of my car, and rushed past the Kennard Mills vehicles half circling the spot where my trailer had once sat. It couldn't be a good thing that the local sawmill team had made it to my place before any sort of firemen. Of course, being the town of Justice had no local first responders of our own and had to rely on other cities or the county for them, that delay shouldn't have surprised me. Pissed me off, sure. Surprised, nope. The reality of living in the middle of nowhere. Justice, Colorado. Population 348.

Maybe 347 after this fire. Where would I live now? I'd have to call my stepbrother and tell him what'd happened, but that idea sent rivers of ice up my spine. My boss would probably put me up for a few weeks while I figured everything out, but that meant moving to the next county over. Something I had no interest in doing. True, Justice was tiny and completely off the beaten trail, but I loved it. I also loved the fact that the Kennard family—who owned the sawmill just about everyone in Justice worked at—ran the place like a military base. Lots of rules, lots of big, burly men in flannel watching your every move, lots of people to keep each other safe. I couldn't go a day without running into a Kennard Mills guy. I'd miss that sense of security if I left.

The smoke blew on the breeze, burning my eyes and drying out my mouth as my thoughts turned to what I'd already lost instead of what I might if I left. *Everything.* I had lost every single thing that I wasn't holding or wearing. From my furniture to my toothbrush...all gone. How did that *happen*?

I hadn't noticed stumbling toward the smoldering remnants of my life, had been too stuck in my thoughts about clothes and beds and those brand-new towels I hadn't even used yet to realize I was moving forward. Yet, I did just that—moved closer to the hot, smoky mess emitting noxious fumes. But before I stepped foot on the dead grass of what I'd jokingly called my front lawn, a pair of strong arms wrapped around me. They pulled me off my feet and against a chest so big and solid, there were only a few men it could belong to. And only one man I both wanted and dreaded it would be.

"Don't go any closer, honey. There's nothing you can save at this point."

Dread won out. That voice, that smell...I knew them. Alder Kennard —owner of Kennard Mills, biggest, toughest looking man I'd ever seen, and star of every one of my fantasies for the past three years—had me in his embrace. He surrounded me, carrying me as if I weighed nothing, making my entire body melt into him as he held me tight.

How many times had I dreamed about that very thing? About him picking me up and carrying me off? Keeping me safe as he called me honey. He may have called every woman in Justice that endearment—I didn't care. So long as he kept touching me, kept rubbing his thumb along my shoulder, kept those hard, hard muscles pressed against me.

I shivered, heat pooling between my legs and my nipples tightening under my thin T-shirt. While my trailer burned to the ground.

Bad timing, Shye.

Reluctantly, I pushed out of Alder's hold until my feet hit the ground again. I had to, because I needed to keep my wits about me. And because the idea of Alder being anything more than a concerned, protective neighbor was a pipe dream. One I couldn't afford to entertain. If he seemed reluctant to let me go, well, that had to be his protective nature. The guy cared about his town and the residents. He might as well have been the mayor, the chief of police, and the fire department all rolled into one huge, handsome package. Him not wanting to see me burned alive had nothing to do with me in particular, no matter how much I wished it did.

Turning, I met those steely blue eyes that seemed to pierce my soul every time he looked my way. And with as much as I stared at him, he tended to look my way a lot. I sucked at covert glances.

"What happened?" I asked, fighting not to fall under his spell.

Alder seemed to reach for me but then checked himself—dropping his arm before he could touch me. Something shadowy passed over his face. "Camden called the office about smoke on the mountain. When we got here, your place was already burning. We notified the sheriff, but—"

"How long?"

He didn't need clarification. No one in Justice would. "I'd guess fifteen minutes before Camden would have been able to see the smoke. Probably close to an hour since we called the sheriff."

Which meant my place had probably been burning for over two hours at that point, about the same length I'd been gone. A hundred and twenty minutes to go from a trailer full of shitty junk that matched my shitty life to nothing at all.

If I thought tears could do anything other than make me feel worse, I would have cried.

"I didn't realize I'd been gone that long," I said, my voice weak.

Alder looked about as sick as I felt. "Jesus, Shye—you had me worried when we couldn't find you. Where've you been?"

"Rock Falls. I was running errands." The reality of my situation slammed into me like a freight train, and I nearly doubled over. "All my stuff. My whole life was in there."

A frown marred the perfectness of his mouth. "Your stuff can be replaced."

That was easy for Alder to say. He'd never wanted for anything. Me? All I did was want. But what could I expect? The Kennard name meant something around these parts.

According to Justice history, the Kennard family had settled this land centuries ago, setting up a sawmill to process the abundance of pine on the hillsides around us. They'd made a fortune right up until the lumber market crashed, then the mountain pine beetle epidemic had almost put them out of business. Almost, until Alder had returned from his stint in the Army and turned the business around.

But really, how he ended up so wealthy didn't matter. He had money, and I had nothing but a debt I doubted I'd ever finish paying off, a body no one would want to touch if they saw the damage to it, and a rental agreement for a trailer older than I was, sitting on a rocky, scrubby mountainside. *Used to* have that trailer, at least. Now I had nothing. Except the scars and the debt that led to them.

A massive boulder of a man stormed around one of the trucks, and I took an instinctive step back, bumping into Alder in the process. I would have been thrilled by the way Alder's hand settled on my hip to support me if it weren't for the fear screaming through my brain. Gage Shepherd— every bearded, muscled bit of him—pounded the earth as he walked, his steps heavy and distinct. His moves harsh. Thick, wild hair, eyes too dark to seem real, and ink running from wrists to throat and everywhere in between completed the picture of the scariest man I'd ever met.

Gage's dog, Rex, followed behind him like always, practically skipping over the rocky ground. The two of them went everywhere together, including a fire, apparently. Rex looked to be a mutt of indeterminate heritage, but he had a quick tail wag for just about anyone and a demeanor that made you want to drop to your knees and rub his belly. Totally opposite of his always-scowling owner.

Next to Alder, Gage almost seemed normal human-sized, though that really said more about Alder's build. Both tall, wide, and thick all over—but opposite as well. Gage's dark hair and beard contrasted with Alder's lighter hair and clean-shaven jaw. The differences weren't simply aesthetic, though. While Alder's size intimidated, he didn't scare me like Gage did. At least, not in a *he's going to hurt me* way, more in an *if I let go for a second, I'd probably fall in love with him* way.

Gage was a different story. The man looked positively lethal, like death coming to snatch you if you so much as put a toe out of line. You could feel the danger clinging to his skin as he walked past, sense the predator in your midst. Gage terrified me in the same way a shark would, and for the same reason. I wasn't top of the food chain with him around.

Gage didn't even bother to flick a glance my way, focusing on Alder instead. "Char marks along the back indicate an accelerant."

Alder's jaw ticked, his eyes going hard. "A fucking arsonist in Justice?"

"We figure out who set the fire, and I'll take care of it."

Alder held Gage's black gaze with ease, obviously comfortable with the threat by his side. "Camden said he had a run-in with a couple of guys earlier today up on this road. Members of that motorcycle club, Soul Suckers. That'd be my guess."

My blood had never turned so cold so fast. Soul Suckers...the motorcycle club with a brand-new clubhouse in the next county. The group I knew far too well because of who my stepbrother was. Who my father had been to them. Up until that point, I'd figured my trailer had burned because of some sort of electrical issue. The place would have been called a dump a decade before I moved in, so it seemed a logical assumption. But Soul Suckers hanging around not long before the blaze? That definitely seemed like a warning. A punishment, even. Something I knew too much about.

Shaking, I took a step away from the two hulking men, putting space between us. "How did Camden see them, and this? What was he doing up here? This isn't technically Justice land."

Alder's heavy brow furrowed as if wanting to argue my point. "Camden's been prepping a new lumber site up the road."

Which meant he'd been out in the woods, the ones I was supposed to keep a watch over. The day kept getting worse. "New site?"

"Miss Hansen sold us eighty acres of her eastern slope."

Most likely because of the trees on that isolated, deeply forested piece of property. The dead ones—the Kennard's current moneymaker. Under Alder's guidance, Kennard Mills took what should have been seen as worthless and made something out of it, from what I understood. Alder saw opportunity in those dead trees.

I saw more death coming, more negatives. Like the fact that all the forests the Kennards harvested were a major forest fire threat because of how dry the dead trees were that clung to the hillsides. And the ugliness of the brown pine needles on what should have been a green slope. But that was all neither here nor there—I had bigger things to worry about, as always.

"How long has your team been coming up here?"

"We've been surveying for about a week." Alder's frown deepened, and he went from seeming concerned to looking almost ready to fight. "What's going on?"

I couldn't control the head shake I gave him. Couldn't stop it from spreading into a tremble that wracked my body either. I'd screwed up somehow. Completely, totally, undeniably. I hadn't paid attention like I'd been expected to, or I would've known the land up the road would be harvested. I'd have noticed the Kennard team in the woods. I'd had one job, one task to complete so they'd leave me alone. And as much as I hated the work I'd been assigned—had always hated it—I'd promised to complete it as a way of paying what I owed. With barely six months left on my sentence, I'd failed, and I'd be forced to pay a price. Again.

"Shye?" Alder's use of my name tore me from my thoughts, reminding me I had a part to play. Lies to tell.

"Sorry. Just...there's nothing to save here." There never had been, not really. Of course, he didn't need to know that. "I should go check in to the motel at Deacon's before it gets too late. I have to work tonight."

But Alder wasn't stupid. "Your home burned down today. I'm sure you can take the night off to deal with all this stuff."

"I have no stuff left, and if I'm going to replace any of it, I need to work. Thanks for your help."

"Shye, stop." Alder grabbed my arm, gently trying to stop me from leaving. But that hold, that demand—no matter how sweet it might be—reminded me of the men who hadn't been gentle or sweet. The ones who'd hurt me. That touch threw me into a place too dark to see past, and something inside of me snapped.

"No," I yelled, yanking my arm away. "Let me go, Alder."

He froze. I'd never seen anything shock Alder Kennard—never seen him as anything other than confident and sure. He didn't look like either of those things anymore. In fact, he almost looked hurt.

"Okay, honey. Whatever you need." And with that, he walked away, heading back toward the fire with Gage at his side.

Heart hurting, stomach sick, I turned and headed to my car. I knew when to retreat. I needed to find a place to hole up, to settle, to breathe. And it wasn't on that damn mountain in front of my burned-out trailer. Or in front of the sheriff, who rolled into the driveway just as I reached the hood of my car. Too late. Always too late, that man.

"What's going on here, Shye?" Tall but thin, Sheriff Baker unfolded himself from his cruiser, his dark boots crunching on the gravel. The same style of boots the cop had worn the night he'd come to tell us my mother had died in a shootout at a strip club outside of Boulder. The same boots that had brought another cop into the house five months later to arrest my stepbrother for manslaughter, a charge later dropped after a hefty payment from the Soul Suckers. The same sort of boots that had nudged me awake after the accident that had destroyed what little sense of normalcy I'd known at that point.

I hated those boots.

Refusing to look him in the eye, I hurried to my car. "My place burned. Probably the electrical—the kitchen outlet tended to spark a bit if you didn't put the plug in just right."

"Electrical fire. I'm sure the insurance will believe that." As if we'd had insurance on that old hunk of junk. "You leaving us then, girl?"

I doubted he meant leaving the clearing in the woods where we stood. "I have to work tonight. I'll figure out what to do about all this tomorrow."

He stared at the trailer for a long minute before turning his head my way, his shrewd eyes catching mine. Searching. Judging. "Okay, then. Nothing we can really do since the fire's burned itself out already." No thanks to him taking so long to get there and obviously not calling for fire support since he'd arrived alone. "I'll come track you down if I need anything."

Of that, I had no doubt. I nodded and slid into my car, slamming the door behind me. My hand shook as I tried to insert the key, and my eyes burned, though not from smoke or fear. No, I didn't cry when I felt scared—I cried when I felt angry. And right then, I was livid with myself for screwing up. Three years—down the drain in an instant.

But there was no use in worrying about how bad my next punishment would be. I had to secure a safe place to stay, someplace to hide out for a few days.

Before I could leave, though, Alder Kennard caught my attention again. I stared at his confident stance, the way his arms bulged as he crossed them over his chest. At the angry, focused expression on his face. I thought I was safe behind the windshield of my car, but he turned before I looked away. Catching me watching him.

I was always watching him, it seemed.

Alder held my gaze, brows lowered, a deep frown marring that handsome face. Gage stood at his side, leaning in and whispering to him, but Alder didn't appear to be giving him a bit of attention. Instead, his eyes stayed locked on mine. Slicing through me. Seeking something I already knew I couldn't give him. In another world, another lifetime maybe, I'd hand over whatever he wanted. I'd give him everything—body, mind, heart. But in my current situation, I had nothing for him except danger. I owed a debt to a motorcycle club, most likely the same one who'd burned my trailer to the ground. There was no escaping that threat.

So I started the engine, and I drove away before I did something stupid like hop back out of my car and ask him for help.

Not even the great Alder Kennard could save me from my fate.

Chapter Three

ALDER

Three days. I hadn't seen Shye in three days, which did nothing but piss me off. That fact and a lack of control on my temper were how I found myself in The Jury Room, a bar and motel on the edge of town owned by my best friend. Also known as the man I was about to punch in the face.

"Tell me."

Deacon shook his head, arms braced against the bar top between us. Unmovable. "Not happening."

I leaned over the bar, getting in his face. Deacon stood about six inches shorter but had a solid thirty pounds of muscle on me. With his longish, messy dark hair, bright green eyes, and a smile for everyone, the man fit the part of the small-town bar owner to a T. But he had a dark side not many people knew about. One I'd seen firsthand while serving with him in a unit of Green Berets. One I made sure never to bring up to people outside the Special Forces.

He was also loyal as the day was long, just not always to me.

"Which room?" I asked, my voice like gravel even to my own ears.

"I don't know what part of not happening you don't understand, but let me explain. I'm not telling you where Shye is."

"Goddammit, Deacon. I pulled you out of too many fucking gunfights for you to bullshit me like this."

Grin gone, my best friend stood firm, refusing to back down. I trusted him with my life—we had been through moments where we'd risked death for each other—but he wasn't a pushover. Especially not with me. And he had a bit of an obsession for reminding me I wasn't the boss of everything in town.

"I know how much you like that little girl, man," he said, his voice calm but firm. "But that doesn't outweigh my responsibility to her. She wants to hide, and I'm willing to bet she needs to. If it was anyone else looking for her, would you want me to tell them she was here?"

Fucker had me there and he knew it, which was why he accepted my single chin raise as an assent.

"Look," he said, relaxing slightly. "I don't know what's up with her, but she asked for my help. I'm sure if she'd been in the right mind—or if I'd asked her—she'd have told me you could know where I stashed her. But she didn't, and I'm not breaking her trust because you've got a hard-on for her."

"I don't have a hard-on for her." A weak argument at best, a lie at worst.

One Deacon didn't buy for a second. "I'm not looking at your dick, man, but I know you."

I sighed, glancing around the dimly lit bar for something, anything, to focus on. But there was nothing to see, nothing but the burn in my gut. She needed me and I couldn't get to her. But Deacon could—he was my only connection to her.

"Is she all right?"

"She's as safe as I can make her." His nod should have calmed me, but it didn't. As safe as he could make her wasn't completely guarded, watched, and impossible to get at—and we both knew it. Though, without knowing who or what she wanted to hide from, there wasn't much we could do. Not beyond what he already was.

"Keep your eyes open for anything, got it? I haven't seen Shye in days, and it's not like her to miss work. If she's scared, I want to know why so I can fix it."

"But you don't have a hard-on for her," Deacon said, a slight smile breaking on his face, his eyes pinning me in place. "Well, from what I understand, she's going back to work tonight."

That perked me up. "Usual shift?"

"No clue. But she mentioned working tonight, so I'd have to assume it."

"Okay." I glanced at the clock over the bar then pivoted on my heel and headed for the door. Six hours—I just had to wait another six hours to see her. But if he was wrong... "Hey, Deac?"

"Yeah, yeah, yeah. If she doesn't go to work, I'll talk to her. See if she minds you coming to see her. Now get the fuck out of my bar before the paying customers show up, you freeloading bastard."

Never mind the fact that he refused to let me pay for anything. I flipped him the bird on my way out the door, for old time's sake. His laugh followed me to the parking lot, which sat empty, the day too young for bar patrons to be showing up. The motel lot next door sat empty too. Shye must have been hiding her car. Smart, but frustrating. I wanted to know what she was so afraid of and how she was handling the stress of losing her home. Make sure she had everything she needed. I didn't want to hurt her —I just needed to see that she was all right.

Six fucking hours to burn.

I headed back to the mill, my mind swirling. I hated not seeing Shye, not knowing if she was truly safe. I trusted Deacon—had since we'd both donned those green berets of the Special Forces—but he stood between me and my girl. That was a hard pill to swallow.

Too pissed to deal with the guys on the floor, I climbed the stairs to my office overlooking the mill and hunkered down. Phone calls, emails, both business and dealing with those fucking Soul Suckers. I kept my computer on and my phone to my ear as much as possible so I could stop thinking about Shye.

An impossibility, really.

Bishop appeared five hours into my six-hour sentence, settling into the chair across from my desk. As usual, the Vice President of Sales and Marketing for Kennard Mills looked sharp and cocky, suited up as if meeting with important people. Which he might have been—I didn't pay much attention to what he did. We sold a lot of fucking lumber, so I knew he handled his job just fine. He also simply could have been showing off.

Bishop had a tendency to do that—it was all that chest-thumping SEAL training in him.

"Workday's over, bro," he said, giving me that salesman smile that garnered him so much attention. Not from me, though.

I kept typing, responding to an email for information on a specific client need. "Still working."

"Until the job is done, or until it's time to head to the truck stop to see Shye?"

"Both." I clicked send and finally turned away from the screen, catching my brother's eyes. "If she's even there."

"She is."

An ache like claws scratching at my chest lit inside of me, followed by the absolute surety that the only way to rid myself of it was to go to her. Immediately.

But I would never live that down, not with Bishop watching. So I anchored my ass in my chair, and I sat back as if I had all the time in the world to shoot the shit with him.

"You've seen her?"

"No, but I sent Finn for an early dinner. He loves their huckleberry pie."

Of course he did. "His addiction issue seems to have been transferred to sugar."

"Better than the alternative."

Truth. But I didn't want to talk about Finn. "We got any leads on the identities of the local Soul Suckers yet?"

"Not much. No one wants to speak out against them, but we'll keep searching."

"I want names, addresses, arrest records... I want to know every fucking weak spot from the president down to their newest prospect."

"I don't understand why we don't just go to their clubhouse and blow the place up."

Typical SEAL versus Green Beret mentality. He ran into combat first, using brute strength to deal with an enemy. I planned and plotted, using sabotage or subterfuge to accomplish my missions. And this was my mission, not his.

"Because without knowing what's coming for us, we could end up pinned down in a gunfight, or they could come after us in an unexpected way. If we know exactly what we're dealing with, we can exploit their weak spots. Force them to their knees before we take them out." I leaned forward, staring into his gray eyes to make sure he got my point. "But when we have all the info? We will blow their motherfucking place up."

Bishop nodded, his jaw tight and his eyes hard. Pissed off, like me. "We're on it."

Yeah, we were. But those fuckers were harder to pin down than some terrorist sects. I'd get it done, though. Shye needed me to, whether she realized it or not.

Speaking of which...

"You in the office tomorrow?" I double-checked the clock before rising to my feet. Twenty minutes before I'd planned to leave, but I was done waiting.

He gave me a quick head shake as he followed me toward the door. "Sales calls. Why? You need me?"

"No, just wanted to make sure I didn't have to see your ugly mug." I dodged the punch he threw and headed down the stairs.

"Hey, Alder?"

"Yeah?"

Frown heavy, Bishop looked down at me. "Be careful, all right? I don't like dealing with this motorcycle club bullshit. These guys don't respect the same things we do."

I nodded, something dark and twisty in my chest. Something too close to memories of bombings and burned-out houses filled with dead civilians to give it life, so I pushed it down and focused on what needed to be done. On the present. "You too, man. Keep the circle tight."

"Always."

A final chin nod and a handful of stairs had me on the mill floor and headed for the door. Work issues, town trouble, and Soul Suckers shit could be forgotten for the moment. It was time to see my girl.

Chapter Four

SHYE

Slinging breakfast platters and country fried steak in a truck stop restaurant hadn't been my ideal way to make a living, but it was what I'd fallen into when I'd moved to Justice three years ago. The hours sucked, the pay was virtually nonexistent, and the tips... Well, they were few and far between. But the job kept me busy, kept my mind off the horror story my life was quickly becoming, and gave me just enough to afford to be independent. Plus, I got to see Alder Kennard. A lot.

The man himself walked in about three-quarters of the way through my shift, long after the dinner rush, when I was sadly the only waitress on the floor. Didn't matter, though—I still stopped and stared at him. How could I not? He moved with a confidence that made most women's heads turn. Mine had been turning in his direction since the first time we'd crossed paths right here in this truck stop. My first day on the job, really.

Heck, maybe I stayed at this job because of Alder. If I left, I might not see him at all.

That night, though—three days after the fire, after moving myself into the tiny motel attached to Deacon's bar, and after running on adrenaline every second of the day, thinking a Soul Sucker would be showing up to drag me back to their clubhouse at any moment—I was too tired to deal with the crush that never went away. Too exhausted to hide my attraction. I might not have truly wanted to, but I needed to stay away from him.

Something nearly impossible considering my position.

"Good to see you, Alder. What can I get you?" I set a cup of coffee down in front of him along with a backup carafe, knowing he'd likely go through the entire thing before he left. Usually, I brought him each cup, stopping to chat, to take advantage of every second I could be in his presence. Tonight, that simply couldn't happen.

He eyed the carafe as if it might jump up and bite him. "Sunrise breakfast platter."

I nodded and spun, heading for the kitchen. Escaping. But he wasn't about to let me go, apparently.

"Shye." The word came out as a demand more than anything, and I bristled.

"Yeah?"

"You going to ask me how I want my eggs?"

Scrambled with a little cheese added in. The exact same way he'd been taking them since that first night we met. Regimented and habitual described Alder to a T, which I'd always assumed came from his military background. But maybe the man just liked cheesy eggs.

"Are you going to change the way you've been having them all these years?"

A slow head shake, his lips pulling into an easy smile that might as well have been a kick to the gut. Good lord, the man was so darn handsome. He had to be ten years older than me, but it didn't matter. He made my knees knock and my panties wet every time he looked my way.

"No, ma'am."

And that voice? Those manners? Dangerous to a girl's restraint. Especially mine.

"Then I'm not asking because I already know." I hurried to the kitchen, ignoring the way his smile fell into a frown. I couldn't with him right then. Couldn't stand next to him and pretend he came into the restaurant for any other reason but the food. I didn't have the strength to deal with my disappointment after losing so much already.

Three days of hell, of feeling completely and utterly alone, had broken something inside of me. My boss had given me time off so I could get myself settled, but that had been a bad plan. I preferred to work—to keep busy—to focus somewhere else. I'd spent three days obsessing over the one thing I wanted to forget about—the knowledge that my stepbrother would likely kill me the next time I saw him.

Something I simply couldn't think about a moment longer.

So I put Alder's order in, and I warmed the coffee cups of the few people left in the dining room, and I avoided the table in the corner where Alder always sat.

Until I couldn't anymore.

"Sunrise breakfast platter." I set his plate of eggs, hash browns, and bacon down first, slipping the smaller one with his toast next to his cup. "You need more coffee?"

He raised an eyebrow and nodded toward the carafe. "I think you got that covered for tonight."

Yeah. Yeah, I did. "If there's nothing else, then..."

But Alder's big, rough hand sliding over mine made the world stop. Made everything else around me disappear. This was...new.

"You okay, Shye?"

Concerned. He sounded concerned about me, as if he really cared.

"I'm fine." Even to my own ears, I didn't sound fine. And Alder seemed to know it.

"I've been worried about you. You haven't been at work."

He'd noticed. He always noticed when I missed a shift, not that it happened often. "My boss gave me a few days off. Because of the fire."

His lips tightened, and that jaw tic I always wanted to run a finger over and smooth fired up. "You get yourself sorted over at Deacon's? Get a place to stay?"

I nodded my answer, too stunned that he'd even thought about me these past few days to speak.

He sighed and squeezed my hand, looking oddly at war with himself. "Good. That's good. You'll be safe there."

As if I'd be safe anywhere with the Soul Suckers possibly after me.

"I should get back to work," I whispered, pulling my hand from his. Wishing the tingles his touch left behind would both never end and stop immediately. Why did this man make me feel so damn much, and why couldn't I get myself to accept that he'd never be mine?

Alder simply nodded and grabbed a fork, refocusing on his dinner instead of me. Giving me an escape. One I wished I didn't have to take.

But work called—people needed more coffee and toast, to know the specials, and to ask if we had any of the huckleberry pie we were famous for. And I had to live my life outside of the dream world where Alder Kennard and I were anything more than acquaintances. And where I wasn't a pawn in the Soul Suckers' twisted games.

———

When the dining area quieted, when all that was left was a small group of high schoolers snacking on buffalo wings plus one Alder Kennard nursing a cup of coffee, I headed to the back to clean up. The overnight cook and waitress would be coming soon, and then I could go back to my motel room and hide. Being on the floor at work—so open and unprotected—had left me slightly shaky and sick. At least, until Alder had walked in. Somehow, I knew I was safe with him around. He'd never let anything happen to me. I wished I could bottle the comfort he inspired and take that essence with me so I could actually get some sleep instead of tossing and turning all night.

Or just have him in my bed.

Not happening. Never happening.

I walked into the empty kitchen, sighing at the silence. The cook had left for his break almost half an hour before, telling me to come find him if customers came. That was fine—in fact, it worked in my favor. I needed time alone, a difficult thing to come across at my job. We'd have guests all through the night, but the worst of my shift was over. The few customers I might see before leaving would be onesie-twosies—truck drivers, cops from Rock Falls, and the occasional family passing through on their way someplace else.

Maybe it was time I did the same.

I'd never thought about running before—not really. Sure, after my dad had died, I'd wondered if there was someplace better for me. Someplace safer. But I'd already made a mistake that had gotten me into hot water, already owed a debt I didn't know how to repay at such a young age, and the Soul Suckers were a national club. No matter where I ran, I knew they'd find me. They still would. No one walked away from them with a debt hanging over their heads. So I'd been moved to Justice, and I'd watched that mountain road for any sign of unusual activity to report to them. I'd worked to pay my debt.

I'd failed spectacularly, though. And eventually, they'd come to make sure I knew it.

I had only a handful of dishes left to load when Alder came through the swinging door from the dining area. So tall, so wide, he took up all the space in the little kitchen. Stole all the air, too. I had to remind myself to breathe when he was that close. Had to force my eyes away from his form, as well. The world funneled down to nothing but him and the stiff frown on his face when he was near, the way his blue eyes watched me. Inspected me. As if he truly *saw* me.

Something I couldn't allow.

I forced myself to look away. "What are you doing back here?"

"Your other guests thought it'd be a fun idea to leave without paying." He set a small stack of bills on the counter beside me. "I made sure to dissuade them from that idea."

And if that didn't epitomize the man—forceful, demanding, but for the right reasons. Always watching out for his friends and neighbors, always taking care of people so they didn't get screwed over. Sometimes, I wished I'd met him before my life had went off the rails. Sometimes, when the reality that he'd never see me the way I wanted him to hit me, I wished I'd never met him at all.

I picked up the cash, waving it at him before slipping it into the pocket of my uniform dress. "That's a little more than their bill."

He shrugged, leaning a hip against the counter and crossing his long legs at the ankle. "I made sure they left you a tip for putting up with them all night."

My smile couldn't have been stopped. "You're horrible."

"Am I really?"

When I looked up, his eyes were still on me. Still staring as if trying to figure something out, to see something inside of me. And heck, I was too tired to hide anymore.

"No," I whispered as I turned off the water. "You're not horrible at all."

Alder pushed off the counter, stalking close. So, so close. But he didn't stop when I expected him to—at a respectable, friendly distance. Oh no, he didn't stop. Not until he stood right in front of me, his hungry eyes holding mine, his body leaning in. Almost...touching.

And then, he did touch.

He tucked my hair behind my ear and nudged my chin up. Forcing me to keep my eyes on his, not that I could look away even if I wanted to. "I worry about you, Shye."

My response came automatically, the lie too easy to tell. "You don't need to."

"I think I do. I think I can't help myself."

I shivered, entranced by his voice, by the look on his face, by how close he stood. The man had owned me since the first moment I met him, since that first day when he'd ordered a cup of coffee and smiled at me. He still owned me in some way, and I was so sick of fighting my desire for him.

I took a deep breath and closed the gap between us, grabbing his arms as I pressed my breasts against that rock-hard chest I'd dreamed about too many times to count. Surrendering to him and praying he didn't make me regret it. "So what are you going to do about it?"

He didn't answer me—didn't need to. He cupped my chin in one huge, rough hand, running his thumb over my lips as he kept his blue eyes locked on mine. Waiting. Looking for something. So I gave him the only thing I could—my approval. In the form of a kiss pressed to his thumb as it passed. His response was immediate.

Eyes gleaming, he dropped down to claim my mouth. I couldn't call what he did a kiss. The word wasn't big enough to encapsulate the way his entire body became involved in the act or how he dominated my lips, my tongue, my mouth. It wasn't a kiss—it was a claiming. He *plundered* me. Hand on my face, one arm sliding around my waist to pin me to him, he attacked my mouth with an intensity that made me gasp. No soft pecks or easy start, no working his way up to anything—he overtook me, taking advantage of my quiet gasp to lick his way inside.

I could have died right then and there with his taste on my tongue and had no regrets.

Heart racing, skin itching with the need to be touched by this man, I let go of all the voices telling me this could never happen, and I kissed him back. He groaned as I threaded my fingers in his hair and tugged him closer, his hands squeezing me hard enough to leave marks. Good, I wanted that. Wanted to see his claim on me. Needed the reminder that for one brief moment, I'd been his. Completely.

But Alder wasn't satisfied with kissing, it seemed. Our tongues tangling, he turned me so my back was to the counter, then reached down to grab me by the thighs and hoist me up. I landed on the stainless steel, my legs spreading on instinct to give the man room to step between them.

He did, and he was so hard against me.

"Give me permission," he said, nibbling over my chin. "I won't take from you, but if you let me...if you want me to." He groaned, his hips jerking against mine almost of their own volition. "Give me permission, honey. Tell me I can feel you. Let me take care of you so I can watch you come."

I nodded even though I had no idea what I was doing, no clue what it was exactly that he wanted to give me. My experience with men—what little I had—had always been about pain and punishment. I'd never been kissed the way Alder kissed me, never gone farther than a simple boob grab that hurt more than aroused. But I'd try, I'd learn. For Alder, I'd figure this whole sex thing out for the first time. So long as he wanted me the way I wanted him.

Whimpering my need, I clung to him as he came back for more, as he continued to own my mouth. The hard ridge of his erection sat wedged between us, his desire obvious. The strong grip of his hands on my flesh, the never-ending kisses that rocked my world on its foundation, the way his body pressed into mine with every breath was proof enough—the man wanted me, and I definitely felt the same.

Unashamed of my need for more, I shifted my hips against him as he pulled me closer. As he wrapped me in his arms and his scent and overwhelmed me with his taste. Soaking—I was soaking wet and probably spreading that to his jeans, but I didn't care. Let him see how much I wanted him, how much he made me feel. Let him know the truth—that there was no other man I'd even looked at in all the years I'd lived in Justice. Only him.

So when he slipped a hand between us, shoving my panties to the side and finding my clit, I simply spread my legs wider. Giving him room to rub, to tease. To finally feel exactly how wet he made me. Something that made him groan.

"That's it, Shye. Fuck, I love the way your little body moves against mine. And you're so damn wet, honey. All for me, right? Is this pussy wet only for me?"

I nodded, gasping as he growled and thrust harder against me. My god, this had to be a dream. A wonderful, heartbreaking dream where I woke up wet and achy between my legs. One where I blindly reached into my nightstand drawer for the only toy I owned, something to help me reach my peak, to relieve the frustration. Any second now, I'd be tossed back into reality and want to cry. Want to curse my wretched brain for playing with my heart and making me think about what I could never have.

But I didn't wake up from some hot dream. Instead, I let my head fall back, and I moaned as Alder moved his attack from my lips to my neck. As he bit and sucked and licked a trail down to my shoulder while continuing his direct attack on my clit.

Death. This was death and bliss and heaven and hell all rolled into one. This was everything.

And then it was more.

Alder lifted me again, keeping his mouth busy on my neck while he carried me as if I weighed nothing. He stalked to the manager's office—a small, closet-like room at the back of the kitchen. The only space with a door and a modicum of privacy. Once inside, he set me on the desk and kicked the door closed before tugging my knees up. And out.

"Alder," I gasped, feeling exposed. Feeling excited.

He ran a hand up the length of my thigh, bunching my uniform skirt as he went, letting his finger brush across my panties. "So fucking wet for me, honey. I can't leave you like that, and I don't want anyone walking in and seeing you on display." He bent down to give me a kiss, biting my lip for good measure and making me jump. "No one else gets to see this pussy, and they certainly don't get to watch as I make you come. Your face, those sweet little sounds you make, are mine. All mine."

He tugged my panties to the side again, running his knuckle over my clit. Sending shock waves down my legs as he teased me. "Tell me this is mine, Shye. Say the words."

"Yours," I gasped when he plunged a finger inside me. Spreading me open. The delicious mix of pleasure and pain making me clench around his thick digit. "All yours."

"Good. Then I'm going to take what you're offering, because I can't hold off anymore." He dropped to his knees, hooking my legs over his shoulders and bringing his face close. Too close. Oh my god, was he going to—

He licked the entire length of my slit before slipping his tongue inside me, not giving me a moment to refuse him. I arched and groaned, biting my lip to keep from screaming. My hands scrabbling at the edges of the desk as I tried to find something to hold on to. Something to keep me anchored on earth.

"Alder," I cried as he moved up to lap at my clit. My thighs shook on his shoulders, my release already so close.

Too much. Too fast. So perfect.

"This is a fucking sweet pussy you've got, Shye," he growled against my sensitive flesh, spreading me open with his thumbs so I could feel his breath. "I always knew it would be. That's why I call you honey. Because I knew this pussy would be the sweetest thing I've ever had on my tongue."

I arched and yelped as he again found my clit, grabbing hold of his head and shamelessly pulling him into me. And like everything else, he took care of me with his filthy mouth, Alder-style. Rough, strong, not giving me a moment to ease into the attack. Owning everything about me with his lips and tongue.

And oh my god, that tongue. It lashed against my clit, throwing in the occasional flat lick to keep me on edge. I writhed, I grabbed his hair and pulled him closer, I chanted his name—I did all the things I'd read about over the years, all the moves that I'd thought were too fake or wild. Instinct...I reacted on instinct alone, wanting more, needing him to make me come, craving it. Demanding it.

"So good, so...Alder. Please."

"Fuck yeah, honey. Give me all that sweetness. So fucking wet, baby, I can't stop licking it up."

And as if the man had somehow studied my body, Alder knew exactly what to do. Finger deep, lips wrapped around my clit, he growled and grunted and suckled hard enough to make me scream. To make me whine and shake.

To make me come.

He kept up his assault as I surrendered, kept drawing out every ounce of pleasure as I gave myself over to the highest of highs. Refusing to give up his place between my legs until I finally had to push him away, too sensitive to let him lick even one more time. He didn't move back far, though, resting his cheek against my thigh and running one finger along the seam between my leg and my pussy.

"Finally mine," he whispered, placing a gentle kiss over my clit and pulling my panties back into place. He hadn't even taken them off. He'd made me come that strong while leaving me basically fully clothed—if the man ever got me naked, he might kill me. And I'd die happily in his arms.

"Yours," I whispered, unable not to. Too wrecked to even think about the reality of that promise. To hide how much I wanted to believe we could actually be together.

With a satisfied sort of sigh, Alder moved up the length of my body, letting his hands wander, kissing me over my uniform until he reached my neck and could sink his teeth into my flesh. Not hard, not painful, but telling—the man wanted to own me, and thankfully, I wanted to be his.

As he moved to drop kisses along my ear, I wrapped my arms around him, holding tight. Still shaking. Still needing more.

"You're trembling," he said, bringing his mouth to mine to give me a soft kiss. "You okay, honey?"

I nodded, kissing him back. Not ready to let go yet. Rolling my hips against where he was still so hard. "What about you?"

Alder simply shook his head, a small smile on his lips as they brushed against mine. "I'm fine. It's not about me tonight, Shye. I don't expect anything from you."

Reality crashed back over me in a blink. He'd given his all but had gotten nothing from me. That was a debt. How did I always end up indebted to some man?

I pushed him back and sat up, frowning. "But you gave me...that. You should get something in return."

"Shye, that's not how this works. It's not a deal or a game where we keep track of points." Alder nuzzled my neck, his hands gripping my hips. "I didn't come here for any of this, but we'll figure it all out."

He didn't come here for *this*. Didn't come for me.

"Oh." I pulled away, suddenly embarrassed. No longer sure of anything other than apparently Alder Kennard had *not* come to the truck stop for me. I pushed him back, sliding to my feet and tugging my uniform back into place. "Then why are you here?"

He stepped closer, grabbing me before I could escape, refusing to let me put even an inch between us. His hands so very strong as he held me. "Because I can't stay away."

That sounded like a dream come true for me. But I wasn't that girl—I didn't get the happily ever after fairy tale. I got the huntsman with a sadistic side instead of a sweet one, and my seven little helpers were demons instead of dwarfs. I got the man who gave me the best orgasm of my life, then told me he hadn't been coming to see me at all.

"Alder—"

He pressed one more kiss to my lips, one more sweet taste, before pulling back to stare down at me. "I've been worried about you. Camden got into that disagreement with some bikers on the Hansen property job —not too far from your trailer. Remember?" He waited for me to nod. "Well, the day of the fire, we found tracks on your property."

Oh no. My stomach knotted, and I dropped my gaze to his shoulder. I couldn't look him in the eye for this, wanting to run, wanting to get away. Wanting so badly not to already know what he was going to say.

"We think they were the ones who set your place on fire."

I locked all the panic—all the terror that statement inspired in me— down tight as I looked up at him. "Why would bikers be interested in me?"

"I don't know." Alder sighed, hands still gripping my hips. Body still so very close to mine. "But it's not safe out there for you, Shye. Even if the insurance replaces your trailer, those woods are dangerous."

He had no idea. "Life is dangerous."

I pulled away from him and opened the office door, needing air. Needing space. If he didn't know about my connection to the Soul Suckers yet, he would soon. He'd figure out how much of a liar I was, how weak and desperate I could be, and then he'd hate me. This, whatever had happened, was already over. He just didn't know it yet.

But I did. "I need to get back to work."

Alder grabbed my arm, stopping me before I could even reach the sink. "Shye, I think—"

The door to the dining room flew open, slamming into the wall behind it. I jumped, but Alder was already spinning me behind him. Facing the threat. Standing between me and...Gage.

"We've got a problem," the big man said, every muscle in his face rigid and locked. "Another fire."

Alder slid his hand down to my hip, pulling me into his body, keeping me close. Keeping us connected. "Where?"

"Camden's place. And he can't track down his wife."

"Fuck." Alder turned and grabbed me around the waist, bending slightly and putting his face right in front of mine as he lowered his voice. "We'll have to finish our stuff later, honey. C'mon. We need to get out there."

It wasn't until he laced his fingers with mine and tugged that the reality of him saying those words to *me* and not Gage sank in.

"Wait," I said as I planted my feet and pulled Alder to a stop. "I'm working. I can't leave."

Alder frowned. "Your shift ends in twenty minutes. Someone can cover for you."

"I can't just disappear. It's *work*."

"Shye, there was a run-in with some bikers up by your place the day of the fire, and Camden was the one who assaulted one of them. This could be retaliation."

Oh god, no. "What did he do?"

"Let's go," Gage yelled from the door to the dining room, glaring at me. "We've got time to talk on the road."

My head shake came without thought or intention. "Alder, let me go. I need to finish my shift."

That jaw tic appeared, his entire face going stony and his eyes locking on mine. Burning, dangerous. Gage may have been a shark in the water, but Alder was worse. You could feel the threat when Gage walked by; Alder hid it. He wasn't hiding that lethalness anymore.

"No." He pulled me against his chest, leaning over me. Dominating me. "Last time I let you go, you disappeared on me for three days. I can't do that again, Shye. I can't spend every minute worrying if you're safe and have what you need. I'll take care of your boss—he owes me a few favors anyway—so you don't have to worry about your job. Trust me, honey. I want to keep you safe, and that means you need to come with me... Now."

Nothing about this situation should have been a turn-on. Nothing Alder said should have made my knees weak, should have warmed me from the inside, reminding me how wet my panties already were. But something in his face, in his hard body against mine, in his words—something made my desire for him explode, and I found myself nodding. Unable to tell the man no.

Not that I wanted to.

Without another word, Alder dragged me through the restaurant and outside as the panic I'd been running under since the fire faded slightly. Safe—I felt safe with Alder. It'd been months since I could remember feeling that way, maybe even years, but the reality of my past wouldn't let me accept it. No one was safe from the Soul Suckers.

The Kennards were good people—law-abiding in their own way. When they figured out what was going on, they'd probably call the sheriff in to investigate. That didn't mean justice; it meant a possible payoff from the Soul Suckers to avoid an investigation and arrests. More debt on my shoulders because I'd been given one job, and I'd failed at it.

This wouldn't be a simple debt of flesh to the Soul Suckers, though. Not something as cheap as a funeral and a few years of living expenses to pay off. They'd take my life for sure this time for causing them to lose a business.

And if I stayed close to Alder, they'd take his too.

Chapter Five

ALDER

Whether I was a king or an asshole, I couldn't tell. I'd kissed Shye Anderson and made her come on my tongue. Had finally gotten to hear the little mewls and sighs as I brought her pleasure. Had I not dragged her little ass out of the truck stop and pretty much forced her to come with me, I'd be in a much better mood.

True, she'd nodded her permission, but only after I'd pushed. Consent under duress wasn't consent, and that fact ate at me. She didn't seem angry or upset. In fact, she'd let me hold her hand the whole way to Cam's place, but still, I worried that I'd crossed a line I shouldn't have.

If I wasn't stuck in the hell of trying to fight a house fire, I might be able to figure out whether I was the hero or the villain in her story.

"We need more water back here!"

I hooked another hose to the water truck with my family name on the side—the one I'd bought to protect the town in moments like this—and directed one of my men toward the biggest flare-up. We all worked continuously, running and carrying water, directing hoses, using axes and saws to open up hot spots so we could try to contain the damage. We risked our lives even though we already knew there would be no putting this fire out.

Like at Shye's trailer, someone had known what they were doing. Justice had no fire department...hell, we didn't even have hydrants except for a couple along the strip of businesses in what we considered town. Three shops, one restaurant that had opened recently, a gas station, a tiny post office, and a few empty buildings—not a lot of tax revenue coming in to pay for things like first responders, so we did without. But someone had known help would be slow if at all, and they had set the sort of fires even my team of employees and our water trucks couldn't handle.

The fire had burned slowly, smoldering through the place until it found a new source of air. A way to breathe. Once fire met oxygen? Inferno. All the water in the world wouldn't save Camden's house. Or his wife, something I kept to myself until someone could confirm if she'd been in there.

First Shye, now Camden. Or had the mark been Leah? I needed to figure it out and fast because there was a slip of a girl sitting in my truck—one I'd been slightly obsessed with for three long, lonely years—and there was no fucking way I'd let anything more happen to her.

My father had always said all the best things were worth the wait, and I had a feeling Shye was the very best thing for me. But I was fucking done waiting. Someone torching her home had thrown my plan to go slow with her, to give her time to come to me, right out the window. And now? Well...she might hate me for what I was going to do, but I had no other choice. Not after the fires, and especially not after I'd finally gotten a taste of that wicked little mouth. And her pussy.

I could still taste her on my lips, and I wanted more. Wanted to slide inside that juicy little heaven and plant my seed deep. Wanted to watch my come run down her thighs after I'd exhausted her body with mine. I'd done the right thing—silently watching over her, practically hiding in the shadows as I waited for her to respond to me for three long years. But the girl was good at hiding, as I'd found out tonight. She'd responded so strongly, with so much passion. She had been wanting me just like I'd been wanting her, so the waiting game was over. It was time to be more direct.

Bishop appeared from the side of the house, his tall body in shadow for a long moment before he edged my way, talking softly so no one overheard him. "It's a little more controlled now. Do we start the search?"

For Leah...who should have been home and inside the very house burning in front of my eyes. "If you can do so safely, yeah. But I don't want the men risking their lives. If she was in there..."

I didn't need to finish my sentence. He knew. The whole damn group did. If Leah had been in there, she wouldn't be making it out alive. And that, her death, would fall squarely on my shoulders.

I took responsibility for our town because 90% of the people living in it either worked directly for me or were there because of my sawmill. Justice, Colorado may as well have been labeled Kennard property. I made sure my guys ran circuits on the roads, keeping an eye on any unusual activity. We collected drunks from The Jury Room and stepped in to help when someone got sick or injured and couldn't work. We also ran our own fire protection team, giving out extinguishers every Christmas and making sure people knew when to change the batteries in their smoke detectors. I'd bought a handful of four-thousand-gallon water trucks to help fight fires, but all of that was useless when someone intentionally set a blaze like the one today. Like the one at Shye's place.

My people were under attack, and no amount of emergency equipment could stop that.

Bishop disappeared back around the rear of the house right as Gage crept up beside me, his face devoid of emotion but his eyes burning with an anger I'd never seen before. I'd also never seen him without Rex on his heels.

"This can't be good," I said, looking around for the dog.

"He's in the truck with your girl. I think he might like her more than me." Gage turned, and I followed, looking toward where I'd parked my truck what seemed like so long ago. Rex was indeed sitting right next to Shye in the cab, the two watching the house burn through the windshield, with a blanket over their shoulders.

"Can't say that I blame him." Shye's eyes met mine, and the fear I saw there—the obvious exhaustion—made my heart lurch. "They shouldn't be here."

"Better here where we can watch over them than alone somewhere out of our reach. Which leads me to my next statement. We've got a problem."

We had a metric fuckton of them, really. "I swear to Christ, man, if you say that to me one more time tonight—"

"Someone nailed a window shut around the back of the house."

It took me a full three seconds to take in his words. "Nailed...which window?"

"Master bedroom."

When I'd fought with the Green Berets, one of my many jobs had been working with Deacon, former sniper with a kill list longer than my goddamned leg. We'd done the sort of work not shown on news stations back home—secretive, black ops, wet work. Part of that had been sabotaging the plans of criminal cells by assassinating the people causing trouble for our government. I knew the drill of a planned hit inside and out. Locate the mark, monitor them to learn their patterns and habits, confirm identity, prep for the mission by securing any escape routes in case things went sideways, and wait until the opportune time to strike, which meant...

"Camden was at The Jury Room with Deacon tonight."

Gage nodded, though I didn't need him to confirm that. Every second Saturday of the month, Deacon hosted a mini poker tournament at the bar. Players came from up to a hundred miles away to get in on the action, and Camden always worked security. He'd been doing it for years.

And whoever set the fire had known that.

"Motherfucker." Rage unlike anything I'd ever felt burned through my blood. Someone had targeted Camden, had watched or asked around. Knew enough to set his fucking house on fire when he was out. That was bad enough, but they'd intentionally trapped Leah inside, which took this to a whole other level. One I hadn't been expecting. One that would start a war between Justice and these fucking road rats.

But first, I needed to take care of the immediate issues. "Where's Camden?"

"Up front. Got Finn babysitting him." Cam's best friend. Smart choice.

"How's he doing?"

"He knows she's in there."

Of course he did. "They trapped her inside to burn."

"Yeah."

And we would kill every last one of them who had planned or acted to make that happen. "We need details. Get Bishop on fire duty. I need you to find out who ordered the job and who set the fire. I want to know everyone involved, down to the cashier that sold them the matches." I stared into the flames, wishing with everything I had that we were wrong. That Leah would come strolling up the driveway after a girls' night out. But we all knew better. Leah didn't go out without Camden, and Cam rarely left her side unless he was working. The two had been together since high school, which was also where Finn had met them. Add in Finn's twin, Elijah, and Bishop's ex Anabeth, and you had the Five Musketeers of Justice. The three boys had been inseparable, Anabeth had been practically family already, and Leah had simply become part of the group when Cam started dating her. I was a lot older than the twins, but I remembered the younger Camden and Leah always hanging at our house.

After high school, Elijah and Finn had gone off to college while Anabeth had headed to Las Vegas to become some sort of medium or psychic. I wasn't real sure. Leah had stuck around town from what I understood, working at the little hardware store on Main Street, while Camden had joined the Marines. The two had stayed together through boot camp and deployments, the girl completely loyal and faithful to the man who might as well have been another brother to me. She'd also stepped in to help once Finn's drug use had come to light, something I'd appreciated seeing as how I had been in the Army at the time and couldn't come home as much as I would have wanted to. I'd liked her, the Kennard family had practically adopted her, and Cam had loved her. Her death would be a dark moment for the entire damn town.

Someone had studied their marks well.

"I want them dead," I said, my voice low and quiet. "We handle the investigation, we track the fuckers down, we kill them. No fucking sheriff or DA. No lawyers. Right?"

"I couldn't agree more. And boss, I don't want to tell you we've got another problem—"

I groaned. "What now?"

"Baker's here."

There wasn't a fire in the world that could blaze as hot as my fury when our lazy, corrupt sheriff came strolling up Camden's driveway.

"Two in a week," he said, ignoring all the activity around him as good men actually did their damn jobs. Something he knew very little about, in my opinion. "That's quite the coincidence, don't you think?"

No, I didn't think. But I wouldn't trust Baker to shine my shoes, let alone investigate a murder. "Awfully late for you, Sheriff Baker. Shouldn't you be at home by now watching *Wheel of Fortune*?"

He scowled, the fire throwing deep shadows on his prissy face. The scar from our first run-in practically fucking glowing. He hadn't been sheriff then, though. Just a deputy. A fact that had probably kept my ass out of prison.

"Just doing my job, Alder. Though, for a logging man, you seem to be real interested in these fires you got going on. What, you ain't got nothing better to do?"

Someday, I'd pop that motherfucker right in the mouth. I'd done it once—while on leave from the Army, when my dad had still been alive and I'd been trying to figure out what to do with a struggling logging business while knowing I needed to get back to my unit. Baker'd come to the house to arrest Finn for supposedly selling narcotics. I'd known it was a sham, he'd known it was a sham, so when he put his hands on my baby brother, I'd lost it and took a swing. Two, really—one to the chest and one to the mouth that left a scar on his top lip. Spent four nights in jail for that one.

Finn had spent seven years in prison, though, all for a trumped-up charge. The kid had used, but he'd never sold. And Baker had known it. But he'd pushed the prosecutor to make an example of Finn Kennard, and he'd fabricated some story about seeing my little brother selling meth. Which was why I couldn't help but hate the motherfucker.

"Is that Miss Anderson in your truck there, Alder?" Baker asked, staring toward where Shye did indeed sit wrapped in a blanket inside my truck. Rex jumped as I watched, his front legs on the dashboard, barking. Smart dog—he'd always hated Baker.

I shot a look to Gage, and he dipped his chin before slowly making his way toward the truck. Gage and my brother Bishop may have been the ones fighting on the same team during their time in the SEALs, but we were all former military. He knew what I wanted without a word, and I knew he'd lay down his life to give it to me. Hell, between him and Bishop, they'd probably do anything to keep Shye and me close at that point. Both loved to bust my balls about my obsession with her. Gage had even been with me the night I'd first met her. He'd known right away that I wanted her to be mine. Nothing would be getting through him.

Once Gage was in position to keep my girl and his dog safe, I granted

Baker my undivided attention. Which meant scowling at him until he couldn't hold my gaze any longer. "You got a problem, Sheriff?"

"Just wondering what y'all got going over here. I know the people of Justice—especially you Kennards—seem to think you're above the law and like to handle things yourselves, but you've never had an arsonist in your midst." He nodded toward my truck. "How long she lived here again?"

The world went red, and not from the flames behind me. "You listen here, Baker. Shye Anderson's got nothing to do with these fires. She's here because I brought her with me to keep her safe. In case you haven't gotten a clue yet, she's been through some shit this week."

"Some shit that could pay out well in insurance money, it seems." He took a step back even as he smirked my way, holding his hands up as if in surrender when I followed him. Practically fucking taunting me. "What about this one? This is Camden Reese's place, isn't it? Anyone home when the fire started?"

"Cam was handling security at the poker tournament for Deacon." The prosecutor couldn't get me on impeding an investigation so long as I told the truth, which I did. I definitely didn't need to tell him a damned thing about Leah—not yet. Especially since he didn't ask about her specifically. That would be my secret for a few more hours. We needed to get inside the house and collect some intel before letting that news out of our circle. If Baker knew there could be a dead girl inside the house, he'd immediately try to take over the investigation. Rumor had it his services could be bought, and if he figured out who was responsible, he'd likely end up in their pocket. We'd never find out who killed her if that happened. Or get our revenge. We needed a little time before the law got involved.

Sheriff Baker watched the fire for a moment before focusing on where Camden sat huddled under a tree with Finn at his side. Both men looking hard, mean, and ready to kill. Which made the next statement out of the good sheriff's mouth that much more ignorant. "I should talk to Camden, see if he—"

I stopped him with a hand to his chest. He wasn't getting near Cam. He especially wasn't getting near Cam when Finn was around. "You want a statement, call him in for one. Better yet, call my brother Elijah in the morning—he's Cam's lawyer and can handle the details for you. Tonight's not the night."

Baker glared, puffing up his chest as if trying to intimidate me. "No matter what you think, Kennard, I'm the law in these parts. Not you."

Wrong answer.

"Says who?" I held his gaze, letting him get a good look at the fury inside of me, making sure he knew who the top dog was in Justice. Because it sure as fuck wasn't him.

Baker hissed a curse as he turned on his heel, retreating like the coward I knew him to be. "I want Camden in my office first thing tomorrow, Alder."

"I'll let Elijah know about your request. I'm sure he'll call with a response." I tipped my head to him, refusing to lock Camden into something I knew wouldn't be happening. At least, not without Elijah by his side to protect him. Especially if we were right about Leah.

Baker needed to get the fuck out of town, and we needed to find Leah's body before anyone else did. And I needed to figure out a way to convince Shye to move in with me so I could keep an eye on her. Because there was no way she was going back to that motel after this. No way in hell.

Fuck, it was going to be such a long night.

———

The glow of the coming dawn had just begun to light up the eastern sky by the time we were able to begin busting into the back of the house. The roof had burned through and a couple of walls had fallen around one side, but we had to use a chainsaw to cut into the master bedroom. The saw screamed in Gage's hands, and three guys kept a constant flow of water on the structure, backing up their teammate. Bishop would be the one to head in, though. It needed to be a Kennard in that building, needed to be my family leading that search.

Finn had wanted to be the one to look for Leah, but none of us thought that was a good idea. Finn may have been sober since he'd gone to prison over a decade before, but whatever had happened to Leah could put that at risk. We needed him solid, which meant he couldn't be the one to find her. We had no idea what they'd done to her before they'd set the fire.

While the boys worked, I stole a moment to head to my truck and check on my girl. Shye had been in and out a few times, always coming straight to my side as soon as she exited the vehicle, but it'd been a couple hours since I'd gotten to smell her hair or touch her skin. I was due.

"Hey," I said when I opened the door. Her sleepy eyes met mine, and her smile made my heart beat a little faster. Fuck, this girl had truly destroyed me in the best way. "How you doing, honey?"

"I'm fine. Everything okay?"

No, not in the least, but she didn't need to know that. "As much as it can be. Do you need anything? Water? A snack? Another blanket?"

She shook her head, rubbing her hand over Rex's head. Damn dog had curled up with his head in her lap...lucky beast.

"I should be asking you that," she said, stealing my attention again. "You're the one out there working. You and your men. What do you need that I can help you with?"

I leaned farther into the truck, stepping onto the running board to better reach those lips I'd been craving. One kiss, two, keeping them nice and soft. Smiling when she kissed me back. "I only need you."

That smile I loved grew. "Charmer."

"I try."

She glanced past me, worrying her lip for a second. Looking anxious. "Is the sheriff still here?"

"Baker? No, he left hours ago."

Her sigh definitely sounded like relief. "Good. He doesn't like me much."

"Yeah, well, that makes two of us. Though I couldn't give a flying fuck if he liked me."

Her head cocked, and her eyebrows pulled down into the cutest confused sort of expression. "Why doesn't he like you?"

"You know that scar on his lip?" I grinned when she nodded. "I gave it to him."

Those dark eyes went wide. "You hit him?"

"He arrested my brother for something he didn't do."

"Which brother?"

"Finn. Do you know him?"

She squinted and nodded distractedly. "Shorter than you, right? Loves huckleberry pie. Your other brother comes in more often, though."

Completely at my request. "Bishop, yeah. There's one more too, though I don't know that you've met him. Finn's twin, Elijah. He's a lawyer down in Denver."

"Four boys in your family?"

"And a girl. Lainie's in college still. She lives with Elijah."

"Five Kennard siblings. I bet holidays were rowdy."

"With four boys, everything was rowdy. Lainie made it ten times worse, though." I grinned when Shye laughed. This was nice, and I didn't want it to end. "What about you? Any family?"

Her smile fell. Crashed, really. "No siblings. After my mom died, my dad married a woman with a son, so I have a stepbrother."

"You two close?"

"Not in the least."

"And your dad?"

"Dead."

One word, and a pained one at that. I wanted to ask her more, but at that moment, Bishop came walking up to the truck. Keeping his steps slow as if he didn't want to interrupt. Smart man.

"We're ready to go in," he said, glancing from me to Shye and back. "Cam's going to need you."

"On my way." I stretched back into the truck, cupped her chin, and gave my girl a better kiss, one that allowed me to get a solid taste of her, one that left her trembling when I was through. "Stay here for me, okay? I need to know you're safe."

"Okay. But I'm here if you need me."

No better words had ever been spoken. "Understood."

One last kiss, and then I hopped down and shut the door, following my brother back toward the house. Back toward the hell of what I knew was about to happen. I sought out my brothers and friends, taking stock of all of them. Making sure they were solid. Tired and sooty, I could handle, but not injured. They all stood watching the fire, waiting for us.

I landed on Cam last.

Camden stood in the middle of the Kennard crew, surrounded by the men he saw as his brothers and friends, his face hard and his body rigid. Gage and Finn stayed close, looking ready to hold him back if needed. Or hold him up. This was going to be difficult for all of us, but no one more than Camden.

When I gave him the all clear, Bishop kicked the wall in, opening a hole into the master bedroom just big enough for him to fit through. Three guys with hoses sprayed through the opening in case the fire flared, and then Bishop pulled on his breathing mask and crawled inside. My chest tightened, my eyes locked on that hole as every instinct screamed at me to follow him.

I couldn't lose my brother.

We'd been in dangerous situations in the past—hell, the two of us had pulled some pretty tough duties while serving our country overseas—but this felt different. Even the danger of the logging industry, the daily threat of falling branches, accidents with the saws, and the occasional forest fires, didn't compare. That house had been compromised by an enemy, and Bishop had to go in alone to clear it. I would rather have been the one to do it.

Thankfully or not, it didn't take Bishop long to come back out. He took off his breathing mask and wiped a gloved hand over his sweaty face. "Door to the hallway is stuck, though whether that's from before the fire or not I won't know until I get on the other side of it."

I stood silent, waiting, needing to know but not wanting to at the same time. Bishop didn't make me wait too long. He eventually took a deep breath and approached Camden, already hanging his head. Looking torn up by what he'd seen. My throat tightened, and I started moving before he even got the words out.

"I'm sorry, man. It looks like she was asleep—"

Camden shrugged everyone off, screaming into the pre-dawn sky like a wild animal. One that had been wounded. Mortally. Finn bent at the waist, both hands fisted against his forehead. Suffering. Clawing my heart right out of my chest with their obvious pain.

And there was nothing I could do to save either of them from their loss. Nothing any of us could do to ease that ache. Except to make sure the people responsible got what was coming to them.

But it was the sight of Shye hopping out of the truck, the fear on her pretty face, that turned my pain to fury. It could have been her so easily. Still could be if I didn't find a way to keep her safe.

"Bishop," I snapped, hurrying toward my girl. "You and Gage take pictures and collect whatever evidence you can. We're going to have to call Sheriff Baker back this morning, but I want to be ten steps ahead of him."

Bishop nodded once. "On it."

"What happened? Why is he...?" Shye trailed off as Camden screamed out in agony, the horrific sound fading into something that sounded like a whine at the end. Something like a pain too strong to push through. Like a call for death to come take him as well.

As Shye shivered and watched Camden fall apart, I wrapped her in my arms, pulling her right off the ground and holding her against me. It made my heart pound a little harder, how she grabbed hold of me easily and wrapped her little body around mine, how she seemed to reach for me for support.

No fucking way would I let her down.

"Camden's wife was in the house. She didn't make it." No sense saying her death had been intentional. Not yet. I didn't want to scare her.

"Oh, no. Leah, right?" Her frown intensified at my nod. "She always seemed really nice when she came to the restaurant with Camden."

"She was nice, and practically part of my family. She'll be missed."

Shye ran a hand through the back of my hair, the touch sending shock waves through my body, pulling me closer as I watched Bishop crawl back through the hole he'd cut. But not even her touch could calm the tension inside of me, the fear of him getting into trouble. This time, two of my other employees followed Bishop into that dark space, their face masks making it impossible for me to tell who was who. That was fine, though. They were Kennard workers—they'd take care of him and each other. Bishop had backup. So I took the time to do exactly what I wanted to— hold my girl and try real fucking hard to breathe. Finally.

We stood that way for hours, it seemed, her body wrapped against mine as I held her off the ground. Something I'd wanted for three long years. Something I'd planned for. I wished I'd accomplished my goal under better circumstances, but I'd take what I could get.

Something scratched inside of me, though. A worry at what was coming. A need to protect everyone, to extinguish the threat against us. I'd been through enough shit to know this would get worse before it got better, which meant I needed to go full out on protection. Especially for Shye. She'd been all alone at that trailer. If they'd have gotten to her while she'd been home, if she'd had to face things alone, I'd have lost her. Not fucking happening.

"Boss," Bishop yelled from inside the house a short while later. "We've got a problem."

I needed people to stop saying that. Shye wiggled out of my hold, so I set her down before yelling, "What kind of problem?"

Bishop popped his head out, looking over the crowd of Kennard Mills employees standing around before focusing in on Shye. He frowned. "Maybe you should come over here."

Oh, hell no. "She's with us."

Shye stiffened, probably uncomfortable being the center of attention because all eyes were suddenly on her. But she was with me, which meant she'd be under Kennard protection. That meant we had to trust her. I wrapped my arms around her shoulders, making my point clear.

Bishop nodded. "Okay, then. I know who set the fire."

"Who?" So we could track him down and light his dick on fire before feeding it to him.

"Spark of the Soul Suckers."

Shye sucked in a quick breath, but I kept my eyes on Bishop. Motherfucking Spark...not like plug. Spark as in flame. Shit, I'd missed that connection. "You better be sure, man."

"I got into the hallway. The jackass tagged the wall." He glanced at Camden. "And barricaded the door. She couldn't have gotten out even if she had been awake."

Camden turned his back on the crew, big, heavy sobs ripping from his chest. His voice a total growl as he said, "I want them dead. Whoever did this, I want them all fucking buried."

Bishop grunted his agreement, and the entire crew nodded. Ready to fight. Ready to seek payback for what these fools had brought down on us.

"What's the plan?" Gage asked me, sounding deadly serious and ready to go to war. Exactly how I needed him to be.

"We take them down."

"You can't," Shye said. "They're a national club—they'll just keep bringing in reinforcements. They'll kill you all."

I shook my head and tugged her closer, looking down into terrified brown eyes. "Not going to happen."

She didn't look convinced. "There has to be some other—"

"Way?" Gage stalked closer, his gaze cold and heavy as it held hers. "Like what, call for help? You think Sheriff Baker's going to go out of his way to solve a murder when the Soul Suckers are involved? He might as well be their mascot for all the leeway he shows them."

Shye cowered against me, igniting my temper, and I turned on my mechanic.

"Ease up, Gage. She doesn't know him like we do."

The man met my glare and took a step back. Flicking one last look at Shye. "What's the next step in this ruck-up?"

"Time for a little joint operational planning." Because we had three branches of the military represented on one team. The Kennard team—Deacon and me with Army Special Forces, Bishop and Gage with the SEALs, and Camden had been a Marine. We had a shit-ton of experience in warfare. "Justice goes on lockdown until we work this shit out. No one gets inside without us knowing, we all avoid our usual patterns, and everyone pairs up to stay safe."

Bishop, covered in ash and soot, said, "Someone better tell Deacon."

"We're headed there now." I tugged Shye with me, wishing there were another way to go about this. To earn her permission before I steamrolled her life. But there wasn't, and leaving her alone even for a second simply wouldn't fly with me.

Once I got her into the truck, I started the engine and turned on the heat before leveling her with a stare. And then I took a deep breath and laid out the rules. "When we get to the motel, I'll sweep your room first to make sure it's safe while you wait in the truck. Anyone walks up on you, you hit the horn. Anything seems off, same thing. Got it?"

Her nod looked stiff, stilted. God, I hated myself for putting that fear in her eyes. I reached for her, unable not to touch. Needing to calm her. "I've got you, Shye. Nothing will happen to you while you're with me."

She didn't look so sure, but she nodded. "Okay."

I leaned in, stealing a kiss. Just one. Because I had a feeling this next part was the one that would make her want to run. "Once I clear your room, you'll have three minutes to get in and grab whatever you want to take with you."

"Why? Where am I going?"

"You're moving in with me, honey."

Chapter Six

SHYE

It was really difficult to avoid someone when you were basically being held prisoner in their house. That might have been a little bit of a stretch. Alder wasn't *truly* holding me captive. He simply refused to allow me to move out, or to leave without him or one of his brothers with me. Some people may have seen that as sort of overprotective and maybe even a little sweet.

Or perhaps those people suffered from Stockholm syndrome.

"You look real pretty today, Shye."

The hound dog look on his face almost broke my resolve not to speak to him, but I held strong. Tough to do considering we were trapped together in his truck. But I wouldn't, couldn't, give in. No puppy dog eyes or compliments would take away my ire at the man. I'd been avoiding him since he'd dragged me back to his home after the fire at Camden's place. Three days of silence, of knowing he stayed right down the hall, of hearing the water running for his morning shower and dreaming about seeing him naked.

Serious Stockholm syndrome, obviously. Because if I compared him to the Soul Suckers, looked at how they'd taken away my free will and put that up against Alder's actions, there wasn't much difference at first glance.

Sure, I had no fear of Alder. Not really. I worried he'd stop looking at me and saying sweet things, or that I'd go walking downstairs one morning and find him saying goodbye to another woman, but that all had to do with my emotions. My body was safe with him. My heart, my mind, my independence...not so much. The Soul Suckers would kill me; Alder would die trying to save me if he could.

Which was why nothing was as important as the fact that my being with Alder put him in danger, but he wouldn't let me leave.

Alder sighed when I didn't answer him, sliding his sunglasses on and driving down his driveway, taking us both to the funeral. Leah's body had been "discovered" by the county fire investigator a few hours after Alder's crew finished up their work at the house. Sheriff Baker had been furious, showing up at Alder's that morning and looking ready to spit nails. I'd hidden in the back hallway as Alder'd told him no one had known Leah was in the house, and to contact his lawyer if he wanted to speak to any of the Kennard Mills guys. Then he'd slammed the door in the sheriff's face, which had made me fall for him that much more.

And yet, I'd resisted acting on it. Even after that kiss. After all the things he'd done to my body in the office at the restaurant. The night I couldn't stop thinking about. I couldn't act on *anything* because, while Alder would never hurt me physically and was only acting in a way to keep me safe, I couldn't promise him the same thing. If I told Alder about my stepbrother, if he knew the threat hanging over me and my debt to the Soul Suckers, he'd either run me off his property and right out of his town...or he'd try to help, and they'd kill him for it.

I could never tell him, so staying mad seemed easier than forgiving him and opening my mouth.

We arrived at the funeral early, but not early enough. Already, a crowd of people congregated near the chairs set up at the gravesite. And by crowd, I meant the whole town. True, that was only a couple hundred people, but still...every one of them appeared to be there to support Camden and say goodbye to Leah. An amazing and yet horribly painful sight.

Alder hopped out of the truck as soon as he threw it into park, racing around the front to open my door. Hand held out for me to grab, his big body taking up so much space, he didn't say a word. Instead, he waited. Not really giving me the choice to take his help or not since he'd have to move if I chose to ignore that outstretched hand, but not demanding I do what he wanted either. Typical.

I took the choice that would bring me the most pleasure. "Thank you."

"You really do look pretty today, honey." He smiled as I slipped my hand into his, looking like a dream in his dark suit and sunglasses. If only...

Bishop walked up right as I stepped out of the truck, a wary sort of smile directed at me. Alder must have told his brother how I wouldn't speak to him. Wonderful. I'd probably get an earful of that Kennard charm trying to get me to break, to speak to Alder, to let go of my stubbornness. Not what I needed because I wanted to let go so badly it hurt, but I wouldn't be responsible for another death.

Alder steadied me as my feet hit the ground but didn't let go of my hand. I didn't let go of his either. It was a day for a truce even if only during the service.

"Hey." Bishop grabbed Alder by the arm and leaned in for some sort of half hug before nodding at me. "Shye. How you doing, babe?"

I ignored the way Alder's hand tightened on mine. "I'm fine, thanks."

"My big brother here treating you well?" He grinned—the smile not quite reaching his eyes—and took me by the elbow, pulling me away from Alder. "You can always come crash at my place if he starts getting on your nerves. I can keep you just as safe as he can. More so, really. I'm a SEAL, baby. He likes to brag about being a Green Beret, but when are they on the news for saving the world? Never."

I glanced back at Alder—a Green Beret? Like, true Army hero stuff? I'd had no idea. Though I also hadn't known Bishop was a SEAL until recently. No wonder they ran Justice like a military base—it practically was one.

"We're good enough not to need to toot our own horns, Bishop." Alder's voice sounded like a warning, all gravelly and low. Dangerous. Heat flooded my neck and face as Bishop pulled me closer. Almost...egging Alder on.

But Bishop ignored his brother and dragged me along with him. "He's been grumpy these last few days, Shye. You two have a fight? Because seriously, the entire Kennard Mills team would give you anything you wanted if you'd help that man get in a better mood."

I glanced over my shoulder again, shivering at the frown on Alder's face. Wondering if he was staring at me behind those mirrored lenses. "Pretty sure I have no bearing on his mood."

Bishop laughed. "Trust me, Shye girl, you've been responsible for everything that man has thought, felt, and done for the last three years."

"That's enough." Alder grabbed my arm, looping my hand over his elbow and pulling me away from his brother. "It's a goddamned funeral."

"Exactly." Bishop looked around, then leaned closer. "They killed Cam's girl. You know how many regrets that man is going to have? Wondering if he should have done this or that, or if he'd changed one thing, would it have made a difference? I'm not living my life like there's not a fucking clock counting down to my death anymore." He gave me a smile before shooting his brother an intense stare. "And you shouldn't either."

Alder didn't say anything, but he tugged me closer, guiding me into the crowd toward two seats in the front row.

And he never let go of my hand.

***

ALDER

The service lasted close to an hour. While I held Shye's hand in mine—refusing to let go for even a moment—numerous people who'd known and loved Leah stood up to tell stories about her life and how much she'd meant to them. Their palpable sense of loss seemed to be shared by everyone in attendance...except for one.

Camden sat silent, his shoulders stiff, back straight, and face hard. While those around him curled in on themselves in pain and grief, Cam seemed to practically vibrate with maleficence. Filled with a rage just waiting to break through. I couldn't blame him. If Shye had been killed in the fire at her trailer, I'd probably have worn the asphalt off the roads tracking down whoever had lit the match. And once I'd found them? I'd have shown them how many ways a Green Beret could kill a man...and bring him back to get information. Yet I only had three years of wanting Shye, one damn good moment of any sort of intimacy, and a few minutes of hand-holding to get me to that point. Camden had close to twenty years of first kisses and first times, two damn decades of loving his woman and being loved in return. He'd lost his *wife*. The man would be a force of nature if he ever got his hands on the person who'd killed Leah.

But Camden wasn't alone. Finn sat on one side, Elijah—who'd driven in from Denver—on the other. Even as the casket began to slip below the ground—as my brothers stepped up to support Camden in his grief—I couldn't help but catalog the differences between the two youngest male Kennards.

Finn had always been smart and driven, much more serious than his identical twin brother. Elijah had been the jokester, the smiling child with the loud laugh and a love for life you felt whenever he walked in the room. Our mom used to say God gave us Elijah to keep Finn from becoming too serious. My dad said God gave us Finn to keep Elijah in line. But drugs and Sheriff Baker had only come calling for Finn, which sent both twins spiraling in different directions.

When Finn went to prison, Elijah'd done everything he could think of to help him. Hell, we all had. The drugs had been hard enough to deal with, but the arrest...the incarceration. Those had altered the family forever. Bishop and I'd both been overseas at the time, but we'd managed to make it home a few times to try to help Finn. Elijah'd been right by his side through the trial, watching as his brother went down for a crime he hadn't committed and being unable to do one damn thing about it. Elijah'd grown harder, more serious and focused. Had switched majors and entered into law school, claiming no one would ever fuck with one of his brothers again. So while Finn had sat in prison, Elijah had become a lawyer. He'd worked for the district attorney, learning the inside secrets of prosecution, then headed out on his own to become one of the most sought-after defense attorneys in the state.

And while Elijah had lost his fun-loving nature, Finn had lost every bit of his ambition. I often wished Finn would find some of Elijah's drive and do something with his life, but he was content working behind the bar at Deacon's and helping out at the mill when we needed him. The man was an artist when it came to woodworking, but he didn't want to make that a career. Always said it would take the joy out of it. He needed more joy in his life...both boys did.

"Alder?"

I startled at Shye's soft voice saying my name, and blood rushed to my cock when I looked up at her. My god, she was so fucking pretty. She stood next to me, her brow furrowed as if concerned, her hand reaching for mine. Everyone around us had left, the casket having been lowered while I'd stared at my brothers who had both also walked away at some point. But she'd waited for me. A fact that hit me like a punch to the chest. Whether because I'd been reminiscing about my youngest brothers or feeling the grief of Leah's murder, my emotions were high. And Shye seemed to know that somehow.

"Are you okay?" she asked, looking so damn worried. I couldn't have that.

"Yeah. Sorry." I grabbed her hand and rose to my feet. "We should probably find Camden."

Shye nodded, still looking at me as if concerned. But she let me lead her through the crowd, let me cling to her hand like a drowning man. People smiled my way and did a double take when they noticed Shye's hand in mine, but no one commented. I couldn't hope they would stay silent for long. We'd be the hottest news on the gossip lines tonight, which was probably a bigger issue for Shye than for me. I'd tell them all she was finally mine if I didn't think she'd run the other way. Or slap me for it. She certainly hadn't been happy with me the last few days.

We found Camden surrounded by my brothers and a few Kennard Mills men under a tree away from the crowd. Shye slowed down as we approached, but I simply kept her hand in mine and dragged her with me.

"Cam." I pulled the smaller man into a hug, having to let go of Shye to do so. "How are you holding up?"

His face stayed blank, his eyes dead but hard. "I'll be better once I know everyone involved in her death is gone."

Finn nodded, and even Elijah seemed to understand the need for retaliation as he asked, "What do we need to get this done?"

"We need intel," I replied. "We need to know everything there is to know about the Soul Suckers—their setup, leaders, business involvement, both legal and illegal. All of it."

Elijah nodded. "I can check with state authorities to see what they know, maybe even move to some Feds I've worked with since they're a national club."

"Yeah, Shye mentioned that." I caught Gage's frown. "What?"

"How'd she know about them?" he asked. "She's not your usual biker bitch."

My stomach tightened, anger flaring at the thought of her being involved with those fuckers. Men like that would eat someone as quiet and soft as her for breakfast. I sought out Shye in the crowd, but she'd moved away from us, heading for my truck, it seemed. "I don't know, but I'll ask her."

"We need more than official records." Bishop paced, passing Gage on each round. "We need the stuff officials don't know about. We need someone on the inside."

"Never going to happen," Gage said. "These clubs are tight—they're all about loyalty and brotherhood. You're not going to turn one member against another without some serious capital on them."

"Unless there's already a fox in the henhouse, or there's a man inside whose loyalty to the club doesn't eclipse loyalties outside of it." I nodded toward Gage. "Your loyalty to Bishop outranks just about everything, I'd guess."

Gage nodded once and held up a fist for Bishop to meet with his own. "Brothers in destruction."

"Damn straight," Bishop said. "So what...we need to find a Soul Sucker who was a SEAL? That might be a little tough. We're motherfucking special."

"Army, Special Forces, SEALs, or a Marine. We've got a ton of brotherhood to lean on in this group." I ran a hand through my hair, still keeping an eye on Shye. If I'd needed someone to watch her while I couldn't, I knew who the first person I'd call would be. And it wouldn't be a man with the same last name as mine. It would be a fellow Green Beret I'd served with. One who already looked out for us in every way he could. The only man outside my family or my crew I'd trust with my life. "We need to talk to Deacon."

Chapter Seven

ALDER

Deacon Manns had been a skinny, immature kid the first time we'd met. Fresh out of boot camp, he'd jumped into my life with a quiet doggedness and simply never left. We'd gone through the Special Operations Training Program together, earned our green berets together, caused a fuckton of sabotage together, and killed a lot of fucking marks together. Well, he'd killed them. I'd gotten him to his station, given him every bit of information I could dig up, and watched his back. He'd been the man with the gun. The sniper in the air. The patient little fuck who could lie in the sand in a desert for three solid days to take a single shot if needed.

When I'd decided to move home after leaving active duty, I'd called Deacon and told him there was a job for him in my mill. He'd told me to fuck off, that I was too bossy for him, and promptly bought the broken-down bar at the county line with the trashy motel attached to it. Five years later and the bar still carried an air of dump to it, but the food was good, the beer was cold, and the place was about as safe as any I could imagine. All because of a man I saw as another brother.

One with a big fucking mouth. "You look like shit. What the fuck crawled on your face and died?"

Though, honestly, I'd been greeted with worse from him. "One of these days, you're going to accept the fact that I'm simply more rugged and manly than you, Deacon."

We bumped shoulders and clasped hands in greeting.

"You bring any friends?" The bar sat empty, as had the parking lot. Not what I'd hoped for after calling in an emergency favor that morning.

"He'll be here soon enough." Deacon poured my favorite bourbon into a rocks glass and slid it across the bar top. "You sure you want to do this?"

"You got any other ideas?"

"Nope." He grabbed his towel and started wiping down bottles. "I'm not sure what you'll get out of it, but it's what I'd do if I had a girl to worry about."

My girl, my friends, my family. I had no idea who the next target would be, so I needed to put these fuckers in the ground. For that, I needed intel, and I was willing to do just about anything to get it.

As I took a sip of my bourbon, the door swung open, and a tall man walked through. I kept my seat, taking him in, waiting. Forming my own judgments about him. Dirty jeans, heavy boots, and the leather vest he wore over a plain black T-shirt screamed motorcycle club rider. His high and tight haircut, forearm American flag tattoo, and Semper Fidelis patch told me the rest.

A Marine...I breathed a little easier at that.

Deacon stayed behind the bar, pulling a beer from the cooler at his knees. When the other man settled onto the stool beside me, he slid the bottle across the bar and nodded. "Alder Kennard, meet Parris."

I held out a hand, shaking his when he returned the offer. "Parris. As in island?"

"The one and only."

Of course his road name was Parris, not Paris. Island...not city. I could work with this. "My buddy Camden says Paradise City wasn't so much a paradise as—"

"A swampy fucking sauna?" Parris chuckled. "I have to admit, I was happy to get the fuck out of there."

"I'll drink to that." I took another sip, thinking over what I wanted to ask. I needn't have bothered.

Parris set his beer down, focusing in on me. "Deacon said a fellow

Marine ran into some trouble with an MC, and that there was a Green Beret around who needed insight on club life to help him get out of it. I assume that's you."

"Yeah, and I definitely need some intel."

"What's the issue?"

If I knew exactly, things would be a little easier. "We've got a club making trouble in town."

"What sort of trouble?"

I made a split-second decision not to tell him about Shye—at least not about her being mine. That would make her a liability, and I didn't trust him enough to open myself up like that.

"They burned down a friend's place first, then my site manager's." I downed the rest of my bourbon, ignoring the way Deacon shot me a glare for treating it like some cheap shot, then tipped my glass for another. "He's the Marine...and his wife died in that fire."

Paris clenched his fist, the only sign anything I'd said had gotten to him. "You're sure this club set it?"

"Yup." I flipped my empty glass over and set it on the bartop before turning to face him. "They nailed her bedroom window shut, barricaded her door from the outside, and tagged the wall with a road name and club logo. It's them, and her death was intentional."

Deacon slid another full glass of bourbon my way before heading down to the end of the bar. Me? I sat and I stewed and I tried to wrap my head around what the fuck was going on. Tried and failed. Which was why I needed a guy like Parris.

"You guys kill one of theirs? Arrest one?" At my head shake, Parris frowned. "You had to have done something. No club would get into shit like murdering civilians without a reason for it. It's too noticeable, you know? Too easy to get picked up for."

"Nothing, especially not like killing someone. My site manager had a run-in with a couple of club members at a job, but it was over in minutes. No cops called, either. Nothing major happened. Just a dispute over who had a right to be on the land in question."

"Where's the job site?"

"Up on the eastern slope of Widow's Ridge. We're harvesting lumber there."

Parris nodded, looking as if his mind was putting together puzzle pieces I still hadn't even seen. "Is it secluded? Far off the main roads?"

I couldn't help but think about Shye up there all the time, how alone that trailer always seemed out on a stretch of road with no neighbors. And right next to where all the trouble had started. "Yeah. Real secluded."

Parris tapped the counter twice before taking a sip of his beer. When he set it down again, he simply said, "Soul Suckers."

Not a question...a statement. "Yeah."

"This property? This job site you got started? You're too close to their kitchen."

"Pardon?"

"Their *kitchen*. They cook and sell meth. That's the Soul Suckers' main income source—high-quality, decent volume. My guess is they've got a kitchen set up off the beaten track. Someplace well off the road where they'd have plenty of notice if anyone got too close." He took another gulp of his beer before setting it down again. "You got too close."

Rage unlike any I'd felt burned inside of me. We'd had our share of drug issues in Justice, including my own brother—hell, the whole damn country seemed to be turning to meth or opiates or some shit to get through the day. But while I'd discovered users in our citizens and had always done my best to help them get clean, I'd never found anyone selling. I'd certainly never expected anyone to be cooking that shit in our town.

And the fact that this had been going on right under my nose pissed me the fuck off. "So this—the fires, the murder—is all about drugs?"

Parris didn't appear as pissed as I felt. "It's about hundreds of thousands of dollars in drugs, yeah."

"Fuck." I hopped off the barstool, pacing the length of the room as my mind spun. Shye had lived up there, close enough to be noticed, for sure. And she'd lived alone. Hell, Miss Hansen, the old lady we'd contracted with to harvest the lumber on that slope, lived alone as well and was in her eighties. I couldn't let anything happen to either of them. I also couldn't let some group of bikers cook meth in my town.

"How do I get rid of them?"

"You're not going to be able to do it in any official way," Parris said.

As if that was an option. "Yeah, well. Considering who our sheriff is, that's pretty much impossible. We take care of our own up here."

Parris gave me an appraising look, nodding as if in approval. Like I'd passed some sort of test.

"Then you gotta go full biker." He set his beer down and shifted to face me fully. "If you want to fight an MC, you gotta think like an MC. These guys won't settle for coming after *you*, fucking up you and your men. They'll come after your businesses, your families. They'll manipulate every weak spot they find. The Soul Suckers are the worst of the worst— the ones even some of the baddest one-percenters leave alone. If you're going to go up against them, you'd better get ready for that unconventional warfare you Green Berets are so famous for. And when it comes to wives and kids, make sure you have your shit together because they won't be left out of the line of fire."

Leah had been the only wife in our main group, and she was already dead because of them. "We don't have wives or kids."

He chuckled. "No? But *you've* got a girl. Or at least, you've got your eye on a girl. Cute little thing—works over at the truck stop waiting tables."

I tried not to react, not to give anything away, but the other man smirked.

"Took me all of five minutes to figure that out when I was checking on you and the town of Justice this afternoon. And yeah, I looked into you when Deacon called. Just because you're a soldier doesn't mean you're someone to do business with. You've got a sweet setup with that lumber mill, good money coming in, and a tight circle of friends and family. I'm pretty sure you could kill a man in the middle of town, and no one would turn you in. But you've got a couple of glaring weak spots—an ex-addict brother and the girl."

He wasn't wrong on any of it, and I hated him for that. "What's your point?"

"My point is you called me here to help, and I'm giving you advice, so don't shit all over it. You telling me your house is in order? Trying to make like you don't have a weakness? It's bullshit. If you want your crew safe, you'd better up your game." He stood, bumping fists with Deacon before heading for the door. But not without throwing out one final warning. "Handle your shit before you take on the Soul Suckers, or you'll regret it. They won't give you a warning, son. They'll come in to kill. Make sure whoever's in the line of fire knows how to handle themselves."

As soon as Parris left, I turned to Deacon, my mind completely overridden with plans and situations and possibilities. But my friend knew me better than anyone else. He didn't say a word, simply reached under the bar, brought out a large, metal box, and unlocked it.

"Suppressor?" he asked, leaving me flat-footed for a whole five seconds before sighing and raising his eyebrows at me. "Do you need a sound suppressor for your gun?"

I blinked, stepping closer. "Yeah. Shye's living with me—that might be best."

He nodded and slid on a pair of plastic gloves. Once covered, he reached into the box, pulling out a Beretta 9mm and screwing the sound-killing cylinder on the end. "This is clean as fuck. You need to go for a kill, try to use this one then get rid of it. No one will trace it to you or me."

I took the gun, being careful not to palm it. Not to leave behind too many fingerprints. "Do I want to know why you have this?"

"You already do." He leveled me with a stare, one I'd seen before. The look he'd worn before every mission we'd ever pulled. Flat, dark, and ready. Yeah, I knew why he had a clean gun that couldn't be traced back to him. For the same reason I'd hang on to it and keep it handy.

To get rid of problems as invisibly as possible.

"Got more of these?" I asked as I sighted down the barrel.

"A few, but I'll place an order."

"Never figured you for a gun seller."

"Never figured you for a murderer, but we all do what we have to do."

There were no words truer than those. And what I had to do was eliminate the threats to my town and my girl. Fast.

So I tucked the Beretta away and held out my fist. "Thanks, man."

"I got your back. Now go take care of your girl, and don't leave her alone again. I'm not picking your sorry ass up off the floor if they get to her."

"Not happening." Ever. No matter what. Shye would be safe, whether she liked my methods or not.

Chapter Eight

SHYE

I hadn't meant to wait up for Alder, but sleep had been impossible. I knew he was out doing something about the Soul Suckers even if he hadn't told me anything. Not that I'd let him. I'd been ignoring him for days, and after the funeral, I'd pretty much barricaded myself in the room he'd moved me in to.

But then he'd left to "handle some shit to do with Leah," and I'd known what that had meant. I hadn't told him to be safe, to be careful, to hurry back... I hadn't even told him goodbye. My regret had grown strong as the hours alone passed, so when he walked in the door just after three in the morning, there I sat. Waiting. For him.

He eyed me warily. "Everything okay?"

I wrapped my hands around my now-cold mug of even colder coffee. "Yeah. Just...couldn't sleep."

He locked the door behind him before heading toward me. Steps slow and precise, he crossed the blue-gray wood floor that had stunned me the first time I'd walked through that same door. The colors created rolling patterns and curved shapes where there should have been nothing but straight lines. Smoky blue battling with the honey tan in a way that made the floors a work of art. Gorgeous, stunning, completely unique. Just like the man who had harvested, milled, and installed the lumber to create the vision.

But something in Alder's gait caught my attention more than the floors, an unnatural hitch I hadn't seen before. He lacked his usual grace. In fact, he seemed almost...stiff.

"Are *you* okay?" I asked, noticing the angry look in his eyes and the twitch in his jaw. Everything about his body screamed restraint, the edge of his temper showing through in the blaze of his eyes. The man appeared to be on the edge, even if he wouldn't admit it.

"I'm fine," he said, looking anything but fine. "It's been a long day is all."

Understatement. The funeral had been enough to exhaust anyone, but then he'd gone to work and out late into the night to deal with "stuff." Of course he was tired.

As I watched, Alder opened the refrigerator and peered inside, not moving to grab anything. Not moving at all. I knew that specific sort of stillness—I'd cooked for men for most of my life. Had soothed them with food when there was nothing else for me to say or do. The man needed to eat but was too overwhelmed to deal with something as simple as choosing what, let alone cooking anything. And after three days of silence, three days of him bending over backward to make me feel comfortable and protected, it was time for me to quit being stubborn and do something to help him.

I hopped up from my seat and hurried over, pushing him out of my way before stepping in front of his hulking form. "Why don't you let me make you something to eat? Omelet sound good?"

"You don't have to cook for me."

I shot him a look as I grabbed the eggs. "And you didn't have to give me a place to stay, but you did."

I didn't mention the fact that he'd forced me to move in with him, that he'd refused any argument I'd offered about not wanting to be a burden or not being able to pay him back. He'd simply taken care of something for me, asking for nothing in return. It was my turn to be grateful.

But when I closed the refrigerator door and turned, all thoughts of anything other than how handsome the man was fled. How...how had he gotten so close? He'd practically pinned me against the appliance, his body eating up the space between us. Looking down at me as if he couldn't believe I stood before him...holding a dozen eggs.

"I didn't give you anything, Shye. I took you. I know you're pissed about that, and I know I deserve every bit of your anger. But as much as I want to be sorry, I'm not." He brushed my hair off my shoulder, his fingers sliding along my neck as if to hold me in place. Or to simply hold on to something. "I'd do anything to keep you safe, my sweet girl. Anything to protect you from what's out there. Even if you hate me for it."

He would, and I knew that. Knew it with every fiber of my being. He'd never hurt me, but I'd been hurting him by being stubborn. Something that needed to end.

"You're a good man." I set down the eggs and grabbed his face when he snorted, forcing him to look me in the eye. "A *good* man. One who wants to take care of others, even when there's no one to take care of you. So sit down, Alder Kennard, and let me take care of you for a minute."

Those blue eyes burned into me, setting something on fire. Something dark and dirty, maybe a little lustful. But I hadn't been kidding about taking care of him, and right then, that meant getting him fed before he fell over.

"Why don't you sit at the counter while I cook?" When he didn't answer, too busy staring at me like I was the meal he *needed* to have, I raised an eyebrow and cocked my head. "Alder, please let me feed you."

Maybe it was the please that broke him, or perhaps he was simply too tired to fight me. Whatever the catalyst, he sighed, his hands coming to rest on my shoulders and his big body leaning into mine. Pulling me closer. Enveloping me in a slow hug that warmed me to my very soul. "Thank you, honey. An omelet would be amazing right now."

He held me in place for a long moment, so comforting and warm. So strong and yet so very close to collapse. I could practically feel the exhaustion rolling off him. I probably should have pulled away to start cooking, but I couldn't. I had a feeling he needed me in his arms more than eggs in his belly. So the hug continued, lasting longer than any I'd ever had and quickly becoming one I'd never forget. But eventually, we had to break apart, albeit reluctantly.

"Go," I said, pulling out of his arms. "Sit and relax while someone else takes care of you for once."

He brushed his lips against my cheek and whispered a soft thanks before letting me go. I took a deep breath when he walked away, trying to regain my composure. To ignore the need to follow him. When he touched me like that, all soft and kind—when that tough exterior broke and I was able to see the man beneath it—I got ideas. Ones involving the two of us getting naked, getting closer, getting intimate with more than just our bodies. Ideas that could never, ever happen.

But I could make him an omelet.

I set about chopping vegetables and meats, picking through leftovers for something to bulk up the meal while I warmed a skillet on the stove. Once I had the pan with the onions and green peppers on the heat, I began breaking eggs into a bowl for whipping. All while ignoring the man behind me. But I felt him—knew he watched me work. And I sort of liked it.

"You look good in my kitchen," he said suddenly, his slow smile spreading when I spun and stared. "Comfortable. You look *comfortable* cooking in my kitchen."

That's not what he meant, and we both knew it. Still, I shrugged and turned back to the eggs, hoping he missed the flush I could feel spreading up my neck and cheeks. "It's an easy kitchen to look good in. Your wood floors are amazing."

"They came from one of our first harvests of beetle kill pine. We used my house for some of the mill's promotional pictures when we moved into that niche."

"What type of wood is that—your beetle kill? And why is it blue?"

"It's pine. Ponderosa pine, to be exact. At least, that's what we try to focus on."

"Why Ponderosa?"

"The wood holds moisture better than lodgepole. The beetles introduce a fungus into the tree, and that smoky color is the stain from it. The more moisture in the wood, the better the fungus grows and spreads, the better the color variations when we mill it."

"Huh. I'd never heard of it before I moved here, though there wasn't much logging going on where I grew up."

"It's become something of a trendy product. One we specialize in. Harvesting can be a bitch, though."

"Because the trees are so dry?"

"Yeah. Ponderosas in our area tend to be centuries old, and they need to stay on the mountain for a handful of years after their death to give the fungus time to stain the wood. Forest fires, falling trees, and landslides as the roots that held the mountains together give way aren't uncommon. Harvesting those trees takes a lot of time and planning, more than most other sorts of trees."

I frowned over my shoulder at him. "How do you deal with all that and still make any money?"

His lips kicked up into a smile that made me catch my breath. "I'm a military man, honey—we plan for all the things that can go wrong and surround ourselves with the best people."

Right. Soldier Alder. No, more than soldier...so much more. Alder had been a Green Beret. I turned back to the skillet and added the rest of the veggies and meats to warm through. "I knew you were in the Army but not...that. Not a Green Beret."

"*That* was a long time ago."

"How long?" I'd never asked his age. Maybe I should have, but it hadn't seemed to matter. Suddenly, I was curious about all things Alder.

Thankfully, Alder didn't seem to mind. "I joined the Army right after high school. Spent fourteen years in it. Been home for five."

"But it stays with you—the training and stuff?"

He sighed, a heavy sound. One that made me turn again to look him over. He sat with his hands flat on the counter in front of him, a heavy frown marring his handsome face.

"You don't have to answer me." I turned back around, adding the eggs to the pan. "I didn't mean to push."

"You didn't push, I just... Yeah, the training stays with you, as does the memory of some of the missions. Good or bad, that sort of thing leaves an impression, especially after so many years in it."

"So fourteen years in the Army and like five home. You're..." I did some quick math in my head as I folded his omelet. "Thirty-seven?"

"Thirty-six. My birthday's in October." He paused, the silence heavy. Weighted almost. I'd known he was older than me, but not how much. I couldn't help but wonder if he thought I was too young for him.

Apparently, he assumed I was wondering if he was too *old* for me. "Does my age bother you?"

"Nope. I'm twenty-three, by the way. I'll be twenty-four in a few months." I turned again to face him, needing to see his face as I added, "Does my age bother *you*?"

He shook his head, his eyes staying on mine. His smile appearing slowly. "Not in the least."

"Then I think we're fine." A bold statement considering *we* weren't anything. Not really. And yet I'd opened my mouth and practically implied we were together.

"Only twenty-three and knows how to make an omelet?" Alder said, sounding more awake than he had moments before and thankfully ignoring my assumption. "You're way ahead of where I was at your age."

"I doubt that." I removed the pan from the flame to give the omelet a chance to set up as I found a plate and fork for him. "My mom made sure I could take care of my family from a young age."

"How old were you when she passed?"

Thoughts of my mom's death—of her murder at the hands of a rival MC while working at the shitty strip club the Soul Suckers ran—always caused an ache in my chest. "Nine."

"Only nine and you had to cook for your dad?"

"Stepdad, technically." I slid the food onto a plate and grabbed a fork, giving the unease of talking about my past a chance to settle so Alder wouldn't see it on my face. "My dad left before I was born, and my mom remarried when I was still a baby. I never knew any other father, so I tend to think of him as my dad. At least I did...when he was alive."

"I'm sorry—I shouldn't have brought up family."

"It's okay. I know how much of a mess I come from—there's no getting past all that."

He smiled up at me as I set the plate in front of him. "Are you joining me?"

"You eat. I'm fine."

God, the way he looked at me—as if he could see right into my thoughts. It made me want to confess my sins and beg for absolution. Luckily, the only sin he wanted to know about seemed to be about my eating habits.

"Did you have dinner?"

I shook my head, unable to look away from him. Unable to think when he stared at me as if I meant something to him, as if my failing to eat personally offended him and was something he needed to take care of.

What I wouldn't give for a man who cared so much about something so basic.

A man exactly like Alder Kennard.

"No dinner? Then you can share this omelet with me."

"I made it for you," I said, my voice barely more than a whisper. The tightness in my chest making it hard to breathe. But Alder heard me. He always seemed to be paying far more attention to me than I expected.

"And I want to share it with you." Alder stood and headed to the row of cabinets, grabbing a second plate and fork before coming back. "Have some."

"I shouldn't."

"Shye." His blue eyes held mine, his face so very serious. So very intense. "Have a meal with me. Please. You've been avoiding me for days, and I'd really like that to stop now. Even if only for a few minutes. I've missed you."

Was there a woman on earth who could refuse him when he looked at them like that? With eyes on fire and a longing on his face unlike any I'd ever seen? If there was, she was a stronger woman than me.

"Okay." My surrender earned me a smile. I followed his lead and took a seat at the dining table, accepting the plate with the chunk of omelet on it that he handed me. "Thank you."

He took a bite, closing his eyes and groaning as he chewed. "I should be the one thanking you. This is amazing."

I shrugged and bit my lip, trying not to preen at his words. "Eat up, then. Though I'm sorry you're having to eat eggs again after your dinner at the truck stop." I frowned. "I didn't think about that when I offered to make you an omelet."

"I didn't have dinner at the truck stop."

"But...you eat there every night."

His fork froze halfway to his mouth, just a pause. One that piqued my interest. What was he thinking?

It didn't take long to find out. "Truth be told, I don't eat at the truck stop every night. Only the ones when you're working."

That was...what? "But...you've been coming in every night for years."

He nodded, his movements slow again. Looking almost nervous. "Three years, but only on the nights that you work. Since the first time I met you."

My heart thumped, his admission a punch to my system that I wasn't prepared for. I had no idea what to say to that. No idea whatsoever. He'd been visiting the truck stop five days a week for three years. Eating that food and drinking their horrible coffee.

Oh. My. God. The coffee.

I sat back, sure I had to have the most shocked look on my face. "You don't actually like the coffee at the truck stop, do you?"

He shook his head, silent. Watching me as the puzzle pieces slipped into place.

"But you drink so much of it."

He coughed, turning away from my stare. "You filling up my cup gives me a chance to talk to you."

Flabbergasted. That was the only word I could think of to explain my reaction to his confession. He ate out five nights a week and drank horrible coffee by the gallon. All to see me.

"Alder—"

"Eat, Shye," he interjected. "Don't think so much about it, just eat with me."

How could I not think about it? About the fact that he'd suffered night after night through horrible coffee and spent so much money on greasy food to be close to me? To talk to me. What man would do such a thing? For three long years?

Alder Kennard would. And at that moment, he wanted me to put aside his sweetness and eat with him. So I ate. No words necessary, no conversation required. My thoughts, though, stayed busy. Focused on him, of course. On his kindness, his care, his actions around me. Every interaction we'd had that I'd thought was just Alder being himself, I reevaluated them all, looking for a pattern. For some sign of his interest in me that I'd missed.

And there were hundreds of them.

The tension built within me, my blood running hot under my skin as my new reality formed around me. As the truth that Alder Kennard wanted me for more than a friendly chat truly settled in. My body responded to his nearness without intention. Heating and throbbing in all the right places. The silence between us felt comfortable, though. Easy. So I pushed all that desire and lust down to be dealt with later. Right at that moment, he wanted us to enjoy a meal together. I could give that to him.

Having someone to sit across from was definitely something I'd missed these last few years. I hadn't really allowed myself to admit my loneliness, though. I'd simply accepted it as part of my penance. One meal with Alder and the idea of eating alone again seemed like another version of my own personal hell. I did my best to enjoy every second, to stay in the moment and be with him. Because it could all end in a matter of hours. Seconds, even. All it took was one Soul Sucker coming to Alder's door, and the blissful feeling of eating dinner with the man would be gone forever.

If it weren't so late, I would have stayed at that table for hours. But neither of us seemed to have the energy even if we both definitely appeared not to want to leave. We sat with empty plates, not moving. Staying together as the minutes ticked closer and closer to dawn. At least until the exhaustion became too much to bear.

Alder's stormy eyes met mine when I yawned, his head cocked. "You don't need to stay up with me. Go on to bed."

I didn't want to, but I couldn't keep my eyes open another minute.

"It *is* late." I stood, grabbing my dirty dish. "I'll clean up my mess—"

His hand on my wrist froze me, his eyes locking me in place. "I'll take care of it. You go get some rest."

"I can—"

This time, he grabbed my hand, weaving his fingers through mine before bringing them to his lips. His kiss searing my skin and making me shiver. "I don't say things I don't mean, Shye. Go on up to bed. I'll clean up."

I nodded, hanging on to him a moment too long. Letting my imagination run wild. This was what it would be like to be with him—late nights, me taking care of him, and Alder looking at me like I was his world. I never wanted to let go.

But there was no way I could hold on to him, no way to make up for what I'd done so that I could even deserve him.

"Goodnight, Alder," I said as I pulled my hand away. Severing our connection once again.

"Goodnight, honey. And thank you for the omelet."

Tormented and knowing I was too confused to sleep, I slipped up the stairs, my skin still burning from his touch, my heart full from his presence. But deep down? There was no way. He'd never understand, and on the off chance he did, he'd never stop trying to seek vengeance for me.

He could *not* know my past, so this chemistry was nothing but a distraction. A temporary one. Once he found out why the Soul Suckers were after me, how I'd helped them protect their business in the woods, he'd hate me.

But I likely had a few more days, at least. A little more time to pretend I had a chance with him. To imagine a future we'd never have. I could take care of him, and he could continue looking at me like I mattered.

Soon enough, though, it'd all end.

And I'd never see him again.

———

ALDER

Shye had made me food. Sitting in my quiet kitchen, the one that still showed signs of her presence, I stared down at my empty plate and tried to wrap my head around that fact. I couldn't remember the last time a woman had cooked for me. Maybe never, really. Definitely not since I'd moved back to Justice after the Army. And she'd done it with a smile on her face, so beautiful I could hardly breathe.

I'd come home from my meeting at Deacon's ready to throw something through a wall, pissed and exhausted and running on empty. The needs around me had all piled up—the need to search out that fucking meth lab, the need to safely burn the place to the ground, and the need to harvest some fucking wood to pay the bills. All while fighting to keep my town safe. So many pieces to manage—something I had years of experience with, and yet the idea had still given me a headache. I'd needed a snack, a good wank session in the shower while I imagined my own personal blonde angel doing devilish things, and a solid night's sleep.

I'd figured Shye would be asleep when I walked in, but finding her awake, as if waiting up for me? In *my* kitchen? That sight had brushed away everything bad about my day. Had made me feel like a fucking king coming home to his queen.

And then things had gotten even better, because she hadn't run away and hid like she'd been doing the past few days. She'd stayed. Seeing her smile as if she were glad I'd walked through the door, getting to touch her, having her cook for me. I could almost pretend she truly was mine. That maybe after a late dinner, I'd take her upstairs and kiss every single inch of her. Sink inside her and pump her full of my cock. I'd been dreaming of it for days, ever since I'd licked her pretty pussy. I'd held myself in check for the past three years, waiting for her to give me a sign. That night in the truck stop kitchen, I'd finally broken down and taken what I wanted. Or started to, at least. And she'd liked it. Had responded with no hesitation or awkwardness—just full-on need and desire.

Tonight, I'd been given a different kind of intimacy. The kind that spoke of connection. Sitting in the quiet and enjoying a meal my girl had prepared, with her sitting across from me, the simple act of eating with one another in a comfortable, casual situation. I never wanted to eat alone again.

I needed to convince her to give us a chance.

Exhausted but too regimented not to clean up after myself, I washed the dishes and put them away, wiping down the counters once I was done. When I had the kitchen back to rights, I turned off the lights and headed upstairs. I had to pass my guest room on the way to my own. Usually, I didn't even glance at the door. A man could only be tempted so much before he caved. Tonight, though, I didn't just look...I stopped. I leaned in and listened.

The soft, rhythmic lilt of her voice slipped through the wood door. Singing. She was singing in there. I hoped that meant she'd found a moment of happiness in all this chaos. Maybe she was growing more comfortable in my house. Maybe even with me.

A man could dream.

Not wanting to be a total creeper—or to kick down her door and pull her into my bed—I headed the rest of the way down the hall. It was harder to do than ever before. I didn't want to leave her alone, didn't want anything in between us. But she deserved her privacy, and I had yet to earn my place in her bed. So I trudged, grumbling under my breath the entire way.

My cell phone rang as I reached my bedroom. Deacon. With a sigh, I swiped to answer.

He didn't wait for a greeting. "Our boy just left."

Our boy...which meant Camden. And, this late? That could only mean he'd needed some serious sobering-up time. "How bad?"

"Bad enough for me to want to call you and make sure you knew."

Fuck. "I'll send Finn over in a few hours to check on him and remind him what's at stake. A little come to Jesus and coffee might be in order."

"Agreed. I like taking the guy's money, but he's been here every single night since Leah's death, often well after closing time. No one wants to watch a good man collapse under his grief, and he's heading down a path that's hard to come back from."

Same as Finn had—which meant we needed to watch my youngest brother as well. This loss would leave a scar too deep to heal if we didn't get in front of things. "I'll take care of it."

"Good. And one more thing? There's chatter about the Soul Suckers, concerning you and Shye."

"What sort of chatter?"

"The sort that makes the talk seem casual but probably means they're looking for her and know you're somehow involved."

A violent rage burned through me. "They won't put their fucking hands on her."

"I get that, and I understand it, but you gotta look at this from the other side. *Why* are they looking for her? What's she mean to them that they'd put any sort of priority on finding her? Because I doubt it's your tie to her that's bringing her into the conversation. If anything, I think it's the other way around. We need to figure out how she's tangled up with the Soul Suckers before we get too deep into this, you know?"

I did know, but I didn't have answers for him. In fact, I hadn't thought too much about Shye's involvement with the club, or even if she'd ever had any. But she'd known they were a national club, and her trailer had been awfully close to where Camden had run into those members. Plus, if the meth lab really was in that area, her place was practically sitting on top of it.

I hated when Deacon made so much damn sense. "We'll get the info. We've hit roadblocks no matter which way we go with trying to get intel on these guys—it's like they're all fucking ghosts—but I'm calling in a few favors. And I'll be getting a team together to head out to the Hansen woods to search for anything that could be considered a kitchen since Parris thinks that's what the deal is out there. Might take me a few days—I don't want to send anyone in unprepared, so we need to acquire a few pieces of hardware."

"Whatcha need?"

"This shit's just chemicals mixed together, right? I figure each man needs some sort of breathing mask in case of fumes. I don't want anyone coming back with jacked-up lungs because I sent them out to hunt down a meth lab."

"I'll take care of the equipment. Give me a day or two to figure out exactly what we need, and I'll get it here."

Deacon always came through, so that was definitely one thing off my plate. "Thanks. I'll prep the guys on what we'll be looking for while we wait."

"Seems like a solid plan." He breathed out, the whoosh coming through the speaker. "And man, I hate to say it, but I wouldn't be a good wingman if I didn't. I know you've got your heart set on that girl, but be careful out there. Until we know how all these pieces come together, she might be more dangerous than we think."

Shye...dangerous? No fucking way. But Deacon and I had worked together for a long time, and I trusted him. If he said I needed to look, I'd fucking look. I'd hate it, but I'd look.

Even if it killed me to do so. "I can take care of things out here. Anything else?"

"Yeah, you owe me ten bucks for the bourbon."

And if I tried to pay him, he'd toss that bill back in my face. "I'm good for it."

"You always say that."

"And I always mean it."

I hung up and tossed my phone next to the bed before falling back on my mattress and closing my eyes. Such a long fucking day. A long week. The fires, Leah's death, Shye's silence and anger with me, the meeting with the biker Marine, Camden's likely fall into alcoholism... I didn't know if there was anything else I could take.

But no matter what Deacon said, thinking about Shye only brought about good feelings. My instincts were solid, and she'd never given me reason to think she was anything other than what she appeared to be. She ignited no worry or distrust with me. Just the warm sensation when she smiled my way, or how hard I got when she laughed. I'd look into her past because it made sense, but I doubted it would matter unless I were so far off base about her that I had a murderer in my house.

I almost laughed at the very idea of that.

Besides, whether she was tangled up in the Soul Suckers or not didn't matter. There was no badness in her, no trickery or ill intention. Shye Anderson was as sweet as they came, and she was mine. I'd do anything to help her or to keep her safe. Anything to keep her with me. Anything to finally get those dark eyes looking at me with want instead of worry. I could picture it—she'd looked at me that way after our kiss. Just for a moment before I'd carried her into the office and ate her pussy like a starving man. That picture—the memory of those big eyes of hers so heated and hungry—was something to fight for. Something to yearn to get back. Didn't hurt that it also made my cock positively leak.

"Fuck." I groaned as I got to my feet and headed for the bathroom. I tugged my clothes off as I went, tossing them in the hamper and turning on the hot water before shutting the door. I needed a shower and a shave so I could think or sleep, whichever happened first.

Good or bad, though, standing naked under the stream of hot water only made my thoughts of Shye come back. And they turned dirtier. My cock jutted out from my hips, painful and thick with my need for the little blonde. I couldn't imagine her being a danger to me. She was a desire, a want that simply wouldn't release me. I couldn't consider her to be something detrimental to my life. I could only focus on how much I longed for her touch. How badly I wanted to keep her with me, to sleep in her bed every night or hold her in mine. I'd fuck her in my shower every morning if she let me, would drop to my knees on the tile and bury my face between her thighs before making her come on my tongue over and over again. All of it—I wanted every part of her.

But for tonight, I only had my hand.

It took me fewer than ten strokes of my cock to hit my peak—three years without the touch of a woman had earned me a first-class masturbator medal. Shye deserved better, though. She deserved to be teased and touched, to be brought to the edge again and again before falling over so her orgasms would be the best she'd ever had. If I got her in my bed, I'd spend half the night with my face in her pussy. Make her come on my tongue and my fingers until she begged me to stop. I'd wring her out good—make sure I had my stroke game on point so she'd crave my cock as much as I craved her touch. It'd take some time, but I'd work my ass off to make sure my girl was always satisfied.

Hell, if I got her in my bed, I'd never let her out.

Chapter Nine

SHYE

Five days after I stopped with the silent treatment and I nearly felt at home at Alder's place. A sort of habitual comfort had settled over me as I'd gone from mute and stubborn to accepting and thankful. But while eating dinner with him every night made my heart practically sing, sleeping down the hall from him was temporary. No matter how much he seemed to want me to stay.

So I did my best to earn my keep even though he protested. I cleaned each day from the ceilings to the baseboards, making sure every inch of his home sparkled. Whenever he noticed, and he definitely noticed, he'd huff and puff and tell me I was a guest, but I felt better knowing I'd done something for him. And of course, I cooked. Breakfasts, dinners, I even packed him lunches. And every day, as I handed him that brown paper bag with whatever food I'd put together for him inside, that hard face of his would soften, and his blue eyes would positively burn as they held mine. I lived for those moments, for the sweet kiss he'd place on my forehead before he whispered thanks. For the way he made me feel needed. Wanted. For the way he simply noticed me. A woman could get used to being noticed and appreciated.

"Another amazing meal." Alder pushed back from the table, setting his napkin on his empty plate.

I bit back a smile. "It's just meatloaf, but I'd hoped you'd like it."

"I loved it. How could I not when you made it for me?" He stood and gathered the plates, brushing off my objection before I even had time to make it. Alder was an equal-partner type of guy—if I cooked, he took care of clean up. Something I'd never experienced before. My father had treated me like a scullery maid at times, claiming he worked to pay for everything, so I needed to do the rest. My stepbrother had been worse. Of course, all the men I'd met in their circle of biker friends tended to see women the same way—as their own personal staff. Cooks, maids, and whores...what else could we be?

Alder never behaved the way they had. But it wasn't just Alder's sweetness that attracted me. He was hot as sin. Tall and muscled, with that dangerous air about him. The one that warned others he could and would take them down if they crossed him. Why that was such a turn-on, I had no idea, but it was. My soaking wet panties and the long, hot showers I took every night with the handheld showerhead between my legs were a testament to that fact.

Five days—I'd been living in a hell of desire for five long days. If only I could stop watching him, but that was an impossibility. The man was a study in human musculature. Alder's entire back clenched and released as he rinsed the dishes and moved them to the dishwasher, his arms bulging at the movements. And his ass—so very bitable—seemed to be a magnet for my eyes. His thick thighs filled out his jeans in a way that spoke of pure strength, and I'd already rubbed myself against what sat behind the zipper. Every long, hard inch, ready for—

Those types of thoughts weren't helping my situation.

"I'm going to run and take a shower." Alder turned, completely distracting me from my pervy thoughts about biting him on his backside. And a few other places. "How about we watch a movie after I'm done?"

"Sure." I coughed, my voice too deep and breathy for casual conversation. "Sounds good."

Alder cocked his head, still watching me. Inspecting me again. "You okay, Shye?"

Of course not. I could normally keep my mind off the idea of him bending me over the table long enough to have a conversation. Tonight was not a normal night. "I'm good. Great. Just...worried about my job."

Because I hadn't been back since the night he'd pulled me out of there. The night of Camden's house fire. The break felt a bit like a vacation, to be honest. One I couldn't afford.

Alder frowned. "I know this is inconvenient, but I need you safe. I've got your boss holding your spot for another two weeks."

"I know." And I did. But it seemed like so much trouble.

"Good." He walked past me, running his hand over my shoulder and sending shivers up my spine. "I'll be down in ten. Why don't you pick something out to watch? We'll see if you can stay up long enough to finish it this time."

"I can't help it if you picked a boring movie last night." I grinned as his laugh boomed through the house, his bitable self heading up the stairs. But my smile fell quickly as my thoughts turned to the farce between us. If only this were *real*. If only I truly belonged to him and this was how my life played out. Sweet hugs when he came home, dinners together, and cuddling on the couch afterward as we watched a movie. Normal couple stuff.

Or would we do that stuff if we were actually together? Maybe instead, he'd take me upstairs right after dinner and shower with me, or throw me on his bed and use my body to do away with the frustration of the day. Maybe all our time would be taken up by our desire for one another—a not-at-all-unpleasant thought.

Impossible, though. A dream. A fairy tale, but I was no princess in the tower. And there was nothing I could do about that.

But I could pretend...for now.

My non-princess self finally left the dining chair I'd been planted in for half the evening, and I turned off the lights in the kitchen before heading for the den. Alder had an extreme movie addiction, both in physical and streaming formats. Action, mystery, comedy, classics—his tastes ran the gamut. He even had some rom-coms and romantic tragedies in his collection. Something that had surprised me the first time I'd seen them. Tonight, I might actually make him watch one.

But as I grabbed the remote from its dedicated home on the table next to Alder's leather couch, lights flared in the window. Someone driving by, it seemed. Alder lived far enough out that seeing others was a rarity, so I watched the lights as they moved closer. As they slowed. As they stopped at Alder's driveway.

"Oh no." Dropping the remote, I raced for the stairs, slipping and sliding on the wood floors. I checked that the front door was locked—it was, Alder always secured the doors when he came in or out—and double-timed it up the steps. I didn't pause, didn't even think about what I was doing or what state Alder would be in until I ran through his bedroom and turned the corner into his bathroom.

And then I froze.

Naked. Alder was naked in the shower. Steam billowed all around him, but there was no ignoring the naked before me. Every dip of muscle, every curve of bone. Naked. Every inch of his hardness. The inches his hand stroked at a leisurely sort of pace. Totally, utterly naked.

I drenched my panties in exactly two-point-one seconds, and his cocky grin when he caught me watching him with my mouth agape certainly didn't help.

"You plan to stand there all night, or are you going to climb in here with me, honey?"

Definitely climb in. Definitely. Except...

"A car."

His brow tightened, and he turned off the water. "What?"

"A car. Outside. I saw a car stop in your driveway."

His smile fell, his face going hard and mean as he yanked the shower door open. Without a word, he raced past me, grabbing a towel to throw around his hips before barreling into his bedroom. I followed, keeping my back to the wall to stay out of his way, my heart thumping fast in my chest. Alder was big enough to be scary on his best day. Pissed off? He was a nightmare. I wasn't afraid of him, though, more of what he'd do if that someone in the driveway turned out to be a trespasser. More of if he'd get hurt dealing with the threat.

When Alder turned from the nightstand, he had a gun in his hand. A gun and a cordless phone. Neither of which I could wrap my head around until he stood right in front of me.

He had. A gun. In his hand.

"Lock my bedroom door behind me and stay up here," he said, pressing the phone into my limp hand. "If I'm not back in three minutes, press and hold five to call Gage."

The words *no, no, no* skated through my head, but I couldn't speak. Couldn't remember what words were, so I couldn't tell Alder how terrified I felt. For him, not me. But my silence gave him no reason to pause. Alder made sure I had the phone in my grip, kissed my forehead, and ran out of the room. Gone to fight whoever dared to cross onto his property.

The thought of fairy tales danced through my head again. Of the stories my mother had read to me. The ones where valiant princes raced off to defend their darling princesses. Those fables that had poisoned my mind as a child and made me want things that were impossible. I'd known for years that I wasn't a princess, but Alder wasn't a prince either. He was the dragon at the gates of the castle, and he would burn you to ash if you threatened what was his. Why that protectiveness was so arousing to me, I might never know. But it was, even if I was playing the part of the cook in the story. The cook could be with the dragon, right? Maybe?

Must. Stop. Thinking. About. Impossible. Things.

Knocking myself out of my panicked—and slightly lustful—stupor, I hurried to close and lock the bedroom door as he'd told me to. Once secured, I crouched between the bed and the wall with his phone clutched in my hand. And then I counted.

One, two, three...

The seconds ticked by slower than I ever would have imagined. By fifty-two, I was edging around the corner of the bed. At eighty-nine, I had my ear pressed to the door. At one-hundred-and-one, a loud bang sounded from somewhere far away, and I jumped. Losing count.

"Please, please, please, be safe." I clung to the phone, listening again. Waiting for some sign that Alder was okay. Terrified he wouldn't be.

If I wouldn't have had my ear to the door, I wouldn't have heard the soft snick from downstairs. I knew that sound—had spent the last few days loving and hating it depending on which way Alder was going. The sound was the latch catching as the front door closed, and that could mean Alder was back. Or someone else had just walked into the house.

Forget three minutes. If Alder needed backup, he needed it now.

With a shaking hand, I unlocked the bedroom door and slowly, quietly opened it. The hall appeared empty, the light on and the path to the staircase clear. Maybe if I leaned out, I could see. I just needed to know who had come through the door. So I leaned and I crept and I slipped a few feet down the hall until I could see most of the front landing, my finger hovering over that number five on the phone the entire time.

Alder stepped into the area at the bottom of the stairs, looking up and catching my gaze. "It was Bishop."

Three words. That was all it took to unravel the knot of fear holding me back. It also unleashed every bit of self-control I'd been hanging on to for these past few days.

I dropped the phone and ran down the stairs, throwing myself at the mostly naked man before me. Needing to feel his flesh against mine and to know he'd returned safe and whole. Wanting it too much to resist. Of course, Alder caught me, pulling me close, wrapping his arms around my body and lifting me right off the floor.

Safe. Both of us are safe.

I didn't even pretend to hold back, didn't even try to stop myself. I pressed my lips to his and dove into a kiss he quickly overtook. Desperation fed my desire and broke all my restraints. I clung to him, my hands fisting his hair and holding him in place. *This*...this was what I needed. The connection between us, the flare of chemistry. Him.

When I whimpered against his lips, Alder slid his tongue into my mouth and groaned. Delicious, and exactly what I wanted. My back hit the wall behind the door, his hips pinning me in place. His hardness wedged between us. I had nothing left, no sense of propriety or worry about what the future would bring. No feelings of not being enough or of being wrong for him. All I had was a deep sense of relief that the man I cared so much about was still alive. That the dragon at the gates was off his leash and safely within the castle walls once more.

My dragon at the gates.

"What do you want, Shye?" Alder's grumbled question as he moved his attention to my neck sent a shot of lust straight between my legs. "I'll give you everything, just tell me what you want. Don't make me guess."

My sweet, sweet dragon. "Everything. I want all of you."

He growled, his hands so rough as they moved to grip my thighs tight. So perfect. "Then show me, honey. Take what you need from me."

I rocked against him, grinding myself all over the hard line of his erection as he moved with me. And when his lips traveled down to my neck, when he bit and kissed and licked a trail to my shoulder, I chanted his name. He liked that for sure. His movements growing rougher with every syllable uttered. He rolled his hips into mine in a way that showed exactly how strong and graceful his body could be, the soft growl he made on every thrust ratcheting the growing pressure inside of me higher until we were nothing but need and desire and friction. I doubted his towel remained around his hips, somehow knew that he stood naked as he pressed against me. And I didn't have a single care about that. I wanted him naked. Wanted him inside me, too.

"Christ. You're just so small." He gripped my thighs harder and higher, pulling me up a little, making me yelp as he rubbed himself right against my clit. "That's the spot, yeah, sweet girl? That's the one that feels good? Gonna make you come like this. Right here against the wall since my fucking bed seems too far away. Do you want that? Want me to make your pussy mine right here?"

Such a deliciously dirty mouth. I nodded into his shoulder, clinging and moving in time with him. There was no break, no pause, no holding back —if it weren't for my yoga pants and panties, we'd be having sex right there against the wall of his entryway. And I would have been thrilled. In fact, I'd never cursed my clothing more in my life.

"So small, so small," Alder chanted, lifting me as if I weighed nothing. "I bet your pussy's small too. Bet I'm going to have to go real slow when I finally get inside you. You're going to squeeze my cock half to death, aren't you, honey?"

I couldn't think enough to answer. Every brush of his body against mine sent shock waves through me, every push making me gasp his name as I chased that feeling. The one that would take me right over the top. So close, so close. A little more…just a little—

"I'm going to have you riding me in no time, little one. I'll lick you until you're so soft and wet and ready, then I'll stuff you full of my cock. I'll train your tight little cunt to take every inch of me."

That did it. Alder's dirty mouth shoved me right over the edge, my orgasm ripping through me. My head hit the wall as I yelped his name, my body bowing as he pushed me through my pleasure, as he growled and stiffened against me. As he came, soaking right through my clothes and leaving me shaking in his arms.

"Jesus fuck," he said, a little breathless, a little handsy still as well. "That was a real nice greeting. I'd take that over dinner on the table any day of the fucking week."

I chuckled, holding him tighter. Unable to stop touching. "I'm sorry I attacked you. I was just so worried."

"I'm not even close to sorry. If you want to greet me that way every day, I'll die a happy man." He pulled back, placing a gentle kiss on my lips. "C'mon. Let's go to bed."

Reality slammed back into me, and I froze. I couldn't sleep with him, couldn't let him see me naked. See the scars and the proof of who owned me.

But Alder was nothing if not perceptive. He laughed, squeezing me once before setting me on my feet. "To sleep, Shye. That was all a little too real for me, and I want to make sure you're safe. If you don't sleep in my bed, I'll end up awake half the night worrying about you."

He grabbed his gun and towel off the floor—yep, definitely naked—set the alarm, and tugged me toward his room, not giving me time to argue. I wasn't even sure if I would have anyway. Sleeping in the same bed with Alder was a dream. One that was apparently about to come true.

Alder dragged me into his room, letting me go only once he'd closed and locked the door behind us. He tucked the gun back in his nightstand before heading to his dresser to don a pair of boxer briefs, the fabric stretching over his naked flesh. Which served as a reminder of my own state of dress.

"I need to change." I tugged at the waistband of my pants when he turned my way. "I'm all wet."

His smoky grin nearly made me want to climb him again. "Wet...with my come and yours."

Darn that filthy mouth. "Yeah."

"Gotta admit, I like the thought of that." He grabbed a white shirt and stalked my way, dropping to his knees and pulling my pants just over my hips before leaning forward to place a kiss on my hip bone. "Can I strip you down, honey?"

My step backward was more instinct than anything, my thoughts going straight to the scars on my back at his words.

"Never mind." He kissed my hip again, those eyes giving nothing away, then rose to his feet. "I don't mean to push so hard. Use my bathroom to change, and then we'll go to bed."

Such a good man, and one I had somehow been blessed to cross paths with. It was going to hurt like hell when he finally turned his back on me.

Happy, excited, and dreading the next few days all at the same time, I scurried into the en suite, closing the door behind me and taking a deep breath. The man drove me mad in the best way, but I couldn't want more than what we had. Shouldn't. I wouldn't get the prince—or the dragon—in the end. I could only hope to borrow him for a bit.

And prepare for the agony of letting him go.

Once I'd stripped and tugged his shirt over my head—sans panties, though the hem ended at my knees so I figured I was covered enough—I opened the door and shut off the light. The sight before me froze me in my tracks.

Alder sat in his bed, the blankets pulled up around his waist, and his deep stare on me. He'd turned off the overhead light, using the small lamp on his nightstand to cast the room in a soft, golden glow. The shadows across his bare chest accentuated his deep muscles, made the hair scattered across the width of him and following the midline down, down, down past his belly button all the more visible. I nearly whimpered at the sight of him.

He held out his hand, and he smiled. At me. "C'mon, honey. Get in here with me."

No thought, no decision, no hesitation. I headed straight for him, climbing onto his big bed and slipping under the covers as he held them up for me. Once I was comfortable, he reached to turn off the light, then slid down deeper. Holding me tight. Making me feel so small and delicate, fragile almost. And protected.

"Sleep, beautiful girl. I'll keep you safe."

And for just a moment, wrapped in his arms with his big body covering mine, his scent completely surrounding me as I closed my eyes against the dark, I almost believed he could.

Chapter Ten

ALDER

I'd never really been all that chipper in the morning, but that was before spending an entire night with Shye in my arms. My girl had slept peacefully against my chest, her hands pillowed on my stomach. I hadn't slept—too wound up to rest, too hard to even try after the little bump and grind session in the hallway. Still the best night of my life, at least so far. I hoped for even better...for more. I hoped like hell for that. But Shye hadn't been ready last night, so I'd held back. Given without taking much for myself. I had long-term plans for her—I could be patient if I had to be. Special Forces had taught me to take my time when planning a mission, and I'd use every skill I had to make sure she stayed mine.

I was in the middle of making breakfast when I heard Shye's soft footsteps on the stairs. The rhythm sounded off, though—too tentative. Too slow. Cautious in a way that screamed she felt uncomfortable for some reason. I couldn't have that.

"Get down here and give me a good morning kiss, honey." I turned, thinking a smile would push her along, but the sight on the stairs stole my smile and my ability to move. Shye stood there in a beam of sunshine, wearing nothing but my white cotton T-shirt. The light seemed to set her hair on fire, soft pinks and oranges burning through the blond strands.

My shirt swallowed her all the way down to her knees—there was no denying that garment belonged to a man in her life. The only man in her life. Me.

Mine.

I choked back the possessive need rising within me, but Shye must have caught it. Or noticed something else that made her nervous. She cocked her head, still standing way too far away from me. Still hiding on the stairs.

"What?" she asked, not moving an inch. "Why are you staring at me like that?"

Like a man in love? Like a man about to grab his woman and secret her away to his bed for a few days? Like a man whose dick pounded in his pants at the very idea of finding its home in the heaven between her legs? Like a man who'd throw every bit of food he'd made into the trash and instead feast on her pretty pussy?

She'd run away if I told her any of that, though. "Because you're beautiful, and because I like seeing you in my clothes. Now, come eat. I'll even let you keep your lips to yourself."

Shye didn't move—looking so fucking adorable as she bit her plump bottom lip—so I turned back to the stove to give her a second to collect herself. Some days, she really lived up to that name of hers. But as I plated the bacon, she slipped in beside me at the counter. At the touch of her hand on my arm, I jerked and looked down at her, seeing the tension in the stiff set of her shoulders. That just wouldn't do.

"What's wrong?"

She shook her head before rising onto the balls of her feet and kissing the one place she could reach—my collarbone. The touch of her lips against my bare skin had the animal inside of me raging to take her, to make her ours. But I was a patient man. I'd waited three long years for her. I could wait out her shyness too.

Still, I wasn't about to ignore an opportunity. I leaned down before she could slip away, dropping a gentle kiss to her lips. Nothing too deep— closed mouth, soft and sweet. Just what she needed, apparently.

Shye smiled when we finally broke apart. "Good morning."

"Did you sleep okay?"

"Like a baby." She headed for the cabinet and began pulling plates and glasses down for us. "Thank you for letting me stay with you. I don't think I would have slept a wink alone."

Letting her—as if I'd given her a choice. "You're welcome, honey. You can stay in my bed whenever you want. I liked having you there."

Her cheeks darkened, her head dropping to stare at the counter, but I saw the smile tugging at her pretty lips. My shy girl.

"Why don't you grab yourself some coffee?" I suggested as I pulled the sausages from the pan. "Breakfast is ready, and I'd like to enjoy it with you before I head into work."

And I needed to get food on the table before I lifted her onto the counter and ate *her* instead.

———

Not thinking about Shye when I was supposed to be working had become difficult, though it definitely got easier that morning. Even if only for a moment.

"The masks are here." Finn hurried up the stairs to my office, followed by Deacon, who carried a cardboard box.

"You got the right kind?" I stood and headed over, my interest in the gear Deacon had found piqued. I couldn't help it—someone brought new hardware in, and I became a kid on Christmas just waiting to play with the new toys.

Something I doubted I'd get to do.

"You trusted me to figure out what we needed to burn down a meth lab. I figured out what we needed to burn down a meth lab. You going to question me now?" Deacon raised an eyebrow and stood back, letting Finn and me dig through the boxful of full-face respirators.

I picked one up, running a finger over the inner filter. Hard-core. "Not really. What do you think, Finn?"

My brother pulled out a mask, lifting it up and down as if checking the weight. "I can have guys in the woods in an hour if you want me to lead them."

A pang of worry knocked me in the gut, one that was more habit than instinct. I always worried about Finn, but I couldn't babysit him every day. I also couldn't blow off work to tackle the job myself.

"Do it."

Finn's eyes snapped to mine. "You're not coming?"

Fuck, I wanted to. "I've got a conference call with a lumber buyer out of Cleveland, and then a friend from the FBI is calling to share what he knows about the Soul Suckers. I trust you and your team to handle this. Just don't do anything if you find the place. Mark it, call it in, and trek back out. We'll make a plan once we get a verified location."

Finn nodded, glancing to Deacon as if for permission. Technically, Deacon was Finn's boss, so that wouldn't have been far from the truth.

Deacon shrugged. "I can handle the bar for a few hours. Go get your G.I. Joe on."

"Take Gage." I might have been fine with Finn going, but I still wasn't stupid enough to send any man out without serious backup, considering the threats against us. "He needs a long walk in the woods."

Finn shot me a smile. "You talking about Gage or Rex?"

"Same thing, kid," Deacon said, holding out his fist. Finn bumped knuckles with his boss before grabbing the box of masks and heading downstairs.

"Think he's going to find something?" Deacon asked, looking toward the stairs as if waiting for Finn to reappear.

"Yup." I had no doubts. A meth lab on that property would make a fuckton of sense considering what I'd learned from Parris and a few other people I'd gotten in contact with. The Soul Suckers were the biggest name in meth around these parts. The kitchen would be there, but so might a few men trying to get it either back in working order or emptying it out.

"Me too." Deacon gave me a smack on the arm before heading for the stairs himself. "And when he does, we'll take it out."

I grunted, my thoughts already swirling. It'd been almost two weeks since the fire at Shye's place. Just thirteen days since we first ran into trouble with the Soul Suckers, and already we had two homes destroyed and one dead friend in Justice. Take it out? If we found the kitchen, we'd fucking raze the place and the forest around it. And if we found any Soul Suckers in the area?

They wouldn't make it off the mountain.

Chapter Eleven

ALDER

That night, I turned down my road in the early evening. I'd been trapped in my office all damn day. The call with the FBI agent hadn't given me anything more than I already knew, so that had been a waste of time. But the worst had been fully work-related. Fucking lumber buyer out of Cleveland took a full two hours to explain in great detail how he had some rich client who thought the fungus stains of my beetle kill pine would be perfect for her kitchen floors, but only if they were more gray than blue and more solid than mottled. I had kept explaining that I couldn't control the damn beetles, but he'd refused to listen. He'd wanted a guarantee of color, which I couldn't provide him. I could only give him first refusal at the next lumber milled.

Truth was, the fungus—and therefore, the color—spread the longer the pines stood dead. The Hansen property had lost most of their trees before I'd come home eight years ago—I would have bet my business those would fit the client's needs, but I couldn't get to them. Not yet. Especially not with what was happening out at the property.

Finn and his team had found what they assumed was the meth kitchen —an old, abandoned barn in a heavily forested part of the ridge. Found it quick, too. If I hadn't known better, I'd have thought Finn knew the place was out there with how Gage described how fast the hunt had gone. Impossible, though. He would have told us if he'd known.

The team had set up a perimeter around the building so they could keep an eye on it without going inside. Once in place, two men would be in the air ready to take out anyone who came near. Snipers on security detail... Since Deacon hadn't gone on the search, that had to have been Gage's idea. I liked it.

Logging was hard enough, though, and adding the destruction of a drug house to our workload seemed almost foolish. Really, it was more of a precaution for the safety of my men who worked in those woods...and a loud fucking warning to the Soul Suckers to get their asses out of Justice. For good. The site would be guarded until we could send a strong enough crew to sweep the property—a crew I definitely *would* be leading—and the old, abandoned barn turned drug lab had to be destroyed. Then, and only then, could we even think of sending our teams up there to harvest.

Tomorrow, maybe the day after. I wanted this shit done, but we needed to monitor the area first. Make sure we had every bit of info we could garner before we stepped inside that kitchen. I'd rather go in filled with knowledge and plans than with guns blazing.

But the workday was finally over, and I craved a little time with my girl before falling back into planning lumber shipments, meth lab destruction, and subterfuge. Shye had been home alone all day. Well, not alone. I'd asked Bishop to handle his sales calls from my house in case of any trouble, so I wasn't surprised to see him sitting on my porch as I pulled into the drive.

"'Sup, brother." He grinned and rocked back in his chair once I'd stepped out of my truck. How the man managed to look like a rattlesnake ready to strike while smiling, I'd never know, but that was the impression he left. Apparently, I needed to watch out for his fangs.

"What's got you so giddy?"

He shrugged. "Your girl made me dinner, that's all."

Motherfucker. There it was—the bite. I shot a look at the door, willing Shye to come out of it. Wondering if she was still in the kitchen...if we'd have dinner together, or if she'd already eaten. If she'd been thinking of me at all today while I'd been obsessing over her. I must have looked as irritated as I felt at the thought of not getting my time with my girl because Bishop laughed.

"You are so far gone, man."

I ran a hand over my hair, unable to argue that. "Any news?"

Bishop got serious real quick. "Soul Suckers tried to stop at Katie's."

The only restaurant in town, recently opened by my little sister's best friend from high school. One sitting in a building I'd offered her rent-free for three years when she'd called to say she missed home and wanted to come back but needed a job. She had absolutely nothing to do with the Soul Suckers bullshit.

"*Tried* to stop?"

"Two guys on bikes made a few loops around Main Street then pulled up outside. Deacon was already there for lunch, so he secured the building when they first passed and kept Katie in the back with him."

Fuck me. "That was damn lucky timing, but I hate relying on luck. Next time, we might not have a man there."

"Which is why I've put the whole town on lockdown until we can set up some perimeters. I figured you wouldn't disagree that it's needed."

"Not a bit. You even got the post office to close?"

"Barney's sorting mail in his garage. Says he can do the pickup in the morning, then take everything home with him. He'll call people if anything important shows up. Otherwise, he'll hold it all until one of us can do his route with him."

"Jesus." I plopped down next to him, staring off over the driveway to the forest beyond. Main Street on lockdown, Katie having to hide in her own restaurant, Barney holding our mail so he didn't have to go out alone, and a motherfucking meth lab in the woods. We were under attack. "You think they're planning a hit on us, don't you?"

"Yup. I think they're going to come after someone here in a bit. Go for a direct blow to make a point. Question is who the focus of that happens to be." He stood, the floorboards groaning under his feet. "Lock up tight, man, and call one of us if anything seems out of the ordinary. You don't need to go chasing people down in a towel again."

Jackass. Still, I nodded, knowing I'd lock my shit down the second I walked inside. I couldn't risk Shye's safety. A thought that reminded me...

"Thanks."

Bishop turned, his brow furrowed. "For what?"

"Staying here today while I went to work. Keeping an eye on Shye."

His grin set my teeth on edge. "Oh no, that pleasure was all mine. She's really something, isn't she?"

Yeah, and that *something* was mine. My brother was the ladies man of the group—bouncing from bed to bed and never settling down. I couldn't blame him—his last girlfriend had really pulled a number on him. Still, he didn't get to bounce into Shye's bed. He didn't even get to fucking *think* about it.

I'd likely kill him if he tried. "Get out of here so I can go spend my evening with *my* girl."

"Yeah, yeah. Keep her all to yourself. A good brother would be willing to share."

"Not on your fucking life."

Bishop grinned and bounded for his truck, casual as ever, but I knew better. The man took his job seriously, took his duties to his brothers even more so, and he wouldn't fail at a task I'd assigned him. I knew I could trust him to be Shye's guard—he'd do whatever it took to make sure nothing happened to her because his brother needed him to. End of discussion. Didn't mean he wouldn't flirt with her every chance he got. Sometimes, you had to take the good with the bad. My brother was definitely both.

Bishop was almost to his truck before he turned back, suddenly looking serious. "She's a sweet girl, that one. Quiet, but definitely kind. I know Deacon's worried about her past, but if she's tied up in the Soul Suckers, it's not intentional. I just can't see it."

Yeah, neither could I. "I know."

He opened his driver's-side door and leaned against the body, still serious. Still thinking. "If she's in trouble, we'll be fighting more than just our shit. We'll need to handle hers as well."

"I know that, too."

"Just making sure. It throws a wrench into our plans, you know? They could come for you or for her, and we won't know until they get here."

Exactly, which was something that had been eating at me. "I'll keep her safe no matter what."

"I know you will, brother. And you've got me and Gage just a text away. He's been staying at my place while he works on that old cabin he's remodeling."

"You let that dog in your house?" Bishop was a bit of a neat freak—muddy paw prints and dog hair would likely drive him to drink.

"Trust me—Rex is the easier roommate to deal with." Bishop slipped inside his truck and rolled down the window as he started the engine. "Good luck."

I needed more than luck.

But as soon as I walked inside, my thoughts of the Soul Suckers, the possible meth lab, and the danger tied up in the two disappeared. Shye stood in the kitchen. No, not stood. Danced. The girl swung her hips and shook her ass in a way that should have been illegal. My blood rushed south, my cock filling to the point of pain in seconds. I couldn't move, couldn't even breathe, too panicked that anything I did would make her stop. I never wanted her to stop.

But she saw me, and when she did, she smiled. Gorgeous, stunning, beautiful...all too mellow for that moment. Something in her expression, in her happy eyes, called to me as much as her shaking ass had. I wanted her joy more than her body, her happiness more than my own. There was only so much I could do to guarantee those, only so much time to take my chance, so I finally gave myself permission to try.

I stalked across the kitchen without thought and grabbed her, pulling her against me. Bringing us together roughly. Her mouth opened on a gasp when I grabbed her ass, and I took advantage. Kissing her deep and rough, the way she deserved to be kissed. Sweet. She tasted so fucking sweet. And when she grabbed my arms and pulled me closer, when she slipped her hands up my neck and secured me to her...I was done.

I wanted her to be mine. Immediately and completely.

Unable to resist a second more, I gripped her thighs and lifted her little body up onto the counter. Still shorter than me, but closer. And just the right height to put my cock level with her pussy. She definitely noticed that fact. She wrapped her legs around my waist, pulling me in. Giving me all the green light I needed. I stepped closer and pulled her to the edge so I could press my cock against her. So I could hear those little mewls and gasps she'd made that night in the kitchen at her work. It felt like months had gone by since then, with nothing but sexual tension and need driving me through the days. But tonight... Tonight, we'd break through all that.

I thrust against her, tugging her into me, watching for any sort of reaction. I could feel the heat of her already. Could practically sense the wetness growing between her legs. Fuck, I wanted to taste it, make her shake and yell and lose control on my tongue. Needed it like air.

"Can't stay away," I mumbled, my fingers digging into the flesh of her ass as I yanked her against me. "Need you too much."

Shye groaned and followed my movements, telling me without words what she wanted. What she needed. I thrust harder, grunting on every press, hanging on to her hips to keep us connected. Turning us into a pair of lusting, needful beings hell-bent on the same goal. Fucking. Not making love, not screwing, not any other euphemism...we'd be fucking tonight. And I couldn't wait for it.

Shye gasped on a particularly rough bump, her head falling back and a groan rumbling through her chest. Laid out before me with her tits pushed up and her nipples hard. So fucking gorgeous, so completely mine, that my leash broke.

"That feel good?" I thrust harder when she nodded, clutching her tight. Making sure she felt every inch of my cock pressing against her. "Fuck, you're already shaking. Are you wet? Is that pretty pussy soaking your panties because of my cock?"

"Alder." My name sounded much like a rebuke, but her body never stopped moving, her hips rolling into mine. The girl wanted me, which worked in my favor because my cock wept for her. He'd have to wait, though. Three years of dreaming of this girl had left me with one particular thing I wanted, and it wasn't shoving my cock inside her. It was watching her fall apart at my hands or my mouth, over and over again. I'd gotten that first taste, stolen a second one just the night before, but I wanted more. So much more.

And Shye seemed ready to let me take it. "Alder, please. Please."

"You beg me like that again, I might just come in my pants," I gritted out, licking up the length of her neck to nibble on her jaw.

"Yes," she gasped, sinking her fingers into my shoulders. Making me hurt in the best way.

"Not yet. I want to get you off first. I need to feel you come. Want to slide my tongue inside you to lick up all that sweet pussy juice. Been craving it." I reached between us, pulling down the soft, stretchy pants she wore. I couldn't take them off without letting her go, which wasn't happening just yet, but I made enough room for me to slip my hand inside. To feel her hot, wet flesh. "Damn, girl, is this all for me? You're positively soaked."

Shye moved as if to retreat, but there was no fucking way. I grabbed her hips and dropped to my knees. Those pants and panties were on the floor a second later, her legs up and over my shoulders, my face right up against her pussy. I hadn't imagined it—that pink flesh was so fucking pretty.

I ran a finger along her lips, circling. Teasing. "I've dreamed about this. Ever since that night at the restaurant when you finally let me have a taste, I've been dying to crawl back between your legs and watch you come apart because of me. Been waiting to taste you again. I'm going to lick this pussy so good, honey."

Shye grabbed my hair as she stared down at me. Mouth open, eyes gleaming. Hungry. My girl looked hungry. I understood that look—I'd been fucking starving for her.

And I was about to eat my fill.

I licked a path where my finger had gone, holding her gaze while I teased her opening with my tongue. Shye bucked and moaned, rolling her hips again, her thighs on my shoulders shaking as I took my time with her. She liked that, it seemed. Once more, I licked along that path, giving her just enough to feel. Not hitting anything important yet.

But my girl had a greedy side. She fisted my hair and tugged, squeezing her legs on my shoulders to pull me closer. "Please, Alder."

It was the please that did me in. "I fucking love to hear you beg for me."

I opened my lips around her clit and sucked, letting my tongue flick the hot little bud for good measure. Shye practically jumped off the counter, writhing and moaning loud enough for people driving by to hear. Good. Let them hear her; let them know this girl was mine, and I would be the only one making this pussy happy from now on. The only one who would know her taste.

Wanting to fucking claim her in some way, I wrapped my arms around her legs and tugged her closer, feasting on her. Desperate to keep her juices on my tongue. To make her shake and buck against me even more.

When I suckled harder, she tightened up, yanking on my hair, chanting something that sounded like my name. Something wordless and more noise than language. Giving me another thing to always strive for—to push her past the point of words, to make her mumble sounds I couldn't understand every fucking time I ate her. Because this wouldn't be the last time—no fucking way.

With a quick intake of breath, she stopped moving—absolutely froze. Hanging on to the cliff of desire and waiting for me to push her over. So I wrapped my lips around my teeth and bit down gently one last time, giving her clit the pressure she needed. Pushing her right over the edge into her orgasm. Teasing her through the pleasure as she shook and curled her body toward me.

I didn't even give her time to finish coming before I picked her up, threw her little body right over my shoulder, and carried her up the stairs with my hand on her ass.

Licking her pussy at the counter was fine—amazing, really, and definitely one of my favorite things to do—but I wanted her riding my cock. I wanted to bury myself inside of her cunt, and for that, she deserved a bed.

———

SHYE

Limp. My body went completely limp under Alder's control. His huge, rough hands squeezing my thighs as he lifted me, his mouth capturing mine in a soul-stealing kiss, his attention bringing me to the brink then shoving me right over the edge. Everything about the man was too big, too much, yet not enough. I wanted more, and I had a feeling he was about to deliver.

When he carried me into his bedroom, Alder didn't even pause. He tossed me on his bed and quickly followed me down. Covering me. Surrounding me completely. The soft, golden glow of his bedside lamp lit up his face, but his eyes burned with something else. Something like care and concern and need and relief. Something I couldn't remember ever seeing from anyone. Just him.

I'd never felt so safe and warm. So cherished. So *wanted*.

"You and me." He nuzzled my neck sweetly, his scruff scratching in a way that made my back arch. "We're going to tear this bed up. Turn the goddamned thing to dust together."

I could certainly hope. "Not with all your clothes in the way."

His deep chuckle made his chest vibrate, and the way his smile spread all slow and hot as he pulled back had me shivering. So much promise in that look. So much challenge too. One I answered.

I moved first, tugging at his shirt as I held his stare. He let me struggle for a second before placing a big, wet kiss on my lips then bounding to his feet. He kept that hungry gaze holding mine as he stripped out of his clothes. Every inch of his hard, muscled form he revealed on his schedule. Every bit of flesh and skin uncovered by his hands. I'd seen his strength but not the full source of it. Not even the previous night when I'd watched him in the shower. Not until he stood next to the bed...naked. So many dips and ridges to focus on, so much power in the makeup of his body. Each muscle defined and obviously taken care of.

I wanted to lick every inch.

And of course, I couldn't help but look down, my eyes focusing on his heavy erection.

Heavy was an understatement.

I'd always noticed how much bigger Alder was than other, more average men—broader, taller and more muscular—and *every inch* of him lived up to that. Without his hand in the way, I got the full image, and it was impressive, to say the least. Long and so very thick, there was no grace to that hard flesh. There was only a blunt tip and broad crown that looked as if it could pound its way right through my body.

I couldn't wait to get that inside me, no matter how scared I might also have been.

"That look on your face is such a turn-on, honey." Alder wrapped his fist around himself, stroking in long, slow pulls. "You look hungry for me. Is that right? Do you need my cock inside you? This will fill you up just right, won't it, Shye?"

Letting go of my fear, I spread my bare legs wider, the chilly air hitting my wet flesh and making me tremble. "I wouldn't know, but I'm looking forward to finding out."

He froze, his eyes practically gleaming even as his brow came down in question. "Wouldn't know... Are you saying you've never—"

I shook my head before he finished asking, suddenly worried that my inexperience would be a deal-breaker. "Not once. I've played with toys, but men... Well, my dad was real strict." I brought my knees together as he stood and stared, wishing I could cover myself once more. Wishing he'd do something. "Is that...okay?"

My quiet question seemed to knock him out of his stupor. He was on me before I could take a breath, his heavy body pinning me down. His hips spreading my legs wider.

"Jesus fuck. Is it okay? It's..." He groaned, rolling his hips against mine, his cock spreading my lips and hitting me in just the right spots as he squeezed me tight. "I shouldn't like that fact as much as I do. First and last, Shye. That's what I'll be for you. Your first and last. I'll claim this sweet pussy as mine if you'll let me." He kissed me softly, his tongue sliding between my lips. The kiss deepened slowly, his body pressing me farther into the mattress as he stopped holding back. So big, so strong. And so very sexy when he pulled away and said, "Tell me this is mine, honey. I'll make sure what we do is so good for you. Give me your pussy, and I'll show you."

I nodded, unable to speak as he worked his body against me. As he pressed and slid and teased. That nod must have been enough, though. His mouth met mine again, and all the sweetness of before vanished. Brutal was the way I would have described his kiss. Overwhelming and passionate worked, too. He dominated my every move, holding me in place as he owned my mouth. As he stoked the fire burning within me that he'd sparked to life.

Alder slid his rough hands up my legs, gripping hard, dragging loud moans from me as they worked over my flesh. So needy, that touch. Covetous.

When he reached my waist, he held on and rolled us over, settling me to straddle his hips. I held myself up with my hands on his chest, my eyes finding his. My thighs spread wide around him. My breath caught at the weight of his stare, the need there. The desire. He pushed against where I was so wet for him, and I knew this was it. That we were about to come together in the most intimate way. But I felt...exposed.

Something that slowed me down. "I don't think I can do this like... this. Up here."

Alder simply held me still, staring at me with a look on his face that made me feel beautiful and wanted. And with his hands holding on to my thighs so tightly, they may as well have been steel bands.

"I'm not a small man." He rolled his hips, making his point as his...oh god, his cock—there was no other word to describe it...pressed against me all the way past my clit. "You can control how deep and how fast I move by being on top. If I get you underneath me right now, there'll be no slow or shallow. I'll go balls deep from the start because I'm so wound up. I've waited too damn long to get you in my bed to be gentle, and I don't want to hurt you."

I believed him. Nothing about Alder Kennard was gentle—not his body, his touch, or his attitude. But I loved that about him. Loved how secure he made me feel. Like with rolling me on top of him, giving me the control to take him inside or not. To set the pace and the depth, the speed. Alder liked to control everything, so I knew how much it meant for him to give me this gift. And I wanted to repay him.

"Okay." I shifted against him, loving the way his eyes darkened and his fingers dug into my flesh as I dragged my wet flesh over him. "Just this time."

"I like the implication of more of this, honey." Alder jackknifed up, moving to lift my shirt as I gasped and clung to the fabric. Knowing what he'd find if he took it off. Afraid it would ruin this moment.

"Please." My voice wobbled, and he froze. "I want to keep it on."

His eyes held mine, so serious and sure. Completely in the moment with me. "Whatever you need, I'll give you, Shye. Whatever makes you more comfortable."

And there it was—that sweetness I loved so much about him. That kindness he kept hidden. I sighed as he let go of my shirt, so ready for him. For more. For this. "Thank you."

"Don't thank me. If it's between sucking on your titties and having you bounce on my cock, my cock will win every time. But someday, I'm going to get my mouth on these." He grabbed my breasts, squeezing hard but not painfully so. Rubbing his thumbs over my nipples before dropping his hands to my waist. "You're so fucking pretty." Alder kissed me sweetly before lying back down, that cocky smile pulling up the corners of his mouth. "Now ride me, beautiful."

Hands on his chest, I did as I was told. Rocking, rolling, dragging my hips over his. Groaning every time that thick head bumped into my clit. Alder kept his hands on my waist, kept his steely blue gaze locked on me. Burning me with a look of pure want. So hot, still so in control even as he let me move how I needed to. As I wanted. Allowing me to use his body to find my own pleasure. But eventually, all my rubbing must have gotten to him, because he grabbed my hips and held me down, arching into me and groaning loudly.

"Shit, honey. I'm going to come all over that hot pussy if you keep that up, and I'd rather come inside you. Let me get a condom."

The idea of something in between us physically hurt. "I'm on birth control, if you want to..."

How did you say it? I'd heard men talk about having sex without a condom, but I wasn't comfortable with the language they'd used. Go bare? Raw? My face heated at the thought of saying such things. Meanwhile, Alder stared, his hands holding me tight. Knowing what I meant without my having to utter the words.

"You sure about that?"

Yes, but... "I guess I should worry about, like, diseases—"

"I'm clean. I haven't been with anyone in a long time."

I couldn't help but ask, "How long?"

He sat up again, the corded muscles of his stomach bunching as he did. Bringing his face right up against mine until all I could see and feel was him. "Over three years. I've been yours since the first time I saw you in the truck stop. Since the night I met you."

Oh...this man was a dream come true. Worry and fear and nervousness disappeared. I kissed *him* that time. Hard and rough and strong, I locked my mouth onto his and pushed him to lie back, lifting my hips so he could wedge a hand between us. So he could rub the head of him over me one last time before slipping the tip inside. I had to break the kiss to breathe, had to moan at the delicious sting of him pressing his way inside. Had to focus on the feeling of him stretching me wide.

There was nothing gentle about his invasion—even slow, he plowed inside, spreading me, making room and leaving me to deal with the tightness of the stretch. It was a good pain, though, because right behind it came a feeling of fullness I'd never experienced. Of completeness I'd never dreamed possible. I let my head fall forward to watch, needing to see where so much sensation came from.

"Fuck, that's so pretty. Can you see it, honey?" Alder used his thumbs to spread my lips, staring down to where he split me open. "Look at your little cunt trying to stretch around me. Might be the hottest fucking thing I've ever seen in my life."

I wanted to agree with him, but at that moment, he pressed a finger to my clit, brushing back and forth in a way that made me see stars. My groan swallowed any words I might have said. I was going to come. He wasn't even all the way inside me, but I was right there on the edge. And he knew it.

"That's it, Shye. I can feel you trembling around my cock already. I want to see how wet you get when you come, how soft and juicy this pussy becomes. Give it to me."

He pressed on my clit, and I was done. Head back, body arched, I screamed my pleasure to the ceiling as every muscle locked down on him. Around him. All over him. Alder hissed something I couldn't understand, grabbed my hips, and thrust up, seating himself inside me even as my body milked his. As I fell forward against his chest and tried to catch my breath while trembling all over.

When I finally stilled, Alder ran his hands over my shirt, still thrusting his hips into me but slowing down. Still so thick and hard inside me. "You good so far?"

Words were too hard, so I simply nodded. His chest vibrated with his quiet chuckle.

"Can you take more?"

I looked into those stormy eyes of his and lost myself for a second. My god, the man was handsome. So rugged, so intense. Everything about him a warning, one I chose to ignore. One I'd run toward instead of away from.

So I nodded again.

He rolled us over, spreading my legs wide and opening me up around him. "I need to go deep, honey. You tell me if it hurts, though." He leaned down to press a tiny kiss to my lips, groaning when I bit his bottom lip before pulling away. "Little tease. You make me me want to pound this pussy, but I won't hurt you. I never want to hurt you."

I believed him, so I wrapped my arms around his neck and held on as he thrust home. As he growled and clung to me and shoved into me so hard, I couldn't stay still. Over and over in and out, he thrust and retreated. Hard and powerful. Loving me the way I'd always dreamed he would.

And when he came, when his body bowed and he groaned through his release, I gave myself over to that tension one last time. Shaking and gasping and biting down on his neck to keep from screaming his name again. Falling so hard into my orgasm, so suddenly, that I didn't care when he rolled to his side and took me with him.

Didn't notice the way he surrounded me with his body. Didn't pay attention when his hands slid from my hip along my spine and to the back of my neck. Under my shirt.

Didn't realize how stupid I was until his muscles went stiff against me as he bent his head to look over my shoulder.

"Shye, honey, how'd you get these scars?"

Chapter Twelve

SHYE

Stupid. I was so damn stupid.

"Shye?" Alder sat up, frowning. How was I supposed to answer him? With the truth? He'd hate me for making the choices I had. So I did the only thing I could think of—I grabbed the sheet and pulled it with me as I crawled off the bed, covering myself as best I could.

Which, apparently, wasn't very well.

"What the fuck is that?" Alder practically leapt up, tugging the sheet away and turning me so he could see my shame. The mark on my back, right over the swell of my hip. The one I'd earned the night my stepbrother taught me what it was to owe the Soul Suckers.

"It's nothing."

Not nothing, but I couldn't force the words out. Couldn't admit to all the wrong I'd done.

"Don't lie to me. That looks an awful lot like the Soul Suckers logo or... Did they fucking brand you?"

That symbol burned into my flesh was a sign of ownership. A reminder of the debt I owed. Worse than the scars, it marked me as property.

Soul Suckers' property. My stepbrother's property

See this, Shye? This is a symbol of ownership—you're ours to do with as we please. And it's forever, sis. No matter where you go, this marks you as Soul Suckers' property.

Not nothing. Everything. "I have to go."

Alder went rigid. "Go where?"

Anywhere. "Home. I have to go home."

"Your trailer's gone, honey." Alder stepped in front of me, looking more concerned than I'd ever seen him. "This is your home now. With me."

You'll stay here and watch for anything unusual. Do you hear me, Shye? You owe us money, and this is how you earn your keep. This is how you start to pay us back. This is your home now, and if you do your job, we might scrape that brand from your hip and call it even.

"No." I pushed past him and hurried out the door, a storm brewing inside of me. One I had no control over. Just like the rest of my life. But this? Staying with Alder or choosing not to? Choosing to protect myself? I could control this. I still had some say.

"Shye," Alder yelled, chasing after me.

"I can't stay here." I rushed into the guest bedroom and slammed the door on him. I even locked it. Put a big slab of wood between us so he couldn't see me fall apart. Couldn't see my truth. I'd screwed up before, and that mistake had gotten my father killed and my body ruined. I'd screwed up a second time, relied on people I'd thought I could trust, and that one had gotten me put into what was essentially indentured servitude. I couldn't screw up again. My mind and body couldn't take any more. And if they came after Alder because of me, I'd never survive it.

One breath, two, slow down for a second and think… Time to move.

I tossed whatever I could in my bag and tugged on some clothes. Alder kept yelling through the door, trying to get me to open it, begging me to talk to him. Threatening to break it down if I didn't let him in. He needn't have bothered—as soon as I had my meager possessions packed up, I threw open the door.

"I'm leaving."

And then I ran past him.

My heart broke a little more with every step, but there was no turning back. He'd seen the marks they'd left on me—he'd figure it out eventually, and when he did? He'd hate me or try to defend me. Either way, I'd be out of his life because if he defended me from the Soul Suckers, they'd come for him. They might even kill him. I couldn't live with that.

"Shye! Stop." Alder clomped down the stairs behind me, but I didn't stop for him. I had more riding on escaping than he did on keeping me there. So I ran outside and headed for my car, not even looking back.

But Alder was fast, and he grabbed me before I reached my destination, spinning me around and looming over me. "What the fuck is going on here, Shye? Why won't you stop and talk to me?"

I opened my mouth, having no idea of what I planned to say, but a floodlight out by the barn suddenly turned on, making the building and field around it glow. We both turned, blinking into the glare. It took me a solid three seconds to figure out what I was seeing, what that light meant. How wrong it was for the field to be lit.

Alder hissed a curse. "Shye, I need you to get back in the house."

"I can't stay here." But I couldn't tear my eyes away from that light—the one I'd never seen lit before. The one that told me something was different...wrong. Oh hell, I'd already failed—they'd come for me, and there was no way Alder would let me deal with them alone. No way to keep him safe. Unless... "We should both go."

But Alder wasn't a man who ran. "I'm not going anywhere, and we'll talk about why you're suddenly gung-ho to run away from me in a little bit. But that's a motion light, which means something's moving out there."

My blood ran cold, my heart racing. We were out of time. "Alder, you should know—"

"Not right now. I need you to get your ass inside the house." He pushed me toward the porch before dropping into a crouch behind my car. Oh god, he wasn't even dressed yet. Baggy gray sweats hung from his hips, but otherwise, he wore nothing. Not even a pair of shoes.

I couldn't leave him behind like that. "Come with me, please."

He shook his head. "Upstairs, in my room. There's a gun in the nightstand, remember? Go get it. Lock the bedroom door, get the gun, and stay put for me."

"Alder, no—"

"Go!"

A sob ripped from my chest, but I went. Racing through the shadows of the porch, stopping only for a moment to look back at the man I had to leave behind. Alone. In danger.

"Go on," he called, looking way more confident than I felt. "Get upstairs and find the gun."

"Alder—"

"Now, Shye. Get that gun and be prepared to shoot."

ALDER

The second I heard Shye close my front door, I finally exhaled the breath I'd been holding.

"Motherfucker. What just happened?"

How this evening had gone from fucking perfect to fucking FUBAR so fast, I had no idea. Finally—*finally*—after three long years, I'd gotten Shye Anderson in my bed. And it had been amazing. Every touch, every breath, every little sound of pleasure I'd dragged from her body—totally unforgettable. Pure pleasure. Until whatever we'd built between us crashed and burned. I needed to get back inside and figure out what the hell had happened, why scars covered her back, why she hid them from me, and who put a fucking brand on her hip. But all that would have to wait. We had company, so my first mission was to keep us both alive.

Crouching low, I crept through the shadows to my truck, slipping inside and grabbing the shotgun from behind the bench seat as I kept an eye on the barn. No movement, no sign of anyone out in the field beside the barn, but that light wasn't exactly sensitive. Someone had to have been somewhere around the door for it to turn on. There was no doubt in my mind—the Soul Suckers had come.

Back in my early days in the Army, I probably would have snuck back to the barn, scoped out the situation, and balls-to-the-walls busted inside. But I'd gone through extensive training to join the Special Forces team and earn my green beret. I'd lived through ambushes and sneak attacks, walked into places and immediately been surrounded by enemy forces. The only reason I'd made it home from a few of those was because I'd had the right training, a damn good team at my side, and men I trusted covering my back. It wasn't time to lone-gunman this shit—it was time to hunker down in a defendable location and call in reinforcements.

Keeping my gun trained on the barn, I backed all the way to my front door. I'd been so focused on stopping Shye, I'd only thrown on my sweats before chasing her outside. I hadn't grabbed my pistol or phone or even a pair of goddamned shoes, something I needed to remedy immediately.

Once inside, I locked the door and shut off all the lights on the first floor. If they were coming for me, they'd have to try to find me in the dark in a house they didn't know. So long as they didn't have night vision goggles, the shadows would be an advantage to me, which made me think that maybe we should buy some night vision goggles. Some military surplus. With Deacon on my side, I had access to some cool toys not many people got to play with. If these guys wanted a war, we'd motherfucking bring one to them.

But first, I needed to deal with whoever was in my barn.

I found my phone in the kitchen and sent a quick text to Gage and Bishop.

I've got company.

Gage replied first.

Five minutes.

"Not soon enough."

I sent one more text with the words *mind the barn at the south end*, then I left my phone on the counter and grabbed my work boots from the closet. No bare feet for this job. Once I had the boots on and tied, I headed through the house to the breaker box. My thoughts on the dark had been valid, and I needed every advantage I could get to make sure backup got to us before the Soul Suckers did. I needed to cut the power to the house, the barn, and all the lights outside. Most properties would have had a separate box in the barns and outbuildings, but I'd made sure to install a kill switch in the house. Just in case.

We were in *just in case* mode, so I powered everything down. The entire valley plummeted into darkness, the land I knew inside and out. The house and barns I'd bought before I'd even left the Army to move home. This was my turf—I had the advantage.

I slipped through the hallway into the bathroom closest to the garage. The one no one ever used. From behind the toilet tank, I pulled out the 9mm Beretta Deacon had given me—the one with the suppressor already mounted. A soldier needed to be prepared, and I'd taken that to heart once the Soul Suckers had started poking around town. I had three other guns hidden on the main floor of the house, but this was the cleanest. The one that couldn't be traced back to me. Between the Beretta and my shotgun, I felt armed enough to make it until Gage and Bishop showed up. I wasn't planning an attack—I was planning to hold the house.

Armed and ready to roll, I crept into the den to keep an eye on the barn through the south-facing windows. Soon enough, my eyes adjusted to the darkness, and stars began to shine through the blanket of black above the property. I stayed in the shadows, still as a stone, peering out over the field to the barn. Waiting on the Soul Suckers to show their faces. Waiting for backup to come. Waiting for what felt like a long damn time.

And then the waiting was over.

Gage and Bishop slipped inside through the garage entrance, the sound of footsteps and squeak of the floor giving them away. Rex's nails clicked on the wood floors as he followed his owner, of course. I'd never been more grateful to see those fuckers or that mutt in my life.

"You stay hidden on your way inside?"

Bishop took a long look over my shoulder, his eyes on the same barn I'd been staring at. "Definitely. Snuck in on the north side in case they're still in the barn."

"All's good?" Gage asked, keeping his voice low.

"So far, but I haven't gone out there yet. I didn't want to leave Shye alone."

"She upstairs?" asked Bishop, and I nodded. "Good. So what's the plan?"

"You stay here with Rex and keep an eye on Shye," I said, handing him the shotgun. "Me and Gage will scout what the fuck is going on out there. Call Finn to have him come be backup for you. We can use an extra set of eyes."

My brother didn't question me. "On it."

"Bishop." I couldn't keep the grit out of my voice, the order. The fear. "She's armed and likely terrified. Don't go up there unless you absolutely have to and take care of yourself if you do."

"No worries, brother. I've got this—I'll keep your girl safe." Bishop stayed low as he crossed to the dark landing, his gun pulled and ready.

"Rex. Follow." Gage pointed to Bishop, and the dog took off for my brother. The two settled into the deepest, blackest corner and practically disappeared into the shadows. Ready to defend my Shye girl.

I prayed like hell Bishop lived up to his promise.

Without a word, Gage and I snuck outside, rounding the house on the north side to stay out of sight of the barn. Once through the woods that practically surrounded my property, we'd have to cross a small, open pasture to get there, but the darkness should cover us well. Still, I gave Gage the hand signal to watch my back, and I went first. My property, my girl...my risk to be at the front.

Gage followed closely, both of us keeping low and moving fast through the high grasses and fences. We reached the barn without incident, both pressing our backs to the wall with our guns pointing at the sky. Easy. Too easy. Either these fucks had one hell of a setup inside, or they were too green to know what was coming.

I seriously hoped for the second option.

A few hand signals thrown, and Gage headed around back while I slipped inside through a side door. The old barn was about as standard as one could be. Built to house horses, it had a large, center aisle and two side aisles divided by rows of stalls. I didn't use the building except to store some extra lumber from when I'd installed my floors, and the stalls were all empty, so there weren't a lot of places to hide. Didn't mean I could be too cavalier, though. One wrong move and I'd be dead. Shye would be alone, left to handle the Soul Suckers without me looking out for her. Not happening.

I crept down a row of empty horse stalls, listening for any sign of life. Any movement. For a brief moment, as the silence reigned and made the pounding of my heart seem as loud as a brass band, I thought maybe they'd gotten past me. Maybe we'd screwed up, and Bishop and Shye were in danger. Maybe we'd missed them. A trained crew could have done it, could have beaten me at my own game and slipped through our net. Hell, it's what I would have planned to do had I been the one staging the attack.

But then I made it to the end of the stalls, and the middle aisle of the barn opened up. Standing in the center stood a man too small to be Gage, and there was no way Bishop had left Shye alone in the house. This had to be our intruder. He stood with what I had to assume was an assault rifle aimed toward the main barn door. Standing, watching, and aiming.

It took me a full ten seconds to figure out he was waiting for someone to ambush as they came through those giant doors, because the very thought of doing something so brash hadn't crossed my mind.

Did he honestly think I was stupid enough to come blasting through the front fucking door?

Apparently, he did, because he never moved, never even shifted his weight. He simply stared and aimed, reminding me of Deacon from his sniper days. Though Deacon would have known a military man wouldn't go through the front door if he thought there was a threat. He also wouldn't have stood out in an open space like that—completely exposed. This Soul Sucker had no clue. I would have called him an idiot, but then a shadow moved along the far wall and my opinion went up a single notch. He'd brought backup. At least he'd done one thing right, though it wouldn't help him. I'd brought backup too, and mine was way deadlier than anyone they had on their team.

I caught sight of Gage as he set up directly across from me, the two of us forming the base of a triangle with the village idiot at the tip, his backup just off to the side. I sent Gage the hand signal that I had the idiot, and he nodded. Time to do bad things for good reasons.

Focused on the backup, Gage moved forward along the wall. Hiding in the shadows, gun raised and ready. Not that he needed it—he didn't need hardware to be destructive. It took Gage all of four seconds to grab the backup around the throat and secure him in a hold that kept him from yelling for help. The second he had the guy, I stepped into the middle aisle and crossed the open space, quick but silent, sneaking up behind the idiot. He wore a Soul Suckers vest—something I hadn't been able to see until I was practically on top of him. Definitely not a surprise, though. And not something that was going to slow me down.

But as I took that final step before reaching the man, just as my focus should have been on the idiot before me, something out of the corner of my eye caught my attention. Something small and blonde and not at all where she should be. Shye. Hiding in the horse stall at the end of the far row. There to witness the worst side of me.

Fuck me.

Unfortunately, the plan was already in motion, the mark identified and in my sights. There was no stopping. No time to pause. Shye was going to see the type of man I was in full, living color. So I kept my eyes trained on the man with the gun. The one who'd come to destroy the woman I knew I was about to lose because of what needed to be done. He had to be destroyed. For her. I'd pay my penance once she was safe.

Striking fast, unable to consider what I looked like to the woman hiding in the shadows across from me, I elbowed the guy in the back of the neck. Man down. With nothing more than muscle memory and solid training fueling my actions, I yanked his gun out of his hands before turning the butt around against him. Two cracks to the face had him lying still in a puddle of blood. His blood.

Mine wouldn't be shed until the woman I loved ripped my fucking heart out for what I'd just done. The woman who was no longer lurking in the shadows.

Man down, indeed.

Chapter Fourteen

SHYE

Every step away from Alder seemed harder to push through. The distance felt wrong, the fear building inside of me exacerbated by the fact that I'd left him alone outside. This was a bad plan, but it was what he wanted, so I forced myself to climb the stairs and hurry into his bedroom.

The scene of my crime, in a way.

Really, I'd committed many crimes against Alder all over Justice. At the truck stop the night we met, when he'd asked me what made me move to town and I'd told him the story my stepbrother had fed me. At the post office when we'd run into each other. At the grocery store in Rock Falls. Every day and night that we'd spent together, I'd committed crimes against him by lying, hiding myself behind the fake life I pretended to live. All while doing the bidding of the motorcycle club that was likely coming to kill him.

But he wanted me to hide, so I'd hide.

Doing what Alder wanted, I locked the door behind me and made my way to his nightstand. It felt wrong going through his things, sneaky almost, but he'd told me to find his gun, so I opened the first drawer I came to. The one I remembered him pulling a gun from the night Bishop had shown up without letting us know. The night I'd first seen him naked.

Not the time to think about that, Shye.

Drawer. Right. Gun, condoms—new box, not even opened—and a piece of paper. I reached for the gun, but something about that last item caught my attention and held it. I hesitated, grappling with myself that looking at it would be overstepping, but there was no stopping me. My curiosity won out, so I grabbed and unfolded the simple white sheet.

A note. From me. One I almost wouldn't have remembered writing had I not seen it. I'd bumped into Alder's truck leaving work one night and hadn't been able to find him inside, so I'd left a note on his windshield, apologizing and promising to pay for the damages. He'd told me the next day that the scrapes on his bumper weren't important, and there was no need to pay him. Why would he have kept that?

Three years. I've been yours since the first time I saw you in the truck stop, honey.

My heart jumped, and I had to fight to keep my tears from falling. Three long years of me lying to him for the Soul Suckers...just a few more months and I should have been free. Maybe we could have built something then. Maybe I could have said goodbye to my past and truly been with him.

Maybe he wouldn't be fighting the Soul Suckers right now.

Tucking the note back inside the drawer, I picked up the gun and discovered one more item. A picture...of me. Someone must have taken it at the festival the sawmill held every year. My hair was shorter, and the shirt I wore I recognized as one I'd thrown away my first winter in Justice —it had to have been taken my first summer in town. Which meant Alder had likely been hanging on to that picture for three years. He hadn't been lying. All that time, I'd seen him as so big and strong, a totally tough man. But the past few days had shown me a side of him I'd missed. A sweet side, one that cared with his whole heart.

One I'd somehow fallen in love with.

Without warning, the lights cut out and the house went silent. Dread crawled up my spine. This was it—the attack had to be on. I gripped the gun tightly and tucked the picture back in the drawer, my hands shaking the whole time. *Calm, Shye. Stay calm.*

Determined to be brave for Alder, I curled up in the corner of the room, hiding behind the bed itself, and laid the gun in my lap. I had a feeling I wouldn't need it. I trusted Alder to keep me safe, which was a new feeling for me. Ever since the death of my dad, since my stepbrother had gotten more involved in the Soul Suckers, I'd been living scared.

Alder made me feel safe.

I'd repaid him by being untruthful.

That couldn't go on a moment longer. And like the dawning of a new day, a light inside my mind shone on the solution. The hiding ended tonight. No more lying. No more dishonesty. I'd tell Alder the truth about my past, about my father and our family link to the Soul Suckers, about my stepbrother's abuse and my debt to him, and about the danger that came right along with me. That way, he could choose if he wanted to be with me or not. The idea of him choosing *not* hurt, but I had to be ready to accept it.

I was also ready to stop hiding.

Gun in hand, I crept toward the window overlooking the pasture. The light outside the barn had gone out, leaving the field blanketed in an inky blackness. My stepbrother could be out there—any number of Soul Suckers could be as well—but what I knew for sure was that Alder was out there. And he needed my help.

Knowing there was no way Alder would have left me alone in the house—and therefore realizing any normal path down the stairs and through the door to the outside was likely blocked—I turned the crank to open the large, wood framed window. It swung out soundlessly, only a screen in my way.

"Learning how to sneak out of the house as a teenager finally comes in handy," I murmured as I flipped the clips holding the screen in place and pulled it inside the room. Once clear, I threw a leg over the edge of the window and shimmied outside. The sloping roof of the side porch gave me a clear path to a spot where I felt confident enough to jump down. Confident, but not unafraid. It took me three deep breaths and a mental pep talk—*you can do this, he needs you, it's all grass down there*—before I could actually take the plunge.

I hit the ground and rolled, nothing screaming in pain. I considered that a win. Once on my feet, I was in motion—running, ducking, keeping myself as out of sight as possible. At least until I froze.

"Lights...shit." Not just lights, but motion detectors. I turned and worked my way around the back of the barn, not wanting to set off the same light that had signaled an intruder to Alder earlier in the evening. I made my way to the horse stalls and started pushing and pulling on each one. Trying to find an opening. Searching for one that hadn't been locked. Alder was good about security, though—every one I came to was secured from inside. At least until the very last one. It was locked but not truly secure. The wood had obviously warped over the years, and the slide bolt didn't have much to hang onto. That was my way in. It took some wiggling, but I managed to slip the bolt back enough to free the top portion of the door.

Jackpot.

A little climbing, a few cuss words I could only say in my head, and what I was sure was a number of splinters on my thigh, and I made it inside the barn. It didn't take me long to see how bad things could have been if I'd gone through the main door, either. Right there in the front of the barn—not fifty feet from where I'd just slipped inside the building— stood a man in a Soul Suckers vest with what looked like a really big, really scary gun pointed at the door. I had a moment of panic wondering if Alder was okay but then I remembered that I'd known better than to go through that door—Alder definitely wouldn't have.

As if my thoughts had pulled him directly from the universe, Alder appeared across barn from me, sneaking around the edge of the opposite aisle. He looked bigger than usual even as he crouched, meaner than ever. He looked downright deadly, and I'd never been happier to see someone in all my life. I mimicked his movements, creeping forward, only taking a step when he did. Stopping when I reached the front of the stall. I tucked myself into the shadows and watched, waiting. Knowing Alder was about to go on the attack and praying like heck that he knew what he was doing. That the Soul Suckers didn't have some sort of trap set up for him. That he could—

A shadow moved past me, not two feet from my face. I held my breath, my heart pounding as it slipped around the corner. As a bushy beard and wide shoulders created darker sections in the shadowy space. Gage. Heading straight for a second Soul Sucker I hadn't even seen. The trap. The two former military men moving in tangent and the Soul Suckers...oblivious.

It took Gage no time at all to grab the Soul Sucker he'd been heading for and...I didn't even know. Kill him? Knock him out? I couldn't tell, mostly because just as Gage took care of that man, Alder moved again.

Striding big and bold into the open space of the barn. Heading right for the man with a gun. For the briefest of moments, I felt his eyes on me. Knowing I'd been spotted. A chill ran up my spine at the lethalness I saw there, the focus and concentration. Alder was a man on a mission. He didn't pause when he noticed me—didn't miss a step or breath. He simply rushed at the remaining Soul Sucker on feet more silent than any I'd ever witnessed and grabbed the gun. Fast, silent, and I had to imagine, deadly.

Alder didn't shoot, though. Instead, he struck the man in the face. Hard. Twice. And then he let the Soul Sucker fall to the floor.

Two down. Two likely dead or soon to be. And I'd witnessed it all.

In the Soul Suckers world, that meant I was a liability. Something to be threatened or destroyed. In Alder's world, that meant I was a capital witness capable of being forced to testify against him. That would never happen. I didn't know for sure if those men were dead, and to be honest, I didn't need to. Alder and Gage were safe. For all I knew, they could be dragging those men out to their car and setting them on their way.

I didn't need to see the cleanup.

I shouldn't see it, actually.

So I snuck back out of the barn the way I'd come in.

Alder could handle himself.

And I could do whatever it took to keep him out of jail.

Including leaving before I knew the ending of this particular chapter and never speaking of it again.

Chapter Fifteen

ALDER

Shye saw me take that man down. She knows how much of an animal I am.

The words repeated in my head, the image of her blond hair disappearing out the stall door into the darkness outside burned into my brain. I'd wanted to run after her, to call her name and have her come to me. To soothe any fears my actions may have incited, but I hadn't. I couldn't let Gage know we'd had a witness, and I couldn't just leave these two ass holes on the floor of my barn. There were things to be done before I could deal with my woman.

But first, I had to make sure she made it to the house. Leaving Gage with the two Soul Suckers, I crept to the large, swinging barn doors and pushed one open. Not a lot—not enough to set off the motion lights— but enough to watch that shining head of hair bounce across the dark field. My girl thought she was sneaky, but that hair practically glowed in the starlight. I kept my eyes on that beacon until I saw her hop onto the side porch. Bishop would spot her—he'd let her inside and keep her safe. Likely after feeling some pretty intense feelings of failure for not having known she was gone.

I would have liked to have seen that.

And then I would have liked to have knocked a few teeth out for him failing to keep her secured.

But not yet. I couldn't go back to the house just yet. Gage and I had things to do still.

Time to focus on the work.

I hoofed it back to the fallen men, my work face back on and my thoughts refocused on the job at hand. Gage sidled up beside me, looking cocky as fuck as he tossed the unconscious backup next to the idiot. He also dropped a battery-operated lantern by the guys and turned it on, kneeling down to take a good look at our visitors.

"I would have gotten him in one hit."

"Yeah, yeah, you say that now." I tucked my Beretta into the back of my pants. Not ideal, but it'd have to do since my holster was still at the house. What I needed to do wasn't a handgun job. The idiot's rifle made a bigger impression. "You secure your side of the barn?"

Gage rose to his feet. "I'm not a bubblegummer."

It took me a second to figure out he meant a new soldier. Jesus, the fucking Navy had some weird slang. They also obviously missed things occasionally, because he'd moved right past Shye without seeing her. Something I wasn't about to call out to him, though.

I nodded my acceptance, staring down at the two Soul Suckers at my feet. Both had their road names on patches sewn onto the front of their vests. The idiot's tag said Beaver, the other... Well, well, well.

"We've got Spark here. As in fire, not plug," I said, pointing the gun at the backup. Gage grunted, knowing where this was going.

"Cam is going to be pissed he didn't get to pull the trigger."

"He'd be even more pissed if we had the guy who killed Leah and let him get away."

"True that. So what now?"

I nudged Beaver with my boot. "You awake there, kid?"

Our idiot friend moaned, so I nudged him again. A little harder this time. "C'mon, man. We don't have all night."

Gage squatted beside the guy, using one meaty hand to hold Beaver's head still. "Maybe a kick to the ribs would wake him up."

"Fuck," Beaver spat, pushing Gage off him before rolling up into a sitting position. Looking way too sure of himself considering we'd laid him out on the floor of my fucking barn.

"Welcome to my home," I said, keeping the gun pointed at him, evaluating options for extracting the information I wanted. "I'd say make yourself comfortable, but it seems like you already did. So I'm sure you'll excuse me if I don't end up behaving like a perfect host."

Beaver glowered up at me, looking defiant, but he also made a rookie move. Fucker set his palms flat on the ground as if about to push himself to his feet. Big mistake. I stomped on his right hand, making sure the ball of my boot sat on his fingers, shifting my weight to that leg to make it hurt just enough.

And then I smiled. "What the fuck are you doing here, Beav?"

The guy grimaced and tried to pull his hand away, but I didn't budge. Instead, I increased the pressure on that foot until I felt the pop of his bones breaking. He bit back the scream I was sure he wanted to let loose, but he couldn't hide the sweat beading on his forehead or how pale his face turned as I ground down on his hand. Nice and slow always hurt so much worse than fast.

"I'll try this again." I pushed the muzzle of the rifle into his temple. "What the fuck are you doing on my property?"

Beaver held his tongue for another few seconds, but the next pop from under my foot had him talking. "The girl. I came to collect what's ours."

Shye. The motherfucker talked about Shye as if she were an object, one the Soul Suckers thought they had a claim on. No fucking way.

"You should have said you'd come for me, son." I dropped down to get in his face. "I'll take your crew on all fucking day, but no one threatens my girl. Your so-called ownership of Shye Anderson is done."

"Our enforcer won't go for that."

"Too fucking bad." I kept my eyes on Beaver as I cocked my head toward Spark. "Hey, Gage. Who were the two guys that set Shye's place on fire?"

"Spark, for sure. Someone was with him, though."

"And who do we have here?" I pointed my gun at Spark.

"That'd be Spark, boss."

"So I assume our friend Beaver here is the other one Camden mentioned." I stood up and pointed the gun in Beaver's face. "Looks like we've got two to take care of."

"I didn't set those fires," Beaver said, his eyes staring unendingly at the end of my gun. "Spark usually runs with Coyote, but he's on another job tonight."

"A job in Justice?" Because if that was the case, we had a lot more to worry about than these two fuckers. Gage shifted closer, probably thinking the same thing. If this Coyote guy was in Justice, we needed to get this show on the road so we could intercept the fucker.

Thankfully, Beaver shook his head. "I don't know where, but not here. Spark and I were the only ones sent to Justice."

To steal Shye from me. I shot Gage a look, knowing it was time to make the call as to what to do with our intruders. Well, what to do with Beaver—Spark had sealed his fate the second he chose to light a match in my town. But even as I questioned the right choice forward, Parris' words from the night I'd met him rang through my head. We had to fight like an MC to beat an MC. The Soul Suckers had sent two men to ambush me and had killed Leah seemingly without a second thought. My Army training told me to send Beaver back to his team with a message.

But this wasn't an Army job.

"Gage." I dropped the rifle behind me and pulled my Beretta from my waistband, taking note of the way Beaver's eyes went wide as I pointed it at him just before I fired. Gage followed suit, ending Spark with a single gunshot to the head. Quiet, fast, and as neat as could be hoped for.

Gage spoke first. "Threat eliminated."

I stared down at Spark and Beaver, my gut churning. Not because of the murders—fuck no, those two were direct threats to me and mine. Nothing more than self-defense, even if the law wouldn't technically see it that way. No, eliminating threats was easy. Knowing there were bigger ones coming our way was a different story. Because they would come looking—once the Soul Suckers figured out these two weren't coming home, they'd send more men to Justice. And we'd have to deal with them too.

They wouldn't find any proof that Beaver and Spark had met their end in my barn, though. By the time Gage and I were done, there'd be no sign that anything had gone down tonight. We'd get rid of the evidence— bodies to guns to bloodstains. In the end, it wouldn't matter. The cops may never figure out what happened, but the Soul Suckers would, even without proof. We'd definitely started a war, and as much as I hated to admit it, the Soul Suckers would use Shye as a pawn in it. She was also a witness. A liability.

I'd thought I was keeping her safe by having her with me. Turned out, I'd put her smack in the middle of the cross hairs.

"Boss?" Gage stood, watching me, waiting. "Want me to take care of this?"

Because there was no way I could focus on such an important task right then. "Yeah. I'll need you to."

He nodded once, face calm and back straight. All that military training he'd gone through as a SEAL coming back to the forefront. Like riding a fucking bike. "Get on up to the house and send Bishop out," he said, taking control. "We can handle cleanup. You deal with Shye. Make sure she's not going to talk about what she saw tonight."

The look he shot me was full of knowledge. Guess the guy hadn't missed her being in the barn after all.

"She won't talk."

He grunted. "You sure?"

"No doubt." And there was none. At least not about her opening her mouth. That didn't mean I wasn't filled with something I didn't know how to handle. Or maybe didn't want to.

"So what's the plan?" Gage asked, and for the first time in a long time, I wasn't really sure. Except for one part.

"I'm going to have to send her away."

Gage didn't speak at first, so I knew he was taking my statement seriously. Mulling it over. Finally, he huffed, the sound somehow chastising. "Safest place for that girl is being looked after by one of us."

I couldn't argue that, but then I looked down at the two dead Soul Suckers, and my confidence faltered. *They had come for her, and their brothers would send more of them.*

"They'll target her because of me." I waved at the two bodies on the floor. "Because of this."

"Don't let them."

Such an easy answer for such a complicated problem. I couldn't control what was coming, couldn't even guess how the Soul Suckers would strike next. But I knew they would come blazing into Justice with a surety that set my blood burning. Keeping Shye with me meant putting her life at risk every single day. I was a selfish bastard for sure, but not that much.

I handed Gage the Beretta for disposal. "I'll do whatever it takes to keep her safe."

Gage watched me with those flat black eyes of his—emotionless and empty—before nodding once. Releasing me. My time in the barn was over, which meant I needed to throw myself into a deeper level of hell. As much as I hated what I knew needed to be done, I turned and headed for the house.

It was time to rip my own heart out.

Chapter Sixteen

SHYE

Bishop did not look happy when he opened the door at the side porch. Neither did the dog at his heels.

Whoops.

"I had to check on him," I said, shivering from both the adrenaline crash after being in the barn and the fear of what Bishop might do. I should have known better—the man gave me a weak smile and stepped back, allowing me inside.

"He's going to kick my ass, you know."

I didn't have the words to answer, not after what I'd just seen. If Alder chose to kick someone's anything, he certainly seemed as if he would win. Even against his own brother.

Bishop looked over my shoulder, obviously ignoring my non answer. "Everything okay out there?"

I paused, thinking back over the last few minutes. Over watching Gage take one man to the ground. Alder yanking the gun away from the other and...

"Yeah," I said, my voice soft. Almost weak. "They've got things under control."

Bishop nodded once, then shut the door. "Get on upstairs then."

He didn't have to tell me twice. I raced across the wood floors and up the stairs, slamming the door to the bedroom behind me and locking it once more. Just as I'd been told to do, I grabbed the gun and slunk into the corner, waiting. Trying hard not to think about what I'd just seen.

Time dragged, minutes turning into what felt like hours as I sat in the dark for some sign of what was going on outside. The first came when the lights clicked on. I blinked against the sudden brightness, rising to my feet but keeping my back against the wall and Alder's gun in my hand. The second came when footsteps approached the door. My stomach dropped at the sound. Alder would be running, he'd hurry to get to me. I knew it like I knew he'd do anything to defend me. These steps sounded slow... almost careful. A trudging beat against the wood floors.

Oh god, what if they'd hurt him? What if there'd been more than just the two in the barn. It could have been an ambush. He could be bleeding on the other side of the door. Or they could have killed him and sent someone else for me. To take what I owed them from my flesh.

Not again.

Aiming the gun at the door, I took a deep breath and prepared to shoot. My dad had taught me how to handle a gun almost as a joke, but those lessons had stuck. I could shoot, and I would. If I had to. I really hoped I didn't have to.

"Shye. Are you okay in there?" Alder's voice broke the silence, and I nearly crumbled in relief. Alive. He was at least alive. But I still had to be sure.

"Alder? The barn?"

"It's over now. Everything will be all right. Why don't you unlock the door for me?"

I set the gun on the bed and rushed to the door, turning the latch and yanking it open almost in one move. I jumped at the man on the other side, wrapping my arms around him as my heart thumped mercilessly hard. I kissed him before I even saw him, clung to the body I'd learned so well. He held me just as tight, his mouth meeting mine with the same frenzy. His tongue sliding past my lips as he pressed me against the wall and gripped my thighs firmly.

I wanted him. Not just lust or desire, I wanted *him*. Every inch. Every moment. Every tic and trait. I wanted the man who kissed me like kissing was an event to be won, who held me like I was a prize. I wanted the happily ever after with my dragon because the prince would never love me as strong. But having him—really having him as mine—meant what I'd dreaded for so long needed to happen. It was honesty time. I hated the thought of laying out all my secrets, of telling him how I'd lied to him, but it was the best thing. The right thing. No future could be built on a false foundation. And I wanted a future with him. Deep down, I always had.

But before I could do or say anything, Alder pulled away, setting me on my feet and putting space between us. Space I wasn't ready for. Space that screamed something was still wrong. He stood there in the hall a solid three feet away from me, looking damn near defeated. A fact that froze my heart.

"What's wrong?"

He couldn't look me in the eye. "You have to go."

My stomach plummeted, a giant fault line opened in my heart, and my breath caught as I whispered, "Why? I swear, I won't say any—"

"I know that, honey. Trust me, I *know* that. But you can't stay here anymore. It's not safe."

The cracks in my heart spread, sending an unbearable ache through my soul. This couldn't be happening. Not then—not when I was finally ready to move forward. "I'm safe with you, Alder. And I promise—I'll listen this time. I'll do what you tell me to. I won't—"

But forward wasn't the direction he wanted to go...at least not with me.

His eyes finally met mine, blazing. Angry. Emotions I'd never seen directed at me. "That's not important, and you know it. I'm sending you to my brother Elijah's place in Denver for a few days. Just until we get you a new trailer on your property. Maybe if I call the insurance company—"

"Why are we talking about insurance?" I choked, tears falling. World crumbling. The future I suddenly knew I wanted disappearing before my eyes. "I don't care about insurance. I want to stay with you."

He shook his head and took another step back. Lining himself up with something sitting in the hallway. Something I hadn't noticed. Something that solidified Alder's decision in my head.

The bag I'd packed when I'd tried to run from him.

He'd already planned this out—the bag, where I would go, probably how I would get there. I had no doubt someone from the mill or one of his brothers would be waiting for me when I went downstairs. Waiting to take me away from Justice. He wasn't going to listen to my arguments.

"I'm sorry. It's for the best." He handed me the bag I'd packed. The one with all of my clothes and stuff, the one I'd thrown together when I'd decided to leave him instead of telling him about my scars.

Ironic—I'd wanted to go and ended up staying. Now, I wanted to stay, and he was forcing me out.

There was only one thing left to say.

"I'll never tell what I saw," I said, and then I walked right past him and headed for the stairs.

Chapter Seventeen

ALDER

I'm a fool."

Bishop's dark chuckle certainly didn't help my mood any. Neither did his smartass response.

"Could have told you that."

I lifted my beer bottle to my lips, swallowing hard to try to battle the throbbing ache in my head. I couldn't stop seeing Shye's face when I'd told her she had to leave. That flash of absolute pain before she'd tried to get me to change my mind. Her begging, looking ready to cry, and then...nothing. Smile gone, light gone. The glimmer I could have sworn was something that could turn into true feelings, gone.

Gage grabbed a beer and joined us at the dining room table, Rex watching him from where he lay by the front door as if waiting to go home. "I'm with Bishop on this one. You're a fool."

Like I needed them to agree with me. Shye had been gone exactly twenty minutes—driven away by my brother Finn as I'd requested—and I'd regretted letting her walk out the door for nineteen and a half of them. Fuck, I hadn't even really explained myself to her. After the sex and the scars and the barn, my mind hadn't been in the right place to deal with that slip of a woman. So I'd sent her away, and I regretted that decision completely.

"I fucked up."

Gage shrugged. "You wanted to protect her."

"She's safest with me. At least, if she were here, I'd keep an eye on her. I'd make sure she had everything she needs."

"So then, why isn't she here?" Gage raised an eyebrow, pinning me with that shark-like gaze. Forcing me to admit it again.

Jackass. "Because I'm a fool."

"We've established that. Now, how about we figure out how to keep these Soul Suckers from using that against you?" Bishop kicked my chair, earning a glare from me. He simply grinned in return before growing serious once more. "I have no interest in burying a brother, even if he is a complete moron when it comes to women."

Gage grunted his agreement. "Ditto."

"I don't see either one of you doing any better," I said, taking another swig from my beer. Bishop flinched, but Gage simply stared right back. Bishop had dated Anabeth Monroe throughout his college years, but that relationship had crashed and burned in a way that had sent him straight into the Navy SEALs program for some reason. I'd already been in the Special Forces by that time— my little brother's dating life hadn't been a top priority. It wasn't until we'd both come home and I'd realized the man refused to allow another woman to get close to him that I saw how much her leaving had hurt him. Sure, I'd seen him out with women since, but no one local, and never more than once.

Gage...well, I'd never seen him with anyone but my brothers or his dog. I didn't even know *if* he dated. Yet these two were the ones giving me relationship advice.

Fool wasn't a strong enough word.

"So what's the plan?" Bishop asked, directing the conversation away from the one I knew he didn't want to have. The one about Anabeth. No matter how many women he picked up on his many travels, how much he'd glossed over their breakup, I knew his heart still hurt for the girl he'd lost.

I also knew I'd end up just like him if I lost Shye.

"Boss?" Gage looked me over, head cocked, eyes hard. Fuck, I needed to focus.

"The plan is that we go on the offensive." I rolled the bottle, staring down at the table. "You have to act like an MC to go against one, and an MC wouldn't let another group just waltz into their territory. They'd fight for it. They'd attack the interlopers."

Bishop sat back, his brow heavy. "Attack how?"

"We go for their money first, and we do it in their style. Not just to shut that kitchen down, but to make a fucking point."

Gage nodded. "So we burn down their business."

"That stretch of woods has a lot of dead pine," Bishop said, always the cautious one. "We start a fire out there, it'll have to be controlled."

"Wouldn't be the first time we had to burn in dry conditions." Gage kicked back, balancing the chair on two legs. Shye would have told him to sit correctly so he didn't break the chair. I'd learned that lesson at the truck stop early on in my obsession, which was why I'd moved to always sit in the corner booth. I hated to disappoint her. Of course, tonight, I'd done worse. I'd hurt her.

Goddammit, I had to stop thinking about her. I took a deep breath, trying to focus on the plan. The sooner this ended, the sooner I brought Shye home. "So we bring Cam's team in to clear the site, then we burn the place down. Between two missing members they sent here and that, they'll know we're not fucking around."

"Cam might want to be the one to light it up," Bishop interjected, making a fuckton of sense. "I know I'd want to get revenge if it was my girl. Wouldn't you?"

Just the idea... "I'd want to bury every motherfucker who dared to touch my Shye."

"Right, and we already took care of Spark. So we bring in Cam to run the blaze, and we prep the site for a burn out." Gage tipped up his bottle, draining his beer before continuing. "And when they come after us for that and our friends in the barn?"

"We take them out one by one, just like we did tonight. No second chances. Their guys disappear in Justice, they'll know why." I gave him a significant look. "But we do it carefully. Nothing can come back on us."

"No witnesses this time," Gage said.

Bishop huffed. "I told you—she slipped out the fucking window. How was I supposed to know she was that crazy?"

Brave. Not crazy. But I wasn't going to correct him. "Right. We take them out—no trace left behind, no witnesses."

Gage shrugged as if I'd told him to change the oil in a Kennard Mills truck, not get rid of some dead bodies, the guns we'd used to kill them, and set up the future scene of a crime. "I'll run any cleanup that needs doing."

Which was why he was such a good man to have on a team. He got shit done, no matter what.

"I'll get in touch with Cam," Bishop said. "We'll set up a team to take care of the kitchen. It will probably take a day to prep, though."

I nodded. "Cleanup tomorrow, burn the next day. Bishop, I want you to stop at Miss Hansen's place. See if she needs any help or if she'd be willing to move closer to town. I don't want her involved in anything."

He nodded. "I'll check in on her."

"You sweet on the old lady?" Gage asked, smiling. "You seem to be the one to check on her a lot."

"I dated her granddaughter, so I know her is all. She's got a soft spot for me." Bishop's face turned stormy. The fact that he hadn't told Gage about Anabeth set me back. She'd been such a huge part of his life, though I guess that was a long time ago. She hadn't been back to Justice in at least a decade. Good thing, too. I'd had to hunt Bishop down the last time he'd run into her. Found him in Vegas, circling the bottom of a bottle and chasing her all over the city. It had taken me two days to clean him up and get him home.

But remembering Anabeth and the pain she'd inflicted on my brother only made me think of my Shye, who would never hurt me. She gave me such joy with her presence and her sweetness, and I'd rewarded her by sending her away. Fuck the planning; I needed to fix things with my girl before I ended up as alone and emotionally closed off as my brother had become. I didn't want a string of one-night stands to keep my dick wet. I wanted dinners at my table, Shye's ass swinging in that wicked way as she danced through our house. I wanted her wrapped in my arms every night and to wake her every morning with my face or my cock in her pussy. I wanted every moment she had to give me, and I wanted it all to start immediately.

Even a fool could see that was the prize worth fighting for.

"We good, then? Plan set?" I glanced from one to the other, wanting to get the conversation back on track so we could call it done. When they both nodded, I rapped my knuckles on the table. "Excellent. Get rid of some bodies and set some fires, boys."

I kicked back my chair and strode for the front door, grabbing my keys as I went.

"Where you going, Alder?" Bishop asked, the smile in his voice obvious. Not that I gave a fuck. Not anymore.

"I'm going to bring my girl home. I'm a fool, but I'm not too stupid to learn from my mistakes."

Gage roared a laugh before pointing at my brother. "Pay up, pretty boy."

"Fuck." Bishop grabbed his wallet, frowning. "Three more minutes, and I would've won the bet."

"You two put money on how long it would take me to go after her?" The jackasses.

Bishop lifted a shoulder, all casual-like. As if betting on my love life was completely normal. Though, I hadn't been on a date in three years—maybe it was.

"You gonna stand here and talk to us, or go get your girl?" Gage asked as he took the bills from my brother. I would have answered, but I was already out the door. Fuck them. They knew where I was going. They also knew better than to be at my house when I got back. I was bringing my girl home, and we'd need some time alone. Naked time. I'd worship every inch of her until she finally forgave me.

I just hoped it worked because I had no idea what else I could do to tell her how sorry I was.

Chapter Eighteen

SHYE

Elijah Kennard differed greatly from his brothers. Especially Alder.

"The instructions for the espresso machine are in the drawer, though I'd be happy to make you a cappuccino or a latte if you'd like. Or Lainie can help you."

I shot a glance at the only sister of the four Kennard brothers. She sat in the living room, legs crossed, foot swinging as she read on a tablet. You'd think that would relax her, but no. With her body stiff and a deep frown firmly in place, anger practically oozed from the pretty blonde. She certainly didn't look as if she wanted to help me with anything. In fact, she looked pissed that I'd invaded her space. Lovely.

"I won't be staying long," I said, my voice more whisper than not. Finn, Elijah's twin and the man who'd driven me out here, had already left to go back to Justice, which meant I was trapped for the moment. I didn't have to stay trapped, though. "I'll probably be out of your hair in the morning."

Elijah's hawklike gaze swept over me, making me feel as if he'd just looked inside my head and found every one of my secrets. Now *that* was a Kennard trait. "My brother said you're to stay here until he takes care of whatever's going on in Justice."

"Alder isn't the boss of me."

Elijah finally smiled, and the similarities between him and Alder came to light. From the cheeks down, he was the spitting image of his brother. And man, did that hurt.

Lainie snorted from her spot in the living room. "You wouldn't be here if you weren't doing what the big boss told you to."

Whatever bravado had moved me to speak disappeared, leaving me empty, my face heating at the accusation.

And just like his brother, Elijah came to my rescue. "Knock it off, Lainie."

I really needed to get away from these white knight Kennards. All of them. "I think I'll head to the guest room. I'm really tired."

Elijah glanced at his watch. Almost one in the morning, if the clock behind him was accurate. "Of course. Do you need anything?"

To get away, and the strength to finally surrender. "I should be fine but thank you. And thanks for letting me stay. I appreciate it."

"Any time."

With a nod to him and a purposeful avoidance of his sister, I hurried down the hall to the little bedroom I'd been shown when I'd arrived. There was nothing special about it—beige walls, tan carpet, nondescript furniture. Nothing special at all and nothing unique. Not like the warmth and splashes of color at Alder's place or the smoky, beetle kill pine floors that stole the show there. Elijah's house, while obviously expensive, felt somehow empty. Temporary, perhaps.

Alder's had felt like home.

But he'd told me to leave, had pushed me right out the door and into Finn's car the second his brother had pulled up in his driveway. He'd never talked about what had happened out at the barn, but that had to be the reason. Something changed because of those moments. Something had come between us. And I had a feeling I knew what. I also had an idea of how I could pay him back for taking care of me the way he had.

How I could pay his penance and prove I would have never told anyone about what he'd done.

Taking a deep breath and praying for calm in the face of one of my greatest fears, I took out my phone and scrolled to the one contact I'd never wanted to have to use again. Then I hit call.

My stepbrother picked up on the second ring. "Well, if it isn't the little troublemaker. We've been looking for you, Shyness."

I had no doubt of that, but it wasn't my immediate concern. "Why'd you burn my trailer down?"

Colt—also known as Pistol, enforcer for the Soul Suckers chapter in Boulder and all-around destroyer of my life—sounded completely casual as he said, "Don't know anything about that, but if I did, I'd say it was payback. You were supposed to keep an eye on our kitchen."

"I did."

"Naw, Shyness. You can't lie to me like that. If you'd been doing your job, we wouldn't have had to send a crew out to deal with that Kennard guy you've been hiding behind."

I'd known they'd figure out I was staying with Alder, but it was still a kick to the gut to hear the confirmation. "Alder has nothing to do with this."

Colt laughed, a harsh, mocking sound that made me want to hang up the phone. Made me want to hide. "Don't try to play ignorant. We know who runs that town. True, we didn't go for him directly at first. Had to deal with that other guy—the one who needed to be taught a lesson about respecting the Soul Suckers and minding his own business. Heard you had a front-row seat to that one—the flames keep you warm, sis?"

The bastard. "Camden. The mill's site manager—that's who you mean. You burned his house down, you sick son of a bitch."

"Don't know what you're talking about. I didn't burn down shit." Because we were on cell phones, and because *he* probably hadn't burned the house down. He'd simply ordered his men to take care of it. And if the harsh laughter in his voice was any indication, he'd enjoyed it. A thought he confirmed when he said, "Sleeping Beauty was a nice touch, no? Take my money, I take your doll. Fair trade."

Doll. He meant Leah. Jesus, only a psychopath would think murder was somehow a fair trade.

My voice cracked as I murmured, "She had nothing to do with you."

"She was a means to an end. Her man got up in my team's face about being out in the woods, and my guys felt disrespected. I'd have let that one go, but he must have notified his boss because your precious Alder set up security in those woods. We can't even get a shipment out of our kitchen right now because of him. But he'll get what's coming to him, no matter what. We always take what we're owed, isn't that right, sis? You know all about payback."

The phone shook against my ear, and I had to take a deep breath to resist the urge to throw it across the room. Payback. I'd been forced to give payback to the club once.

For men involved with the Soul Suckers MC, payback usually meant a fine or a beat down, depending on the severity of the inciting incident. The worst punishment was to have your patch taken away, to be kicked out of the club. But for the women who hung around and were involved with the riders, payback came in a different form. If a woman betrayed the club, she paid with her body.

I'd been a virgin when my dad had died, and his name and rank in the club had protected me just enough to avoid being raped. But Colt had pressed that I needed to make amends for my role in his stepdad's death, that my debt had to be paid. And since I wasn't blood to the guy, Colt had argued the protection my father's name had afforded me was null and void. The club's leaders had agreed, so I'd been given the choice. Pussy or flesh.

I hadn't been willing to spread my legs for the club, so I'd ended up being forced to pay in flesh. Literally. Colt had used a bullwhip on me, had covered my back in scars as payback for my big mistake. They had served as reminders of how it had been my fault his stepfather—the president of his chapter—had died. Every inch of mottled flesh, including the ownership brand on my hip, given by the man on the other end of the phone.

I couldn't let Alder get involved in my mess.

"So what's up, Shyness?" Colt asked, pulling me from my thoughts. "You sick of hiding? Planning on coming in to take your punishment for failing us? Or are we going to have to come pick you up? Prez already sent a team to Justice, you know."

I did know. Or at least, I assumed that was why those two men had been in the barn. Soul Suckers on Alder's property, in his town. This couldn't go on.

"I'm not in Justice anymore."

"That's real unfortunate. You wasted our time, sis. But since you're not there, we can add the hours and gas mileage of sending a couple of guys straight to you to your bill. Hell, maybe I'll give them the okay to take what you owe them directly." His words sent a shiver of fear up my spine, but this...this was how the Soul Suckers operated. What they expected. And if I was going to keep them away from Justice, I had to accept it.

Everyone had a debt to pay, and the time to protect the only currency I had left was over.

"I'll come in on my own, but on one condition."

"You're not in a position to make demands. Besides, I can't promise to keep that pussy safe this time. You lost us a lot of money."

He thought I wanted to protect my body, when in actuality, I wanted Alder safe. That might actually work in my favor—I had a commodity to surrender to them. Something to offer in exchange. The thought of it made me sick, but I'd do what needed to be done.

I closed my eyes and reached deep for every shred of courage I had. I wasn't a virgin anymore. I'd spent one amazing, sensual night with Alder, which would simply have to be enough to get me through what was coming. I could pay my debt back with the one thing the club hadn't been able to take from me and fight from the inside to keep them all away from Justice. From Alder.

"I understand what needs to be paid, and I'm not trying to keep the guys from taking what's owed. I have a different condition, one we can talk about in person." Because if I gave him too much time to think, he'd strike before I even made it in. I needed to set this up just right, to work through how I could convince him to let me pay Alder's debt on top of my own. How I could be assigned the penance for Alder's transgressions.

Anything to keep him safe.

Colt grunted, sounding far too happy for my liking as he replied, "Yeah, well, we'll see about that once you're here. Don't go running your mouth now, either. We don't want to make your punishment any worse than it already is, do we?"

"I won't talk." A lie. If it meant saving Alder, if I thought anyone could actually do anything about the club, I'd tell the whole world all I knew about the Soul Suckers. Not the two dead ones back at Alder's place, but the rest. Loyalty to the club had meant everything to my dad, but Colt had taken it too far. With me, with Camden, with Leah...and now with Alder. Way too far.

The Kennards were the only men who deserved my loyalty and my silence.

"Get your ass to the clubhouse," Colt said, his voice like gravel. "I've got some new toys to play with, and I want to try them out on you."

My back burned at the thought, and a single tear fell down my cheek. But I stayed standing, kept my shoulders back, kept my chin up. If I was going into hell, it would be on my own two feet...

And for my own reasons.

"I'll be there tomorrow."

Chapter Nineteen

ALDER

The drive to Elijah's usually took a solid two hours without traffic. I made it in ninety minutes. It helped that there were no cars on the road so late at night. It also helped that I broke every speed limit to get to my girl faster.

My truck engine roared through the city streets of Denver as I finally made it to Elijah's neighborhood, the heavy rumble breaking the silence of the night. Or morning, depending on how you saw the hour, I supposed. Shye would normally be asleep already, but I doubted that was the case. The night had been too packed with emotion and adrenaline, too filled with stress. She'd be awake and likely hurting, all because I'd made a bad decision. One that I would do anything to make up to her.

And me? The ache of losing her still ate at me, but the flame of rage burning in my gut over what had happened earlier that evening overpowered it. The Soul Suckers wanted to come after me? Wanted to try to show me who was boss? I'd let them, and then I'd rip them down one by one until my girl, my family, my business, and my entire fucking town were safe once more. No options, no second chances, no warnings. And no way would they ever get close to Shye again.

After way too long in the truck, my tires finally rolled onto Elijah's driveway. Lights glowed through the windows, telling me more than just Shye was likely awake. Not what I'd been hoping for. I wasn't in the mood to deal with my sister's inevitable attitude. If Lainie decided to throw one of her "what about me" fits, I'd have to ignore her and deal with her shit another day. I needed to see Shye.

My girl's soft smile on my mind, I threw the truck into park and raced inside, not bothering to knock. Elijah must have known I'd be coming because he sat in the kitchen with Lainie, both of them looking as if they'd been expecting me. Elijah even shot me a sarcastic smile, looking so much like a healthier, younger version of Finn it almost made me pause. Almost...

"Second door on the right," he said, nodding his head toward the stairs. "Try not to break anything, okay?"

I didn't even attempt to make such a ridiculous promise. Instead, I ran up the stairs, taking them two at a time. Needing to see my girl. I'd beg if I had to, drop to my knees and crawl for her if she wanted me to. Whatever it took, I'd fix this thing between us.

When I reached her door, I didn't pause. I simply barreled through it, ignoring the crunch of the handle hitting drywall that I'd probably have to pay to get fixed. Didn't matter. All I cared about was Shye, which was why I froze the second my eyes landed on her. And why my gut suddenly felt as if I'd swallowed a bucket full of lead.

This might be harder than I thought.

Looking completely unfazed by my entrance, Shye sat on the edge of the bed wearing one of my T-shirts, her eyes rimmed in red and her face streaky. Jesus fuck, I'd made her cry at least twice in the past few hours. She looked exhausted and wrung out, like her emotions had tried to consume her and she'd had to fight to stay alive. I'd never allow myself forgiveness for putting her through that, but I'd beg for hers.

"I'm an asshole."

Her brown eyes refused to meet mine, and she didn't move except to respond with a soft, "Correct."

"An ignorant, selfish asshole who wasn't thinking."

"Still not arguing with you."

I wanted her to look at me, to give me some sort of sign that she hadn't walled herself off from me completely. But she gave me nothing. Not a sigh, a look, a shiver. Not a damned signal of any kind. It was time to get real honest with her. "Tonight, those two men broke into the barn as part of an ambush. The Soul Suckers are coming for me because our harvest on Widow's Ridge shut down their meth lab." Deep breath. Deep, deep breath. "I had to take them out."

Dead eyes finally met mine, empty and flat. Not my Shye at all. "I know."

Her simple response stopped me cold. "You do?"

She nodded and rose to her feet, inching closer. Setting my heart on fire with every fucking step. "My stepbrother is the enforcer for the Boulder club. My father—stepfather, really—was president at one time." Closer still, no longer looking in my eyes. "I swear I never wanted to be involved in any of this."

The pain in her voice killed me. Ripped my heart right out of my chest. "Involved in what, honey?"

She shook her head, looking completely heartbroken and scared. "I was just supposed to let them know if anyone came snooping around my side of the ridge. Nothing else."

Truth slammed into me like a fist to the chest, nearly knocking me backward. "You knew the meth lab was there."

She shook her head. "Not specifically, no. But I knew something had to be out there if they were putting me in that trailer to watch. I didn't want to know what exactly, so I never asked."

My thoughts scrambled. She knew. She *knew* they were up to something, and she never told me. Never asked for help. She never said—

"They would have killed me if I'd told anyone," she murmured, as if reading my thoughts. "That's why I'm so good at keeping secrets. I have to be." Slowly, hands shaking, she pulled my shirt over her head and turned, showing me her back. Confusion spun straight into rage as I put together the pieces of what I was seeing. What I'd felt with my own hands earlier in the evening. The reason why she'd run from me.

"They whipped you."

"Thirty lashes or thirty men. That was the choice I was given to pay for the damage I'd wreaked on the club. When you owe a debt, you have to pay it back, and my only currency was flesh or sex." She turned, showing me the brand on her hip. Two shallow, sharp S's side by side—Soul Suckers. "I chose flesh again the second time, not because I wanted to, but because I had no other way to do it."

"What sort of debts?" I reached for her, needing to touch her, feel her. Wanting to hold her. And my god did it half kill me when she jumped away from me, too skittish to let me close to her.

"I killed my father." She tugged her shirt on, covering herself once more. "It was a car accident—T-boned by a semitruck—but I was driving, and the police deemed it my fault for running a yellow light. Since he wasn't my biological father, the club decided I wasn't allowed any sort of family protection. I thought my stepbrother would step in for me. He knew me—had met me when my father married his mom years before. I assumed he'd explain what had happened and how it wasn't intentional, but he told me the club came before family. So he set the punishment." She shook her head and curled in on herself that much more. "Set it and carried it out."

Her stepbrother was a dead man, but I'd get to that. "And having to watch the meth lab?"

Her face turned stormy, her eyes burning with anger. "I didn't come out of the accident unscathed. The Soul Suckers paid for my father's funeral and my living expenses while I recovered. Nine months of housing and doctor bills—with interest, my final debt came to four years labor." Her shoulders relaxed again, her anger fading. "I had six months left when all this started. That's why they burned my trailer down—I didn't do the job I'd been assigned."

"Fuck, Shye. Why didn't you—"

I spun, grabbing my hair and pacing the small room. I didn't need to finish my question because I already knew the answer. She *couldn't* have told me anything. They'd already broken her down—taken her life away from her and abused her to the point that she only saw one road to her survival. She wouldn't have anything left to give, any way to protect herself, and she wouldn't want to see anyone else stuck in the same quagmire. Her silence was a sign of self-preservation and altruism, not deception.

Shye must have thought my pacing meant something negative, though, instead of me finally seeing the entire picture of her life. Tears fell from her pretty eyes, and she turned her back to me. Hiding again.

"I know what I've done, Alder. I know how bad it all is. I'm going to make it up to you, though. I'm going to Boulder to see my stepbrother—"

"Fuck that." I grabbed her, held her. Stopped her from throwing everything away. "You're coming home with me. I want you safe, and that means you're under my watch from now on."

"I can't," she said, looking almost panicked. "They're already coming for you for payback. Once they realize the two from tonight won't make it home, they'll attack harder."

"I don't care."

"I do, but I can fix it. I can do this, Alder. I can go see Colt and convince him to let me pay for my mistakes. I can take responsibility for you finding the kitchen and for the two men tonight. I can fix all of it."

Digging my heart out with a spoon, this girl. As if I'd ever let her put herself in the line of fire for me. "Over my dead body. It's not happening."

"Alder—"

"Goddammit, Shye." I tugged her body against mine, unable to hold back another second. Too terrified of her walking away from me, from us, to be gentle. "Do you think I'm going to let you go there, knowing those fuckers are likely to beat or rape you? Do you really think I'm the type of man who'd allow that to happen to someone?"

She shook her head, eyes watery again. "You're not, but I'll take the punishments so you'll be safe. So they'll leave everyone in Justice alone."

"They won't let either of us *just go*. They've got their sights set on us now and being reasonable isn't how they operate."

"But it's all my fault. If I tell them that, if I let them take what they want from me—"

"No." Fuck no. Just the thought of them taking anything from her made me want to set the world on fire. "This isn't something you need to fix. Is it your fault your stepdad died? Even if you were driving the car, you didn't kill him on purpose. Is it your fault the people who should have protected you and taken care of you chose to abuse you instead? Or that Camden lost his temper with those bikers, or that I refuse to turn my back and let them cook meth on that mountain?" I took a deep breath and looked down at her. "Or that I killed those men in the barn tonight?"

"No, but—"

"None of this is *your* fault."

She choked on a sob, dropping her head against my chest. "They'll kill you. If you try to protect me from them, they will *kill* you."

Fuck, those tears broke my heart. I wrapped my arms around her, squeezing her tight. Doing my best to hold her together. "No, honey. They won't. They'll try, just like earlier tonight, but they won't succeed. I won't let them."

Big, questioning eyes looked up at me. Filled with so much doubt. "How can you be so sure?"

"Because I've already got plans in place to deal with them and a strong team around me. I'm a goddamned Green Beret. Deacon too. Bishop and Gage are SEALS, and Cam's a Marine. They took Leah from us because we weren't ready for an attack—that won't happen again. We'll be the ones attacking."

She shook her head. "They sent two men after you."

"And they're both taken care of. End of story." I shushed her when those wide eyes met mine and the color drained from her face. "I don't want to put you at risk by telling you more, but we eliminated that threat. There's nothing for anyone to find. No way for someone to pin this on me or my team."

She stood silent for a long time, watching me. Slowly regaining her color and seeming almost to settle. "I saw you attack the Soul Suckers who came to the house tonight."

"And I'd do it again. They were there to knock me out of the way and take you back to their president." I leaned closer, making sure she understood my sincerity as I said, "No one will ever hurt you, honey. I won't let them."

She took a deep, shaky breath, still looking so damn worried...but she wasn't running. In fact, she had a strong hold on me. Clinging to my arms as she asked, "Aren't you scared?"

"Of them? No. Of losing you? Terrified." Just the thought had my hands shaking, my body leaning over hers to gain more contact. "I can handle this. I promise you—me and my team can deal with the bullshit they try. Trust me to take care of you." I ran my nose along her cheek, holding tight. Almost afraid to let her go. "Don't leave me, Shye."

She coughed a laugh, running her hand up my face to cup my cheeks and pull me down to her level. "Leave you? I thought you'd be leaving me after all this."

Crazy girl. "I love you too damn much to ever walk away from you."

She gasped, and I took full advantage of her open mouth by pressing mine to it and sliding my tongue inside. That kiss turned into more, both of us quickly bringing our bodies together. Trying to feel one another again. Trying to reconnect.

The second I had Shye's arms and legs wrapped around me, I grabbed her ass and moved. I might have rushed to get her underneath me, but once I laid her on the bed, I took my time. Worshiping her body the way it deserved. Small kisses, little licks, a full-body rubdown—all of it done nice and slow. Making my point hit home that she was mine, that I'd given her my heart, and that I'd always work to take care of her. That nothing would ever come between us again.

"Alder." She pushed me back, breathing hard and looking adorably mussed and ready to be fucked. "What about Elijah and Lainie?"

"They're not my priority right now." I went in for another kiss, which she allowed before pulling away from me.

"They might hear us," she said, sounding almost scandalized.

I could only grin. "Good. Let's teach them both a thing or two."

And then I stripped her down, tugging my own clothes off once I had her naked and ready for me. Recovering her body with mine so there was nothing between us.

Nudging my way inside her tight, wet heat felt more like coming home than anything ever had. I savored the moment, rocking slow, keeping our mouths fused together as I used my body to show her how perfect she was for me. How hard I'd strive to be perfect for her.

When I had her clawing at my back, begging for more and harder and faster, I moved down her body. Kissing, licking, rubbing my way to the feast between her thighs. And then I dove in for a taste.

She told me she loved me the first time I made her come on my tongue, promised me forever the fourth. And when I slid my cock back inside her, when I nearly collapsed with the relief of being joined to her again, I knew this was it for us. She'd be mine. Forever. Just as I'd be hers.

Sex always felt good, but there were different levels of good. With Shye, sex had been amazing—emotional and hot at the same time. Knowing I would always be the only man to know the taste of her, the squeeze of her pussy around my cock, the way she arched and clung to me as she grew closer to her release, had added an extra kick to it. Our make-up sex blew that *and* everything I'd ever experienced out of the water.

"Alder, please." Shye tugged on my shoulders and tilted her hips, trying to make me move faster. To pull me deeper inside her tight, warm pussy. I gave in to that request, pumping hard, dragging her up the bed with the force of my thrusts. Chasing my own release as I watched for signs of her next one.

When I had her completely at my mercy, begging and chanting sounds that should have been words as her body shook beneath me, I slid a hand between us and thumbed her clit. She exploded around me, screaming my name and digging her nails into my back. A beautiful, shaking mass of *my girl* sucking me deeper. With her pussy still milking my cock, I followed her right over that peak, coming hard inside her tight little body. Surrendering the only way I ever would...to her, for her, and because of her.

Later, after too many minutes had passed in the quiet of the two of us wrapped around one another, I felt the telltale sign of Shye thinking too much. True, she curled into my body and let me hold her against me, but she felt way too stiff for someone who'd just gotten fucked the way she had. Something still wasn't right.

"What's wrong, Shye?"

She sighed and pressed her forehead against my chest, taking a long time to finally speak. "I'm still worried. I mean, what are you going to do about all this? The Soul Suckers will come after both of us. They'll come after the town."

"Don't even think it. They're not getting anywhere near you."

"I'm not just worried about me."

"And neither am I." I rolled her underneath me once more. "Justice is not up for sale, especially not to some biker gang with a propensity for arson. They roll into town, we'll kick their asses out. They strike at us, we'll strike right back. They come for me, I'll shut them down. They come for you, I'll blow their fucking world apart."

"I'm not worth it."

Those words gutted me, the tone pouring salt over the wound.

"You're worth everything to me." I ran my tongue along her lips, tasting her. Nibbling that plump bottom lip before pulling back. "No one will ever hurt you again, honey. I'll bury anyone who even thinks about it."

She kept her eyes on mine, kept her arms holding me tight around the neck. That look, the way she seemed to truly *need* me, made me want to flip her over and fuck her until she couldn't breathe. But she wasn't ready for that yet. And me? I still needed to make sure she was mine. Or rather… that I was hers. That she wanted me as much as I wanted her.

"Come home with me," I pleaded, barely more than a whisper against her lips. "I promise I'll take care of you. That I'll keep you safe. I need you, honey. Give me my girl back."

She leaned up to kiss me, squeezing me tight and pulling me on top of her as she responded with a simple, "Yes."

And that was all I needed from her to know we'd be fine.

Chapter Twenty

ALDER

Shye was still asleep when I crept out of bed and headed downstairs. I needed to make a call, to set a few things up. Things she couldn't know about. The sort of things I only trusted one person with.

Phone in hand, I settled in against the kitchen counter, looking out the window. There were too many lights here, not enough stars. That was okay for a night or two, but Justice was my home. The place I had put down roots. The town where I would marry the girl sleeping upstairs and raise our kids.

Only one thing I saw standing in the way of that, so dialing the familiar number was real fucking easy.

"I was wondering if you'd be calling," Deacon said as soon as he answered the phone. "Heard you drove out to Elijah's to get your girl. Everything okay?"

Perfect, and yet... "She's good, but I need a favor."

"Name it." All business. No bullshit. Exactly what I expected, and why I'd called him.

"I need you to call Parris and set up another meeting."

Deacon paused, the silence dragging a beat too long. "Got a reason for that request?"

"Shye's stepbrother." Colt. The enforcer. "He's the link between her and the Soul Suckers. I intend to break that link."

"You looking for information or something more?"

Good question—and one I had no trouble answering. "Information. I'll be taking care of the *something more* personally."

"Planning on filling me in?"

Yeah, I would. Her story wasn't mine to tell, but I could give him enough. A taste of the rage fueling my decision. "He whipped her, left her scarred, and he plans to bring her back to the club to pay a debt. I don't think I need to tell you how a woman pays for anything with a man like that."

Deacon's voice dropped lower, rumbling like a growl. "You sure the fuck don't."

"So then you understand what I need."

Names, addresses, habits, friends, who he fucked, who he owed money to, where he bought his fucking groceries, how often he took a shit. All of it. A full dossier on the sick bastard.

So I could find a way to take him out.

I didn't need to tell Deacon any of that, though. He knew. "Text me everything you know about him, and I'll make the call. I'll take on the debt of owing Parris a favor for it, too."

A favor might as well have been a golden ticket in the MC world. That was something we'd both figured out fast. "You don't have to do that."

"Yeah, I do. And when the time comes to break the link, I'll be beside you."

Of that, I had no doubt. "Hooah, brother."

"I'll let you know when I have something." He ended the call without a goodbye. I didn't mind—I had enough to deal with without having to worry about manners and shit. I needed to dig up information on Shye's stepbrother, needed to develop a plan of assault, needed to cover all my bases. Then I needed to skin the fucker alive for what he'd done to her. What he still might *try* to do. Because there was no way he'd succeed in getting his hands on her. He'd have to go through me first, and I wasn't a man who'd go down easy.

"Alder?" Shye slipped down the stairs, looking so fucking sexy and rumpled in my shirt that my breath actually caught in my throat. "What are you doing?"

Everything I can to keep you safe. "Nothing, honey. Just checking my phone. Why aren't you in bed?"

I held out my hand to her, pulling her close when she grabbed it. Needing to feel her against me. She snuggled into my chest and sighed, so damn small in comparison to me. So delicate. My fragile girl with a spine of steel.

"I woke up in a weird room all alone," she said, keeping her voice soft. Sounding almost nervous. "And I was afraid you'd left."

Oh, fuck no. I tipped her chin up, looking into the most beautiful brown eyes in the world. "Never. You're mine now, and I'm yours. I'm not going anywhere."

Her smile had never seemed brighter. "Good. Then let's go back to bed. It's too early for you to be up, and there's no way I can figure out that fancy coffee machine thing."

My laugh rumbled softly as I stood and followed her to the stairs. "I stayed here once for a meeting with a client and nearly threw the fucking thing out the window."

"Really?"

"Yep. Lainie was pissed."

Shye's lips twisted into a sort of frown. "I don't think she likes me."

Lainie's story was one for another day. "She doesn't like anything to do with me or Bishop, but she won't bother you." She'd better not, at least.

I herded Shye into the bed, rolling her halfway underneath me once we were under the covers. Breathing her in as I rocked my hips against her, dragging my cock over her thigh.

"You tired, honey? Because I'm pretty sure I can keep you occupied if you can't sleep."

Shye's soft laugh turned to a groan when I yanked up her shirt and sucked hard on her small, tight nipple. So sweet, my girl. Every inch of her. And I wanted to taste them all.

Arching her back and spreading her legs, she moaned, "Alder," in a breathy sort of tone.

Yeah. I'd never get tired of hearing her gasp my name like that. Like she *needed* me. Just as I needed her.

I popped off her nipple and moved down, kissing her stomach and spreading her legs wider as I went. "I wonder if your pussy tastes any different now."

She gripped my hair, tugging as I teased the seam of her thigh with my tongue. "Different how?"

"Don't know, but you're not a virgin anymore. Virgin pussy might taste different than owned-by-Alder-Kennard pussy."

Her body shook with her giggle. "You already tasted me tonight. You should know if it's different."

"I wasn't paying attention then. I will be this time."

"You're crazy. There's no difference."

"Maybe. Maybe not." I spread her with my thumbs, taking a good, long lick of her cunt. "I know a way to find out."

And I did.

Find out.

A few times.

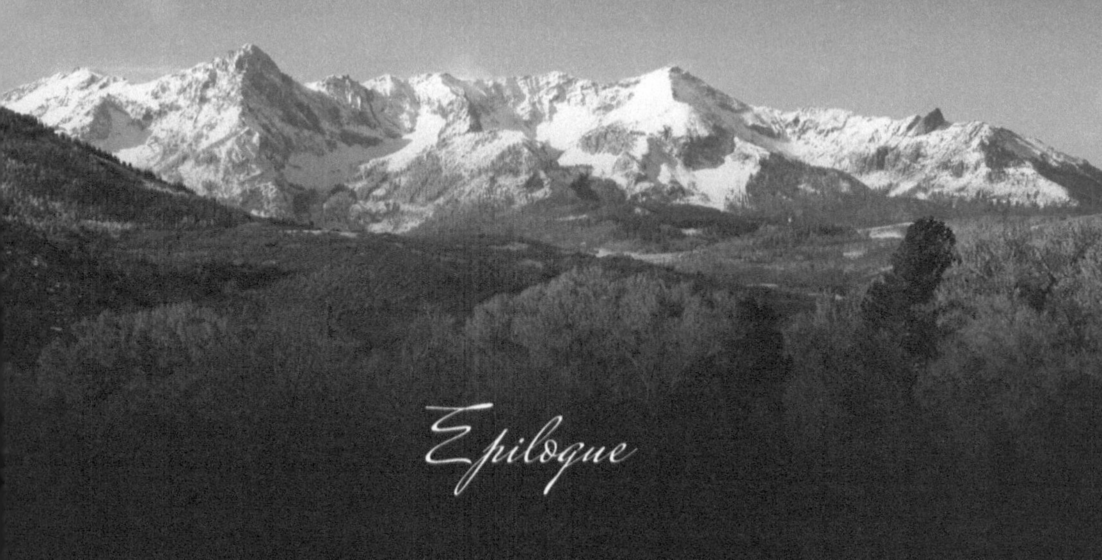

Epilogue

SHYE

It wasn't every day that the Kennard team set a forest on fire. Okay, not a forest. Just a section of one. One with an old barn that had been retrofitted to be an illegal chem lab of sorts. One they shouldn't have known about. So I guess you could say it wasn't every day that the Kennard team set fire to a meth lab. But on that afternoon, a mere two days after Alder had come for me at Elijah's house, that was exactly what the boys were doing.

Alder and I had spent that first day together in that guest-room bed, loving and being loved together, but eventually, he'd needed to return to work. To get back to killing the Soul Suckers' business in Justice. So I'd climbed into his truck, and we'd spent a leisurely three hours on backroads heading home to Justice, talking and laughing and getting to know one another better.

And ignoring the thousands of phone calls, voicemails, and text messages from Colt.

Alder had said we'd get my number changed, but we both knew that wouldn't be enough to break Colt's hold on me. I'd turned my phone off that first day and hadn't turned it back on yet. Which was how I ended up sitting in the silence of Alder's house—my house now, too, I guessed—

alone and with nothing to do except cling to the cordless phone from Alder's room. My room now, too. Things were changing so fast.

Some things stayed the same, like Alder making sure I had someone to watch over me. Finn sat outside on the porch, keeping guard. I didn't know much about the youngest Kennard brother except that he was a recovering addict who loved the huckleberry pie at the truck stop. He hadn't spoken much on our trip to Denver together and even less since he'd shown up that morning. In fact, Finn had been outside since Alder had left for Widow's Ridge, leaving me alone in the house for hours.

Exhaustion weighed heavy on my shoulders, but I couldn't even *think* of going to sleep. Not knowing Alder was out there doing something that would certainly bring hell to his front door. Not with how worried I was that things would go wrong and I'd never see him again. The Soul Suckers could have booby-trapped the woods. They could have been lying in wait. Alder had said I didn't need to worry, but without him...

I couldn't think of that, so instead, I lifted Alder's heavy mug and took a sip of the coffee I'd brewed for him before he'd left with Bishop. I sipped, I worried, and I stared at the front door, willing Alder to walk through it, sitting in that silent house and waiting for some sort of news. Waiting through the torture of not knowing anything. I'd chosen to stay back, had decided I didn't need to see that kitchen burn to close any doors on my past. I'd already seen Alder in soldier mode—he could handle this one without me there to distract him.

The first sign that I was about to learn what had happened out on the ridge came in the form of a rumble. A truck driving on the road, moving closer, and finally turning into the driveway. Then footsteps on the porch as Finn moved in front of the door. I kept my seat, too afraid to hope that Alder had pulled up. Telling myself that it would be Bishop or Gage instead, coming to tell Finn and me that something had gone wrong and Alder wouldn't be coming home. Fearing it.

Seconds dragged, every sound heightened and making my head throb. Voices, more footsteps, and then nothing. Silence for several long minutes. I finally stood, still staring at that blasted slab of wood keeping me away from the outdoors. Still waiting.

But then Alder opened the door, walked inside, and the world righted itself. I had a brief moment of relaxation before I took a good, hard look at him. Relaxation gone. My sweet, loving Alder was gone, replaced with the cold, hard soldier I remembered from the night in the barn. The one who'd grabbed the gun from the Soul Sucker and pounded the handle against the man's face. The one who'd been all business. The one who'd killed...for me.

And yet, I'd never seen him look so mean as he did right there in the doorway.

I couldn't move, frozen in place by the hardness he exuded even though I wanted to run to him. Fearing how he would react. He looked bigger and rougher than usual, more military than I'd ever seen him. I'd always known he'd been in the Army, and he'd definitely acted like a soldier at times, but this was different. The man before me was all business, completely focused and ready to destroy anything in his path to complete his mission. From his heavy brown boots over his jeans to the neckline of his black T-shirt, he looked every bit like a man who would sooner end your life than listen to you mouth off. And he couldn't take his eyes off me.

"All done?" I finally asked when the silence grew too heavy.

He nodded, still staring. His body tense and his eyes devouring me with a fierceness that made goose bumps appear on my arms. I didn't know whether to be aroused or scared—maybe neither. Maybe both. I fidgeted with the coffee mug, bouncing slightly on the balls of my feet but not moving. The prey to his predator, too afraid to make a mistake and end up in his jaws. Too afraid not to.

But even prey had to take a chance at some point.

"Alder," I whispered, my entire body trembling with the warring desires of safety and lust. One said to run away, the other to run toward. I couldn't decide which instinct to follow, so I waited for him to tell me. To give me some sign of what he needed. What he wanted. I set down the mug.

Alder cocked his head, probably at the plea in my voice. Watching me. Waiting for *something*. An animal finally off his leash. My dragon at the gates set free and hungry for me. I whimpered at the thought, and he finally broke.

"You going to get over here and love me, honey? Or am I going to have to bend you over that counter and eat your pussy nice and slow to remind you that you're mine?"

And just like that, my choice appeared. The only one that made sense.

I was in motion before I could even think of moving. Running toward him in my bare feet, eating up the space between us, and jumping into his arms. He smelled of the forest and smoke, a harsh reminder of where he'd been and why. But when he grabbed me, when he picked me up and carried me as if I weighed nothing, I simply melted into his strong body and let him.

His, indeed. "I was so worried."

"No need. I can handle this—*my team* and I can handle this." His eyes burned with the fire of a confidence I'd never known but that he obviously had in spades. "You'll be safe. Just stick with me, Shye, and we'll pull through. I promise you that. We *will* destroy this club. No one will hurt you ever again."

And as much as I knew they were just words, I had to believe him. Because he'd never given me any reason not to. Because he was still the biggest, strongest man I'd ever seen. And I had faith in him.

"I love you, Alder."

"I love you too, honey. So fucking much. Now, let's get back to talking about how I'm going to eat that pussy of yours."

My sweet-talker, my protector, my dragon at the gates. It didn't matter what I thought of him as, so long as he was mine.

———

REPARATION

kristin harte

Reparation

Everyone left threads untied in their lives. Mine just happened to be the kind that could make you stumble, could make you fall flat on your face. Could leave a trip line handy for the enemies who would use it against you.

My girl needed safety and security, and I hadn't given that to her. Not really. Not yet, at least.

To secure her future, I needed to put mine in jeopardy.

I needed to do some killing.

Chapter 1

ALDER

The evidence of someone else's depravity had become the ultimate sign of my failure as a man.

Scars. They riddled her body, covered her back in a mishmash of raised flesh that made my blood burn hot with rage. Every line, every lash, was a bitter reminder that I'd failed her. Even though I hadn't known her when those marks had been created, I saw them as my own personal defeat. The man who had hurt her, who had broken her skin and made her bleed, who had branded her as if she were nothing more than livestock, was still alive. Still a threat to us. Still pulling strings that endangered my girl, my town, and my family.

Still instilling fear in the woman I loved more than life itself on an almost daily basis.

I never knew what sort of mood my Shye would be in when I got home from work. She was a happy person at her heart—kind and loving, nurturing almost to a fault. She'd normally have a smile on her face and a few words for me about how she'd missed me. She'd ask me about my day and give me a little hug and a kiss. Those days were my favorite because I got to tell her how much I missed her, too. How much she meant to me.

Got to run my hands over her curves and feel her hot little body pressed against mine.

But every once in a while, maybe one day out of fifteen, she wouldn't be waiting in the kitchen for me. She wouldn't be smiling or happy or ready for me to paw all over her. She'd be tucked into a dark corner or curled up under a blanket. Her face would be blank or maybe tear-streaked, her muscles tense. I'd come home to find my girl trapped in memories I couldn't rescue her from and surrounded by demons I couldn't slay for her.

I knew today would be one of the bad days the second I pulled up to the house.

"She's been quiet." Three words. That was all Finn needed to say for me to understand exactly what I was walking into.

"Thanks. I'll take care of her." I hurried up the steps and across the porch, leaving my brother to head home without a goodbye. My mind was already focused on my girl, on what she needed, on finding a way to pull her from her fear cycle as quickly as possible. I opened the front door slowly and called, "Shye?"

Nothing. No response. Which wasn't like her. She had to be hiding somewhere in the house. Not from me—never that. Thank Christ the woman didn't fear *me* because I think that would have broken my heart to have to see. No, what Shye feared she wouldn't find inside of me. Not ever.

I headed to Shye's normal hiding spot, crossing the smoke-gray floors with quick but quiet steps. She adored my beetle kill pine floors and the neutral colors of my little house in the woods. She said it had felt like a home to her right from the start, which was what I'd wanted. I would have changed anything—ripped the whole damn structure down and started over for her—but she'd loved my place from the moment she'd moved in. So it was now our place, but she had her preferences on where she spent her time. Her spaces that seemed more comfortable for her. One of those was the entertainment room—big, soft couches with matching armchairs furnished the room, a respectably sized television hung on one wall, and my books lined shelves that circled the rest of the room and framed the large windows looking out over the valley. Dark and comfortable, the room had always been my favorite one in the house. Shye must have agreed.

I found Shye curled up in one of the leather armchairs, a soft blanket covering her and a book left open in her lap. She looked completely relaxed at first glance. Just a woman staring out the window at the beautiful fall day outside. But then she turned slightly, just enough for me to see the red rimming her eyes and the paleness of her face. The pinkish tinge along her cheeks from the tears. She'd been crying. Again.

"Honey? Are you okay?"

She finally faced me and gave me the wateriest smile known to man. "I didn't hear you come in."

Because she was probably stuck in the rut of reliving memories. Of the years between when her dad had died and when I'd snatched her away from her solitary life. Of how her stepbrother had tortured her, beaten her, and threatened her very life.

All things I needed to deal with at some point. Soon. But first...

"You look cold."

She shrugged, still not holding my gaze. "It was a little chilly earlier."

"Why don't I draw you a bath? We can sit and chat for a bit while you warm up."

"You don't have to do that."

"I want to. Besides, I always enjoy getting you naked."

She laughed, still sounding too soft to be normal. Too far away. Still lost in her thoughts. I'd tug her out of them, though. Soon. I paid attention to her—knew her signs of struggle and her wants almost as well as she did. I knew what she needed most of all, too, and I'd provide that for her. I hadn't yet—not really. Not completely. But I was a determined motherfucker. Steadfast and sure. I'd get there.

I followed Shye upstairs, my head swimming with plans and thoughts and intel on the issue at hand. I couldn't tell her what I was going to do— she'd try to stop me. Be so worried something would go wrong that she'd beg me not to try. And I'd listen to her because all I wanted was to make her happy. To give her what she wanted. But need had to outweigh want, and what she *needed* was safety and security. Stability. That meant getting rid of the metaphorical quicksand beneath our feet.

Once the bath was run, I stripped out of my clothes and slowly, lovingly removed hers as well. Seeing her naked always revved my engine, but the flatness in her eyes, the emptiness, kept me from taking my foot off the brake. She needed me, but not in that way. Not yet, at least. Later, she'd want my weight on her body and my arms around her. She'd want me to love her good and slow, want to lose track of everything but me. She'd want to spend a few hours being us.

Right then, there was someone else in the room. The ghost of a memory haunting her, crowding us. So, I'd wait, and I'd do my best to break the hold of that energy. I'd make sure she knew I would always take care of her, and I'd give her time to forget once more.

So instead of kisses and touches and pushing her toward a physical peak of pleasure, I settled her between my legs in the hot water and started washing. I took care of my girl because she needed it. Needed me to be soft with her for a bit.

I was washing her hair when she murmured, "You are the sweetest man."

No, I was a man who paid attention and was so fucking grateful for the gifts she gave me, but I wouldn't argue with her. Not then. "You deserve sweetness. Now, what got you upset today?"

"I'm not—"

"Shye."

She sighed, leaning back against me as I ran my fingers through her wet hair. "Colt's birthday is today."

Colt. Her stepbrother. Also known as a Soul Suckers enforcer with the road name Pistol. Also known as the motherfucker who had tried to force Shye to fuck thirty men for some sort of screwed-up payment after her dad had died in a car accident. And when she'd refused, he'd put the scars on her back instead. Thirty men or thirty lashes.

Colt didn't deserve to celebrate another birthday.

I rinsed the shampoo from her hair and leaned her forward, staying silent. Giving her the chance to tell me more. At least, until she flinched when I touched her back.

"Alder—"

"I love you, honey." I kissed along her shoulder, tracing the lines of brutality with my lips. Showing love where she'd once been shown hate. Not stopping until she had relaxed again in my hold.

She finally sighed. "I know you do."

There was no way she understood how much, so I kissed her scars again. "Every inch of you."

"Those are some ugly inches."

"You're beautiful. Always."

"And you're a charmer."

"I still try."

"You still succeed." She turned, straddling me. Facing me in the tub even as the water sloshed over the sides. Looking more like her normal self. "I'm sorry I get so upset."

"Don't you dare apologize to me."

"You shouldn't have to pick up my pieces when I fall apart."

Aw, fuck no. "Shye, you make me happier than I ever thought possible. So, yes, I *should* have to. I should worry and care for and do everything I can to keep you happy because there is nothing I love more than seeing you smile."

And there it was—her real smile. The one she saved just for me. The one that told me I'd locked that ghost up tight. For now.

"I know I already said this, but I hope you know I mean it when I tell you that you are the *sweetest* man."

Not even close. "Just giving back what you give me. Now, come on— let's get out of this tub and put some clothes on. I feel like taking you out."

The excited smile on her face felt like a punch in the gut. I'd been so busy lately with work and taking care of the town that I hadn't spent as much time spoiling her as she deserved. I'd start fixing that tonight.

Shye stepped out of the tub, grabbing two towels and handing me one as she asked, "Where are we going?"

As if we had a lot of options. "I was thinking we could go to The Baker's Cottage for dinner, and afterward maybe head over to that country bar in Crystal Falls for a little dancing."

"You've never taken me dancing before."

I hadn't, but I suddenly wanted to spend a few hours with her wrapped in my arms. Wanted to rock her side to side as we moved across the hardwood floor. Wanted to forget that Camden had quit the mill and left town, that Bishop had basically done the same with as much time as he spent in Vegas with Anabeth, and that Gage and Katie had killed the county sheriff last week, which had meant Deacon and I had been forced to make some pretty last-minute decisions on the body disposal of a relatively public figure. She needed to get her mind off her past, and I needed to get my mind off my present.

"Maybe not, but that doesn't mean I can't do it tonight. C'mon, honey. Put on a pretty dress. I want to show you off a little. Make sure every man in the county knows you're mine."

Her laugh warmed my heart, but my own grin fell the second she walked out of the bathroom. We'd go out tonight. I'd buy her a nice dinner, take her dancing. Charm the panties right off her and make sure she laughed and blushed a few times. And when I got her home, I'd have her calling my name and coming on my cock for sure.

But, tomorrow...

Tomorrow, I'd start putting things in motion.

My girl needed safety and security.

Which meant I needed to do some killing.

Chapter 2

ALDER

Being pulled from sleep in the middle of the night had never been my favorite thing. As a kid, it had usually been because one of my siblings was having a nightmare. When I'd grown old enough to help my dad take care of the town as all Kennard men were bound to do, he'd tended to wake me up because there'd been an issue that needed handling. Some sort of emergency that couldn't wait until morning.

When I'd headed off for the military, wake-up calls were because of incoming enemies or missions that needed to be enacted right away. Or simply because the officer in charge had felt like being a prick. That had also happened in my earlier years, though I'd become the prick later on. Turnabout being fair play and all.

Once I'd moved home, if I was woken up in the middle of the night, it was usually because of a problem in town that needed my attention. Right back to my teenage years, just with me fully in charge. Fully responsible for the lives of the people who called Justice home.

So, yeah, all bad reasons to be pulled from sleep. Because of my history, I tended not to like being woken up. At least, I hadn't until I moved my girl in to my house and my bed. Three years of wanting her, wondering what loving her would be like, and I'd learned my answer. I'd also learned to enjoy being woken up by her. The woman had a tendency to pull me from sleep with her hands on my flesh, her dirty words softly whispered in my ear, and her body primed for me. Great nights, but not the best. My favorite was when she woke me with her lips wrapped around my cock. Just like tonight.

"Damn, honey." I groaned and arched hard, sliding into the sweet, hot heaven of her mouth as I came fully awake. She hummed around me and sucked harder, taking me deep. Fuck, I was going to come. Likely only two minutes in, and I might as well have been a horny teenager with how much control I had. Or didn't have.

But Christ, I wanted to make this last. Wanted to enjoy a few extra minutes of her loving me that way. Wanted to burn the image and feelings into my memory—the way her hair tickled across my abs with every bob of her head, how she kept her hands braced against my hips for leverage. The wet heat of her mouth enveloping me. So good. Too good for any man to resist. That girl was too much but not enough all at once, and I was right there with her. Loving every second of heaven and hell she gave me.

And when she suctioned those lips that were made for doing exactly what she was doing, I finally lost my damn mind. With pleasure rocketing through my gut and tightening my balls, my leash snapped. But I didn't want to come in her mouth.

"Get up here." I grabbed her under the arms and dragged her up the length of me, capturing her mouth as soon as I had her where I wanted her. She wiggled those sinful hips over mine until I was lined up just right, then sank back, taking me inside her. She couldn't take me quick, though. My girl had been a virgin when I'd met her, and she was a lot smaller than me. Every time we had sex, I had to be careful, to nudge my way inside slowly. To give her time to stretch around me so she didn't hiss in pain. That first minute or so when we joined was always a test of my control— the heat, the tightness, the way she'd gasp and hold her breath as I worked my way deeper. All challenges I needed to overcome so I didn't come on the spot.

But the best, my absolute favorite and most mind-blowing thing my girl did was to close her eyes and purr as I finally worked my way in deep. She fucking *purred* like a cat. That noise always came right as I slid in all the way. Just as I ended up completely surrounded by her heat. That sound made me want to come so hard, every time. I'd been the man who introduced her to sex, and knowing she enjoyed it—that she was able to give herself over to her pleasure with me—was everything. I'd never deserve her, but I'd work myself to the bone to make her happy. And right then, making my girl happy meant making her come.

"Alder, please." Shye sat up straight, her hair falling over her shoulders in golden waves, my T-shirt covering the parts of her she didn't like me to see. I knew what she wanted—what she loved. My mouth. Or, more specifically, my words. As much as she'd likely never admit it, she loved when I talked dirty to her. And I loved watching her go wild on my cock when I said the right things.

"That's it, honey. Ride me hard. Let me watch your little cunt take my cock deep."

She bounced harder, moaning loudly. I slipped a hand between us, pressing on her clit with my thumb as she worked hard on top of me. As she brought us both right to the edge of release and then let herself go. The feel of her coming, the way her pussy clenched around me and practically milked my cock, was too good to resist. Too much. I'd been fighting wanting to come long enough. I thrust up hard, groaning as I filled her. As I came inside her heat.

"Fuck." I took a deep breath and yanked her up my body, kissing her nice and strong when I had her wrapped up in my arms. "I love it when you wake me up with your mouth."

"I know." She giggled and curled up on me, clinging to my arms as she caught her breath. "You tell me that every time I do it."

I did. "Just want to make sure you know how happy you make me."

She lifted her head and brought her mouth to mine, giving me one of those sweet, sweet kisses that almost made my heart stop. Her smile when she pulled away restarted it, though. "I'm glad I do because I feel the same way about you."

"Good. Then we're a matched set." I patted her ass and helped her stand, knowing she'd want to clean herself up a little before we went back to sleep. After we'd both taken care of what we needed to, I dragged her little ass back under the covers and tucked her against my chest. "You good now, honey?"

She hummed her assent. "Dinner, dancing, and late-night loving. This has been the best night ever."

My chuckle shook the mattress. "I'm glad you enjoyed it."

She released a big sigh and snuggled closer. "I never expected to be this happy."

That comment stole all the air from my lungs. "You didn't think I'd make you happy?"

"I didn't think you'd do anything with me. After my dad died, after the accident, I never expected..." She sighed, rubbing her face against my chest. Hiding. "You were a surprise to me, that's all I meant."

But it wasn't, and we both knew it. She hadn't expected to be happy because her stepbrother had made her life miserable and threatened her at every turn. He'd treated her like an object, like something he owned. Something he could abuse without consequences. And deep down, I knew she still worried he'd come back for her. I did too—which was why I never left her alone. If she wasn't with me, one of my men was with her. I kept her safe.

But danger lurked, and there were things I couldn't control or see coming. A thought that had been building inside of me since the motorcycle club her stepbrother was part of had burned her trailer to the ground. They'd started a war with Justice, bringing a battle straight to my door, and I was going to have to finish it. Especially if I wanted to keep them as far away from Shye as possible, which I did. I wanted to make sure the men of the Soul Suckers never ever even crossed paths with her again.

And then? When I finally made sure there was nothing hanging over Shye's head that scared her? When I cleared the path for her to have the happiest life possible without fear? I'd marry her. I wanted to already, craved it like nothing else, no matter how little time we'd actually been together. I'd wanted her for three years before she had even given me a chance. I wasn't about to waste more time waiting. But first, I needed to eradicate the threat to her.

Which meant I needed to break the connection between Shye and the Soul Suckers.

ALDER

In the morning, the thoughts lingering in my head weren't good ones. They weren't memories of a fun night out with my girl or the feel of her lips wrapped around me. I didn't wake up to bask in the residual happy vibes that had surrounded me the night before. No joy lingered, no sense of being sated mattered. My thoughts that morning had gone full dark.

They were deadly.

Murderous, even.

Shye hadn't slept well after she'd woken me up. In fact, she'd seemed to have nightmares for the rest of the night, whimpering in her sleep until I squeezed her tight and whispered into her ear to remind her that I was with her. That nothing would take her away from me. She'd settle for a little while, falling back into a restless sleep until the cycle started all over again.

I was exhausted, but even more than that, I was pissed. My girl deserved to rest calmly. She deserved the peace of knowing she was taken care of, that there was nothing out to get her. No demons waiting to snatch her away from the life she loved. She deserved to feel safe, and the fact that she didn't rested solely on my shoulders. Which meant I had a job to do. One I'd spent months preparing for at that point. I'd been studying hard, but the final exam was coming. And soon.

I followed Shye to The Baker's Cottage, the restaurant where she worked as a waitress a few days a week. Not that she needed to—I'd promised to provide anything and everything she needed. But Shye liked pulling her own weight, and I respected that. I'd refused to let her keep working out at the county line truck stop, though. I couldn't keep an eye on her there, so I'd made sure Katie—a local girl who'd recently moved home from Denver—had everything she'd needed to open a restaurant in town. Then I'd convinced her Shye would be the perfect waitress for her new business. My girl was a hard worker—I'd already seen that. She was also kind and pretty, the perfect person to serve grumpy old loggers coming down off the mountains every night. And those men all worked for me—I didn't have to worry about wandering hands or propositions.

Thankfully, the women got along and were even developing a friendship. I considered that a huge win. Justice got a restaurant, Shye got a job, and my team got a convenient cluster of women and one child who needed protection all in the same area—Katie, my Shye, Mercy, who owned the hardware store in town, and her young son. And with the relationship blooming between Katie and my brother's best friend, Gage —a former Navy SEAL with an attitude almost as wide as his shoulders—I knew those women would be protected well. Especially when I couldn't be there...like today.

Gage was sitting at the bar in the restaurant when I walked in with Shye. No Rex, though. His ever-present canine companion was such a regular sight that it struck me as unusual not to see him at his master's side.

That fact put me right on edge. "What's up, man?"

Gage gave me a head nod but didn't rise to his feet, didn't say a word either. He simply sat and looked ready to spit nails. It didn't take long to figure out why.

A man walked out of the restroom—one I didn't recognize in the slightest. One whose stiff jeans, dark collared shirt, and thick, black glasses made him appear slightly...out of place. Like a costume. Clark Kent in place of Superman or some shit.

"You must be Alder Kennard," the stranger said, beelining toward me. "Zane Grogan. I'm the undersheriff to Sheriff Baker, though, I guess I'm sort of acting sheriff right now, what with him being missing and all." His smile reminded me of Bishop's when he was getting ready to bust your balls—like a rattlesnake prepared to strike. Fortunately, I'd been dealing with my brother and his antics for most of my life. I knew how to handle the undersheriff. But first, I needed to make sure my girl was out of the way.

I patted Shye on the ass and leaned down to give her a quick kiss on the cheek, keeping my body between hers and the interloper's. "Go on back, honey. I'll pick you up later."

"Have a good day. Come see me at lunch if you can."

"Promise." I shot Gage a look, which brought him off his stool. He ambled closer, directing Shye into the kitchen. Whispering to her and making her smile. Shye hurried across the restaurant with Gage, scurrying past the undersheriff, looking small and almost scared as he followed her with his eyes. Unacceptable—him looking and her being scared.

"Like what you see there, Grogan?"

Zane turned his ice-blue gaze back my way, the look on his face shrewd. Calculating. "I do, actually. Nice place Justice has in this Baker's Cottage. Can't say I've ever had the occasion to come out here before, so I had no idea what to expect when Mark—sorry, Sheriff Baker—told me his niece had opened a restaurant here. It's more than I thought it would be."

Yeah. Baker's niece owned the restaurant. She'd also helped kill her uncle after he'd tried and failed to kidnap her for the Soul Suckers. I had a hunch Gage—who was back at the bar looking like a boulder waiting to crush whatever was in its path—had actually pulled the trigger. Not that it would matter if Undersheriff Grogan started digging too deep. I didn't want either of them going down for that sort of crime.

"Something I can do for you, Sheriff?"

"Undersheriff, still. At least, until Baker's body is found."

"I didn't know the investigation into his disappearance had been upgraded to a homicide."

"It hasn't. Not yet, at least." He grinned, showing way too many teeth. Not a rattlesnake about to strike. More like someone trying way too hard to seem friendly. "But Mark was a good man—solid and sure. I can't imagine any other reason why he'd suddenly disappear unless there was foul play involved."

I could imagine plenty of reasons, most of them because good, solid, and sure were the least accurate words to describe Mark Baker that had ever been spoken. "I see. So, what brings you to Justice?"

"Just driving through, really. I'd been hoping to see Mark's niece—maybe talk to her about her uncle—but your bearded guard dog over there claims she's not around."

No way was Katie not in the back, likely with Rex at her side, which meant Gage was running interference. Smart man. "Looks like you'll have to schedule your conversation for another day. Sorry you wasted your trip."

"Not a waste." He grabbed a bag from the counter—one of Katie's bagged lunches—and a to-go cup of coffee. "Your friend supplied me with this takeout, and I got to meet you."

Something about that sounded more ominous than the words themselves seemed. "Some reason you were looking for me?"

"Not really. Just wondering what's been going on around here lately. I've heard a few rumors."

"What sorts of rumors?"

He shrugged as if this was some sort of casual conversation. "Things about the town being dangerous. About some missing men. Good men. Like the sheriff."

Good? The only men missing were riders in the Soul Suckers motorcycle club who'd come to take Shye from me. And the ones who'd tried to kidnap my brother's girl, Anabeth. And a few who'd attacked Katie on orders of her uncle. Not so good in my opinion. "Can't tell you anything about missing men. That Soul Suckers motorcycle gang has been around a lot, though—maybe you should be looking at them."

His slow smile might as well have been a threat crossing his face. "Oh, I've looked at them already. Had a nice long conversation with a man named Pistol. He had a lot of stories to tell me about you and your girl. Her name's Shye, right?"

If Gage hadn't jumped in to press his hand against my chest, I likely would have ended up in jail for murdering the county undersheriff right then and there.

"Alder." Gage physically pushed me back. "Don't do it."

My attention wasn't on him, though. "You bring that name into this town again, and it won't matter who's around—I'll drop you where you stand."

Grogan didn't look surprised by my anger. "Is that a threat, Alder Kennard?"

"It's a fucking promise." I shoved Gage off me and headed for the kitchen, needing to make sure my girl was okay, to know that motherfucker Pistol hadn't somehow gotten past me. Suddenly wishing I could take Shye home with me and pack our stuff. I'd never run from a goddamned thing in my life, but I'd never had so much to lose either. If it were just me, I'd fight to the death. But having Shye by my side? That changed everything. I wanted to keep her safe, and safe might mean not in Justice.

"Hang on," Grogan hollered, holding up his hands. "I just wanted to talk to you, Kennard."

"Yeah, well, talk is cheap." I stopped at the door to the kitchen, making sure to hold the fucker's gaze as I said, "Get out of my town, Undersheriff Grogan."

"You're not the law around here."

I laughed. Loud and long. I practically fucking guffawed my way back across the restaurant. "You know, I heard that from Sheriff Baker just a few months ago. Those exact same words." My laughter stopped. "He was wrong then, and you're wrong now. I'm the only law in this fucking town."

Grogan didn't back down. "I want to talk to you about the Soul Suckers."

"Unless that talk includes details of how you're arresting those murdering motherfuckers, I've got nothing to say."

His lips went thin, his eyes hard. "I can't arrest them. Not without some sort of case to give the DA."

"Like I said..." I held out my arms and backed away. "Have a safe drive out of town, Undersheriff Grogan. Next time, call before you cross into Justice. We're awfully busy over here."

Before I could disappear into the back, Zane fucking Grogan tried one last time. "Mark Baker was a friend of mine, you know."

"You should be more careful who you call friend, because I can guarantee you this—that man would have sold you out in a heartbeat. Just like he sold out everyone else around him."

And with that, I slammed through the swinging door into the kitchen, leaving the undersheriff with Gage.

Shye stood waiting for me. "Are you okay?"

I didn't answer, just picked her up and carried her to the back hallway where I could be alone with her. Where I could break even if for only a second without anyone else seeing it.

"Alder, baby. You're scaring me."

Just one more thing to add to my pile of how I'd failed her. I stopped, leaning her against a wall and sliding my hands down her legs. Caging her against the concrete wall with my body as I tried to catch my breath. "I don't mean to."

"I know." She tugged on my hair, making me grumble. She knew how much I loved it when she did that. "What happened?"

"Nothing, honey."

"Alder." My name was a rebuke on her lips. One I couldn't fully ignore.

"Nothing happened. Yet."

She gave me a hard, worried look. "I don't know if I like that *yet*."

If she knew what was involved in that *yet*, she definitely wouldn't. "It'll be fine, okay? I promise."

She stared me down, so very beautiful and fragile. Blessing me with her smile and her caring eyes and her body wrapped around mine. She was everything I could have asked God for back before wars and battle and the nastiness of life made it hard for me to believe he existed. Shye made me believe again—her goodness, her trust. Her simple faith that she put in me without question. The woman loved me, no doubt in my mind about that. Loved me in a way I would never deserve. But I'd sure as hell try.

"I love you, Shye," I whispered, unable to hold back.

Her smile grew, lighting up the whole damn hallway. "I know you do."

"I don't think you know how much."

"I do, Alder. I really do."

Words I so wanted to hear, just in a different place. Or hell, in this place. If she said them to me with a preacher beside us, we could do the deed wherever she wanted. So long as at the end of it, she was mine in big capital letters. Legal-like.

I was the law in Justice, but not for this. Not for county records and paperwork. For her, I wanted official. I wanted everything.

I wanted her tied to me forever. But to get that, I needed to knock a few things out of our way first.

Chapter 4

ALDER

It took me almost an hour to be able to leave Shye with Gage and Katie. Took me thirty minutes to get to the mill as I backtracked and looped through the streets of Justice to make sure the undersheriff wasn't lying in wait somewhere. Thankfully, I'd had the good presence of mind to text Deacon the second I'd left the restaurant. No flowery words or wishes of good morning. Just a simple *get your ass to the mill*.

He'd understand the message.

It took Deacon a lot less time to get there than I would have expected seeing as how it was still early morning and he tended to be a night owl. So little time, in fact, that he was waiting for me in my office when I finally rolled in.

"I'm surprised you're awake already."

He shot me a look that said he wasn't in the mood to joke and pushed a cup of coffee across my desk. "Some jackass texted me a message to get my ass here right as I was going to sleep, but seeing as how my ass is attached to the rest of me, you get the whole package."

I dropped into my seat behind the desk and grabbed the coffee. I had a thermos full that Shye had made for me this morning, but I was not a man to turn down a cup. "Thanks."

"You're welcome, jackass." He took a sip of his coffee, watching me over the rim of his cup with those almost unnervingly green eyes. I knew what he was waiting for—an explanation for why I'd dragged him down here. He could complain all he wanted, but he was my best friend. I knew he'd show up if I asked...or demanded, as it were. I also knew there was no one else I wanted by my side as I took care of what I needed to. Knew the man as a soldier and a friend. Knew he'd make sure we did what we needed to on any mission—no questions asked—and got out clean. Which was why I'd called him instead of one of my brothers.

"It's time."

He barely responded to my statement, just a slight head nod before pulling the coffee cup away from his face. "You got a plan?"

"I think so."

That earned me a reaction. A single eyebrow raise that looked like a question mark on his face. "You think, or you know?"

I gave that the time it deserved, let all the data Gage had dug up for us on Pistol's life play through my mind, let the information we'd acquired from a biker named Parris fill in the gaps. Allowed all the pieces of the puzzle time to slide into place in my mind and create a solid picture. One I could use to maneuver right into Pistol's life.

"I know," I said, leaning forward. "I've spent enough time looking over details and learning shit I never wanted to think about. Some things may be on the fly, but the base of my plan is solid. We can take care of the problem."

"You're sure it won't come back on Shye somehow?"

I loved that he was thinking about my girl, and that proved he had my best interests at heart. Because if there was any blowback Shye's way, I'd never get over it. "I'll make sure it doesn't."

That question mark eyebrow dropped back into place, and Deacon took another sip of his coffee before saying, "Then I'm in. When do we move out?"

"Tonight."

We spent the next few hours going over the intel we'd acquired on Pistol. Deacon reviewed my base plan, expanding it, taking into account certain bits of information I'd seen as inconsequential but he saw as important. When we were finished, we'd managed to blow through an entire pot of coffee, a box of cookies from the wife of one of my employees, three pens, and a marker that ended up being thrown at the wall during a particularly stressful discussion about post-mission cleanup. But in the end, we had a clear and concise plan of attack. One that would likely take a few days to carry out.

Which meant I needed to leave town for a bit. And Shye.

I trudged home at the end of the day, dreading the conversation I needed to have with Shye. Knowing she'd tell me it was fine—that she'd be okay without me for a few days. Also knowing she'd be lying.

"Alder," she said as soon as I came through the front door, turning away from the stove and hurrying toward me. But my girl was smart and real damn observant, especially when it came to me. That smile fell the closer she came. "What's wrong?"

See? Smart. "I love you, honey. No matter what."

She felt stiff as I wrapped my arms around her. I couldn't blame her. That answer had been shit, but I wasn't ready to lay everything out for her. Not yet. I needed to hold her, to know she was safe. Then I could throw a big old wrench into the gears of our life together.

"Tell me." She tugged on my hair, kissing my neck as she whispered again, "Tell me."

There wasn't enough breath in my lungs. "I have to go away for a few days."

"Why?"

I shook my head, refusing to lie to her. Not willing to tell her either. "I've got Finn coming to stay here at the house with you."

"Alder." An admonishment on her lips. One that hurt more than I thought it could.

I grabbed her face and tugged her closer, pressing my lips against her ear. "You know I can't tell you. I can't bring you into this."

She gripped my wrists, shaking. Trembling. "When?"

"Tonight. Soon."

"Okay."

And that was it—one word, and I had her approval. Her trust. Her... everything. I didn't deserve it. But she knew what sort of man I was— knew when we got together that I was a soldier. A protector. She'd watched me almost as much as I'd watched her for those three years where we circled one another. She came into this relationship knowing I'd do anything to protect her.

And I would.

Anything.

"C'mon," she said with a sigh when I didn't offer up more information. "I made dinner. Let's get you fed before you have to go do...whatever."

I snagged her wrist before she could walk away. "You all right, honey?"

"I will be. Once you're back home with me. Safe."

Yeah, I understood that.

Dinner was a quiet affair, just the two of us trying hard not to think about what was coming. Afterward, I loaded the dishwasher and scrubbed the pans. Normal—nothing unusual to that except the suffocating tension surrounding us. When Finn arrived, he took one look at Shye and disappeared into the entertainment room, claiming he needed to check the scores on some game. I had a feeling he was simply trying to give us space, so I let him go without another word and headed upstairs to pack. Shye followed me, silent. Watchful. Worried.

I checked my jump bag for anything that might be missing and tossed it on the bed. Then I went for my weapons. Thankfully, I had most of those organized in such a way that I could grab a bag or a trunk and take the whole damn thing with me. But there were a few, a handful of items, that were stored separately since they received so little use. A few explosives, some night vision equipment, and armored body wear got added to the pile. My *just in case things go to shit* section, as it were.

Shye must have been thinking along the same lines. She suddenly came up behind me, her little body wrapping around mine. Her arms snaking their way across my chest and her head nestling against my spine.

"I love you, Alder."

My heart nearly cracked under the sweetness of those words, and I grabbed one of her hands to pull it to my lips. One kiss, two. Clinging to her as much as I could. "I love you too, honey. More than anything in the world."

"You don't need to do this."

I turned around, needing to see her face. To meet her eyes. No matter how much the tears in them killed me. "I do, though. It's time to clean up the last of this mess, and I'm the only man to do that. Okay?"

Her goddamned lip trembled, shattering something inside of me into pure pain. "I don't want to lose you."

"You won't."

"What if you don't make it home?"

"I will. No matter what, I'll make it home to you. Always." I pulled her into my arms, practically cradling her small body against my chest. Meaning every word of my promise to her. "I'm doing this for us, Shye. And once it's over—once I know you're safe—I'm going to marry you, and we're going to spend the rest of our lives wrapped up just like this. You and me. And maybe a dog."

She snorted a sort of laugh. "You think so, huh?"

"I know so, though the dog is only a possibility. I didn't like Rex taking so much of your time when we had him those few days." I gave her a soft kiss, wanting a taste of her but holding back. Knowing she needed words more right then. Serious ones—no more joking around. "I'll take care of the threat against you, then we can begin our lives together. Once I do my job as your man."

"Oh, Alder." She rose up to kiss me again, to lay the softest press of her lips against mine before dropping back down. "I'd marry you today if you asked."

That, at least, was a bright spot to my day. "I'd ask you right now if I had this shit handled. So, be ready, beautiful. I'll have a question for you when I come home."

I grabbed my bags, knowing it was time to get rolling. Deacon would be waiting for me at the Jury Room. The sooner I left, the sooner I got shit handled. And the sooner I could come home to my girl and the life I'd always wanted.

Shye followed me to the front door and out onto the porch. Watching as I loaded up my truck. Looking like a goddamned angel leaning against the post at the top of the stairs as the last of the sunlight peeking over the mountains and trees bathed her in a golden glow.

How was I supposed to say goodbye to her?

How could I not, knowing what was lurking in the shadows?

Once I had my truck ready to go, I hurried back to the porch. Back to her. I gave her one last deep kiss—making sure to run my hands over her ass just because I could—before pulling away. Before walking down the steps. Before leaving her. But I'd be coming back, and then...

"Be ready, honey."

"For what?"

I shot her a grin. "For me to ask you to marry me the second I come home."

"Oh, I will be, but you'd better be ready too."

"What for?"

She spun on her heel and flounced her way back toward the door, only answering me once she was practically inside again. "For me to say yes."

I couldn't hold back my grin. Yeah, I'd be ready for that. There was just one obstacle in my way, and I'd be taking care of that. It was time.

Time to kill her stepbrother.

Chapter 5

ALDER

Well, ain't this the perfect little hideaway?" Deacon looked out the side window, his face in shadow. "This guy set us up good, didn't he?"

"He sure did." I turned the corner one last time before parking along the curb on a quiet stretch of residential street one block over from our goal. "Let's go on foot for now. We'll come back for the stuff."

No sense giving our quarry a heads-up that something was going on—taillights were hard as hell to hide.

"Sounds like a plan." Deacon hopped out of the truck, shutting the door quietly as he looked around the dark and nearly deserted neighborhood. Yeah. Our guy had set up his own murder well, even if he didn't know it yet.

Pistol, aka Colt, aka dead man walking, lived in a single-story ranch house just outside the city limits of Boulder. His place sat back from the street with large, overgrown bushes all around it and huge trees shading most of the property. Shabby would have been a good way to describe the property—neglected worked too. He fit right in, though. The neighborhood itself had obviously taken a turn for the worse over the years as there were plenty of empty homes lining his street, along with ones that looked to be in need of some serious rehab.

Lucky for us, our research had discovered there was an empty place right across the road from Pistol's. Like most of the houses on the street, our temporary home sat back from the road and was shaded by large, old trees and overgrown bushes. I doubted anyone could even see the place from the street. The situation was one we would have wished for back in Special Forces—easy move-in, easy access to the target for monitoring, easy extraction. The only hard part would be having the patience to wait for the right time to strike. This was no standard government mission—this involved my woman, and finding the control not to go racing across the street to snap the neck of the fucker who instilled fear in her heart was probably the hardest thing I'd ever had to do.

Deacon handled the actual break-in—he always had been handy that way—so I took care of humping the equipment in, cutting through yards and staying off the sidewalks, just in case. As soon as we'd gotten ourselves relatively settled, we set up our equipment for capturing pictures, video, and sound from Pistol's place. Legal? Hell no. Neither was what I planned to do to him once we had enough intel to make our move.

The next morning, as Pistol headed off to his weekly lunch meeting with his club president—thank you, Gage, for all your research—I snuck inside his place to install a few bugs. I didn't think we'd get anything useful from them, but verifying targets and intel was old hat to Deacon and me. Almost habit. We'd listen and watch for a day or two before taking action.

Which meant time away from my girl, and that didn't exactly put me in the best mood. Something my partner in this endeavor didn't appreciate.

That first full day was a long one.

"Here," Deacon said on that first morning in the house as he shoved a cup of coffee and a donut from one of those chain places in my face. "I picked up breakfast while on my perimeter watch."

No way that coffee was as good as Shye's. "I'm not hungry."

"No, but you're an asshole. Have some sugar—maybe your mood will improve."

The only thing that would improve my mood was finishing this mission and getting back home to my girl. An impossibility at the moment. I couldn't even text her without worrying about her somehow being tied to this. No one could know we were in Boulder—according to our friends and Shye, we were in Vegas for a guys' weekend away. We even had Bishop making a few purchases along the way with a couple of credit cards we'd sent him, just to cover our bases. If anyone ever asked, there was a paper trail that Alder Kennard and Deacon Manns were hanging out on the Strip. So long as no one went looking for camera feeds, what happened in Vegas would stay in Vegas.

So, yeah. I was cranky. Deacon was likely tired of dealing with me already.

I took the fucking coffee and donut. "Thanks."

"That's better." He took a sip of his coffee before settling into his spot against the front window. He would have liked to be higher up—a second-story window or the roof, even—but we didn't have that option with the house we were squatting in. No matter. If the time came, he'd get a shot off. That wasn't what we wanted—I preferred to deal with the bastard face-to-face. Let him see what was coming for him instead of giving him the gift of a quick death. Plus, shooting across a street, no matter what sort of noise suppressing device Deacon had on that long-range rifle, could attract attention. We definitely didn't want that, but I'd take Pistol out any way I could. So long as neither Deacon nor I could be pinned with his murder, I figured it'd be a good kill. I'd rather make it a perfect one, though.

"Think Camden's coming back?" Deacon asked out of the blue, tearing my attention from the house across the street.

"Yeah," I said after giving the question the thought it deserved. "Someday. He's as Justice as they come."

"What happened to him…it changes a man. Might make him a different person than you know."

True. The Soul Suckers had burned down Camden's home while he'd been out, trapping his wife inside and killing her in the process. We'd taken out one of the fuckers who'd done it, but the other—a Soul Sucker with the road name Coyote—was still out there. Camden knew it, knew one of the men responsible for Leah's death was still breathing, and that fact had eaten at him until he'd snapped. The scar from Leah's murder still ran deep with me. I couldn't even imagine how deep it ran with him. If those fuckers had gotten to Shye like they'd tried…

"Fuck." I shook my head when Deacon looked up. "Just...worried about Shye."

"Finn's with her."

My youngest brother—one of a set of twins—and a former drug addict. "Yeah."

And yet, doubt ate at me—was I doing the right thing? Was Shye safe? Had I made good decisions for her, for the town, for everyone? The death of Camden's wife had thrown me for a loop, and Camden putting the blame of that death on me before he'd left town had put a substantial chink in my confidence. What if all my decisions were wrong? What if—

"Stop it." Deacon pointed a finger at me when I looked his way. "I know you too fucking well and can almost smell your thoughts burning up in that head of yours. Stop doubting yourself. No one could have predicted what happened to Shye's trailer or Camden's house. No one. Not even the great and powerful Alder Kennard."

Jackass. "I should have left you with Shye and brought Finn with me. At least he doesn't talk as much."

"Yeah, but then I'd be alone with your woman."

"You saying you'd try to steal her from me?"

"A man can't steal what doesn't want to be stolen. But I'm one charming motherfucker. Even Felicia says so."

A woman from Rock Falls whom Deacon had been spending a little time with. "You've had what...three dates? I'd hold off on assuming your charm is working."

"I'll have you know sleepovers are happening. I've got this in the bag."

"Yeah, well...bags rip, motherfucker. You'd better be reinforcing that thing."

"That what you do with Shye? Reinforce?"

My girl didn't seem to need to be reminded of how much she meant to me, but I still did it. Every day. "Damn right, it is."

"You're whipped."

"So be it. I'm happy."

"See? I told you the sugar would put you in a better mood." He shot me a grin before taking another sip of his coffee and adjusting his rifle to sight down the scope. Christ, the man had attitude to spare. And I was the luckiest fucker on the planet for having him by my side.

———

"You think Finn's going to stay sober?" I asked, breaking the silence as the sun began to sink below the treetops. We'd been at this all day—watching, waiting, listening to the nothing of another man's life. We hadn't learned anything new except Pistol liked lemons in his water and peanuts in his beer. Vital, this shit. Totally vital.

Deacon, lounging half under the front window, shrugged, not taking his eyes off the house across the street. "Depends on how bad he wants it."

"Seems to want it pretty bad."

"Seems to. For now." He sat up a little, cracking his neck. "You worried about something in particular?"

"Anabeth." Our other brother's girl. Bishop and Anabeth had been hot and heavy back in school, but then she'd disappeared on him. I knew how much that had gutted him because I'd been the one to pick his sorry ass up out of the Las Vegas gutter after he'd tried tracking her down. She'd come back recently, and we finally knew she'd left because of her and Finn's drug use. Bishop worried about Finn dragging her back into that life—my worries went in the other direction.

"She doesn't use."

"I know that." I did. I knew it. And yet... "But there's a memory there each person is dealing with, and there's also Bishop's anger. I've never seen him as pissed as the day he punched Finn."

"Not to condone violence—" Deacon shot me a sarcastic sort of smile "—but Finn deserved that shot. If for nothing else than keeping her drug use secret from B. Finn knew Bishop wanted to marry that girl—that goes beyond friendship. The code between married people surpasses everything."

"Even between brothers?"

"Yes."

"Between brothers-in-arms?"

His face went serious. "Yeah, it does. I know where I sit when it comes to Shye. She'll always outrank me with you. I know it, I accept it, and I'm thrilled you found her. She's a part of you, and I'll do anything to keep her safe for you." He rose to his feet and stretched. "Except sit on this hard floor for another goddamned second. My ass is never going to forgive me for this."

The man was king of the subject change, but his words still hit home. "You know I'd feel the same way if things were reversed."

"I do. Which is why I'm glad I don't have anyone yet—you'd be all demanding and shit to keep her safe. It'd drive me crazy." He patted me on the shoulder as he walked past. "I'm grabbing a pillow to sit on. My ass deserves it."

Yeah. It did. As did the rest of him—he deserved the best because he was the best friend a man could ask for. And he always would be.

———

I was going to kill Deacon.

"Seriously, though. Shye's just so small."

"Deacon."

"I just don't understand it. You're so much bigger than she is. How does it work?"

"Christ. I'm not talking about this."

Deacon rose to his feet and hurried out of the room, leaving me alone for the first time in a number of hours. He returned way too soon, dropping a pad of paper and a marker in my lap. "What the fuck is this?"

"You said you didn't want to talk about it."

My sex life with Shye? Not a bit. "Yeah. So?"

"So, don't talk. Draw. Stick figures will do. I need to understand the logistics of how—Ow. Fuck, man, that hurt."

I flipped the pad of paper off my lap and grinned, pretty fucking proud of hitting my target dead on. "You're not the only one with good aim."

Deacon rubbed his forehead before bringing his hand down to look at it. "You threw that with the cap off."

"Sure did."

"That's permanent marker."

Not really. He'd get that black slash off eventually. "Don't ask about my sex life."

———

Day two passed much as day one had with one massive change. Pistol had company.

"What do you think is going on?" Deacon asked after the third car had come and gone.

"I know what you do." Which was nothing. Nada. Zip. The bugs were still picking up conversations, but it was like the fuckers were speaking in code. All I could understand was some sort of shipment was coming in a few hours, one Pistol was excited for. "Could be drugs."

"My bet's on weapons."

"Doesn't seem like his bag."

"Maybe not, but neither does drugs."

"Both bring money."

"That definitely seems more like his thing. He's an opportunistic fuck."

Deacon wasn't wrong. Pistol worried more about how much money the club had coming in than I would have expected for someone in his position. He wasn't a treasurer—he was an enforcer. The muscle of his crew. The money thing had to be because of something internal with his club. An event or punishment or responsibility we'd never have access to unless he blabbed about it at home, something I highly doubted would happen. Guys in motorcycle clubs—especially ones who'd grown up in them as Pistol had—were notoriously tight-lipped.

Still, something about the plans for tonight didn't sit right with me. Something more than the money aspect. It took me a while to start to pin down what, though.

"This seems more personal," I finally said. "Like something *he* wants, not something for the club."

"But the club is setting him up with whatever it is."

A gift. A present. A token for a job well done...that's what this was. The way Pistol talked about it, the way the other guys had come and offered it. Pistol was getting rewarded for something.

"He's done something the club is happy about. That's what this is. They're going—"

Just then, a car pulled up outside Pistol's house. Deacon and I barely breathed as we stared out the front window. The sun had almost set on the day, the shadows growing deep around our property and Pistol's. There was enough light to see, though. Enough to spot the four guys who stepped out of the vehicle. Big guys—fighters. Likely club muscle.

But what made my blood run cold was when they yanked a fifth person out from the back seat. Dragged, really. Because that person didn't fit with the others. At all.

Small in stature and build.

Definitely feminine.

Bound.

They'd kidnapped someone.

And that someone looked enough like my woman to turn my blood to ice.

Thirty men or thirty lashes.

"Well, shit," Deacon said before grabbing the burner phone he'd been keeping beside him.

"What are you doing?"

He kept his eyes on the screen as his thumbs flew over the buttons. "Making sure Finn and your girl are okay."

"That's not Shye." I met his gaze dead on when his eyes darted to mine. "I know my girl—that's not her. She's taller than Shye is."

Deacon set the phone down, looking out the window again. I could almost see the anguish on his face, the worry for that girl. She threw a wrench into our plans. A big one. One I would need to deal with before we could finish what we came here for.

I rose to my feet and headed for my weapons bag, my mind focusing in on the job at hand. On the mission that had just been shoved to the forefront of our goals. First rule of planning was that priorities shifted, and you needed to be able to shift with them.

Time to shift.

"What are you doing?" Deacon stayed on the floor by the front of the house, still sort of watching out the window. Paying attention to me, though. Ready to back me up. Good.

I slipped on my leather gloves then grabbed the night vision goggles I'd packed and a couple of small hand grenades. Not enough bang to blow up Pistol's house completely, but enough to startle the fuck out of him if I needed to. I had a feeling I'd need to.

"Alder?"

I loaded my backup gun and made sure I had extra ammunition on me. Slid my hunting knife into the strap on my thigh. Popped a box of matches in another pocket—matches always came in handy on jobs like this. When I was done, when I felt ready to take on the enemy, I gave Deacon my attention once more. "You thought that was Shye."

"I did."

"It could have been. It likely was once."

Deacon frowned. "It's not today, though."

No. But the *could haves* and the *dids* and the *never agains* weren't going to let me go. The memory of Shye flinching away from my touch and hiding herself—her scars—from me wouldn't leave my thoughts. I had a feeling I knew what was about to happen in that house, to that blonde, and there was no fucking way I could sit back and do nothing.

So it was time to move. "I don't want anyone else ending up like my girl—with scars on her body and fear so deep down inside, she feels she has to hide herself from the world. I won't sit back and do nothing while that useless excuse for a human makes another woman bleed. I can't allow it."

Deacon sat silent for a moment before rising to his feet. He set down his long-range rifle and grabbed a handgun from his stash, going through the same preparatory process I just had. Sighting down his guns, sliding extra ammo into strategic pockets, grabbing the tools he felt he'd need for the battle ahead.

The one that wasn't really his to fight. "What are you doing?"

He shrugged. "Whatever the fuck you tell me to."

"We said no witnesses, which I was fine with until now. The girl wasn't in the plan, but I won't let her be collateral damage."

"Then she won't be, and we'll deal with how to keep things quiet once we get her out of there." He snagged an apple from his bag and took a huge bite. "Saddle up, cowboy. It's time to rescue a damsel in distress."

There was only one thing to say to a statement like that.

"Hooah."

Chapter 6

ALDER

Two of the men who'd pulled up at Pistol's left soon after they dropped the girl off inside the house, leaving her and three targets. So long as they didn't have greater firepower than Deacon and me—or catch sight of us coming before we were on them—this mission would be going in the success column. That wasn't being cocky, arrogant, or overconfident—we'd dealt with these fuckers enough to know their skills —or lack thereof. We'd already put a number of them in the ground. We had this.

And as I thought of Shye and the scars running up and down her back, I knew we *had* to have this. There could be no failure.

Deacon and I snuck out through the back door and slipped around the side of our borrowed house. The sun had set a little more, and the shadows had deepened. The only streetlights in this part of town were at the intersections, which would leave our end of the block nice and dark once night had fallen all the way. Just what we would need by the time we were finished with what was about to come.

Cleaning up dead bodies was easiest in the dark. No doubt there.

The two remaining Soul Suckers sat on the back porch, smoking cigarettes and talking softly to one another. As if this was a normal night, a totally typical evening for them. Kidnap a woman, drop her off for Pistol to do with as he wished...and then what? Would they kill her? Take her back to their clubhouse to be drugged and used as club pussy? Worse? Because as bad as this was, in the world of sexual slavery, there was always worse.

Deacon and I stood at the corner of Pistol's house, listening. Waiting for our chance to take these two fuckers out and clear the path inside. It happened faster than either of us had likely been expecting.

"I need to take a piss," Soul Sucker One said as he rose to his feet. The sound of his footsteps moved toward the yard, though. Not into the house. Something his partner seemed to confirm for us.

"There's a john inside."

"Nah. I don't want to interrupt Pistol. The man's been a fucking pain in my ass for weeks—let him work out some of that frustration."

Number Two chuckled as Number One headed across the yard toward the detached garage. Deacon gave me the hand signals to lay out his plan—he'd follow Number One, and I would need to take out Number Two—before slipping along the fence line toward the opposite side of the garage where One had gone. If Two was watching, I had about three seconds to take him out before he alerted One and Pistol that we were there. If he was paying attention—

He wasn't.

Deacon made it to the corner of the garage and disappeared around it, leaving me time to approach the porch with care instead of balls the wall. Two didn't see me coming—not until the last possible second, which was exactly what I wanted. I wanted his eyes on me, wanted to get a solid look at my target before firing. One shot. A small thump bouncing through the air as my supresser did its job. A quiet grunt was Two's last sound.

One down, one to dispose of.

Normally, I wouldn't shoot someone in what I considered a public place. Too messy. But the bullets I had in my gun were meant for this sort of work. They'd puncture flesh just like a standard round, but that was about all that was standard. There'd be no through-and-through shots with these, no second wound as the bullet exited the body. They entered and then exploded like a tiny bomb, ripping through flesh and sending shrapnel all through the immediate area. Effective for killing and way less cleanup. Something I had needed to keep at the forefront of my mind during planning and that Deacon had made sure I was prepared for. I had to get my ass back to Shye and keep it there, which meant sloppy mistakes that could lead the authorities to my door weren't allowed.

I dragged Two toward the back of the garage, figuring Deacon had already taken care of his target as well. I wasn't wrong about that. I found my partner standing in the doorway to the crumbling old structure, looking way more casual than a man on a mission should.

"Took you long enough," he said, giving me a grin. "Need some help with that, old man?"

If looks could kill, he'd likely be dead. "Just get out of the doorway, jackass."

He stepped back, still grinning, and swept his arm to the side in invitation. I hefted my load inside and dropped it on top of the other body already laid out on the floor.

"How are we handling them?"

Deacon strolled up, staring down at the two bodies we'd definitely need to get rid of. "I say we burn the place. Easy, effective, but it brings immediate attention to the attack."

True. And we didn't want to be anywhere around here when that sort of information got out. "Let's deal with Pistol first, then make the final cleanup decision. I don't want to lock into one thing if this situation gets messy."

"There's a girl inside there. An innocent, most likely. It's already messy."

Truth. But there wasn't a lot I could do about that. "Ready?"

"Always. Let's go break the link between the Soul Suckers and your woman."

My thoughts exactly.

We didn't even make it inside the back door of the house before we heard it. Loud, thumping music, some sort of rhythmic snap that didn't quite fit the beat, and the girl. Screaming. Crying.

Fucking begging.

All I could think of was Shye; all I could imagine was her inside that house. Tears staining her pretty face. Anguished pleas for Pistol—her own stepbrother of a number of years—to stop hurting her.

The rage inside of me could have fueled the entire town of Justice for a year, it burned so bright and hot. It made me move, made my steps strong and sure, made me enter the house without a thought spared for keeping quiet. Fuck that. Let Pistol know we were coming for him. If he did, he might stop whatever he was doing in there, and the girl might get a break. I had a feeling no one had given Shye a break.

"Alder, wait." Deacon grabbed my arm, getting right up into my face when I shoved him off me. "That's not your girl in there."

"I know that."

"Then slow the fuck down."

The girl screamed again, and I heard Shye in her voice. Heard the woman I loved crying for mercy. I couldn't go slow. It simply wasn't an option.

I raced down the hallway, Deacon muttering a quiet *Fuck* behind me before he followed. The door at the end sat closed, the music and other sounds coming from behind it. I knew the setup of the house—that was Pistol's spare room. A space filled with his toys, his weapons. Not an ideal spot to try to take him out, but I had no other choice. I'd been in a lion's den before. I'd managed to bust my ass back out of it. I'd do it again—and this time, I had one hell of a motivation.

Shye.

The door swung open as soon as I kicked it, the wood holding the handle shattering into thousands of slivers and chunks. It might as well have been in slow motion for how my brain processed that, because as soon as I had a visual inside the room, my world went sideways.

The girl stood naked against what looked like a St. Andrew's Cross. Her back to me. Pistol between us with a whip in his hand. But I barely saw him, hardly even glanced his way because my eyes were locked on her.

Blond, like Shye.

Super petite, like Shye.

Scared and shaking, like Shye.

Crying, like Shye.

Bleeding, like Shye.

Every plan I'd ever come up with, every moment of military training I'd gone through, slammed through my brain in a split second. There was only one option here. One chance to set things right. If I missed this opportunity, if I didn't follow through with this, if Pistol somehow got away from me—this would be Shye's future. Her past revisited. More scars would be added to her body, more tears would stain her pretty face. More of her blood would be spilled because I wasn't able to keep her safe.

"No fucking way." I lunged for Pistol, the world suddenly no longer in slow motion and, instead, speeding past. I caught the bastard around the throat and pulled him back, locking him in my hold as Deacon stormed in behind me. Before he could even take a step in my direction, I nodded toward the cross. "Take care of her."

Deacon reacted without pause, no argument needed. He rushed to the cross and started working the straps holding the girl in place. Whispering to her. Likely trying to calm her down. Not that she'd ever be calm again after what she'd been through. I'd seen those types of scars firsthand—both the internal and external ones. My Shye was a strong woman, but what her stepbrother had done to her had broken something that could never truly be fixed. Left her with jagged pieces that slipped and cut at the most random of times. Left her with memories that coated her happiness in shadow.

Calm wouldn't be in her lexicon for a while.

As soon as Deacon freed the girl from her restraints, he directed her out of the room, leaving me alone with Pistol. Likely staying close enough to step in if I needed him to. Not that I would. This was my time—my kill. My moment to get Pistol to make reparation for what he'd done.

"Looks like you weren't expecting me," I said, tightening my hold as he tried to wrestle his way out of it. "That wasn't too smart."

Pistol choked out a laugh, still fighting hard against my grip. "You're the one without smarts. You think I'm alone here?"

"Nah, you have two guys with you outside." I leaned closer, making sure my lips brushed his ear as I whispered, "Or, at least, you *had* two guys outside before my partner and I got to them."

Pistol stilled for just a second, those words probably settling into his mind and stirring up the primordial beast that kept scum like him alive. The one that brawled and strained and refused to go down without a fight. The one that had to see the end coming and would likely soon do everything it could to get away from me.

Not happening.

I braced my feet and gripped Pistol harder around the throat, cutting off most of his air supply. Most, but not all. I had things to say, things that might need a response. Just for fun. Still, I tugged him close and kept my choke hold strong, not willing to let him get a single second of reprieve from me. He had so few left anyway.

Still, Pistol tried. His feet even slipped right out from under him as he attempted to work his way free of my hold. Attempted...and failed. He had nothing but a will to live. I had years of training behind me, the knowledge that even though the act of killing him was wrong, the motivation was right, and the love of a good woman guiding me. He had no shot.

And he knew it. Or he would. I didn't feel the need to beat around the motherfucking bush on that particular aspect of my plan.

I gave him a little more space to breathe—fucker didn't even know to drop his chin for air, so I had to spoon-feed him that release—and said, "You're a dead man, Pistol."

And just as I expected, he spouted off as if he had a shot in hell at getting out of that room alive. "You think you're going to get away with this? My brothers will know who you are. They'll come for you."

"I don't think they will. I don't think you're as valuable to them as you think you are. They've sent what...ten men to Justice? Some on your orders, right? Ordering men to take me out, to kidnap Shye, to snag Katie. You keep sending men in. How many have come back?"

"Fuck you." Pistol jerked again, his fingernails digging into my arm. "What the fuck do you want?"

As if he had something to trade. "Nothing. I want nothing from you. See, this isn't about the Soul Suckers or the fires or the men who keep coming and causing trouble. This is about Shye and what you owe her. You fucked up when you laid a hand on her. Or should I say a whip?"

He laughed, a sad little choking sound. "You're doing all this for pussy? Man, and I thought you were smart. Though I do miss her hanging around here. She was a good little bleeder—you have no idea how many times I've gotten off to thinking about her blood dripping onto my floor. Right here."

When looking for a way to kill with zero mess, a choke hold focused on impeding blood flow instead of airway constriction, one my fellow soldiers and I called a rear naked, was a good call. Quick, simple, real fucking hard to defend against without having trained for it—that hold was an all-around winner for quiet murders. You had to be close, though. Had to have some strength in your arms and get your body into just the right position. Had to know precisely how to grip the target around the throat to block the blood flow to the brain and arch your back just so.

Thankfully, I had extensive training in such a thing.

Muscle memory took over, years of repetition moving my arms into position. I fixed my grip on the bastard's throat—left hand gripping my right bicep, right hand gripping the back of his head—before arching my body. And then I counted.

Five seconds until the lack of blood flow to the brain caused Pistol's movements to grow slower and clumsier.

Ten seconds until he lost consciousness and hung heavy in my arms.

If I'd been a good man, I'd have stopped. If I'd been a good man, I'd have called the authorities to take him to jail on kidnapping charges for the girl. If I'd been a good man, I wouldn't have tightened my hold, continuing to count down as his brain died a quick death.

I'd long since stopped considering myself a good man.

One final jerk at the minute mark and I finally released him. Pistol dropped like a rag to the floor. Not breathing. Dead.

And I would never ever feel guilty about that.

I walked out to find Deacon standing in the living room with bloodied towels at his feet and the girl wrapped in a blanket on the couch. He must have taken care of the damage Pistol had done to her back while I'd been taking care of Pistol. Good.

She shot a fear-filled glance my way, looking less like Shye now that the beast inside of me had been quieted. She was a witness to what we'd done, though. Something which we'd need to handle. But first...

"We'll put him in the garage with the other two, and then we burn it. Burn it all down. We're done here."

Chapter F

ALDER

The girl proved to be more of a problem than we'd expected.

"But I don't have anywhere to go."

I brushed past her, tossing another bag in the back of the truck. We were loading up to ship out—just Deacon and me. "We're taking you home. That's where you'll go."

"She doesn't have one," Deacon said, suddenly standing in my way. He'd spent more time with her than I had, so the seriousness of his expression shouldn't have been unexpected. "She has no home and no family. She grew up in another club, one just like the Soul Suckers. You know what that means."

I did. They probably had treated her like a servant girl—she had to cook for them, clean for them, and, more than likely, spread her legs for them. Not the sort of life anyone deserved to be forced into. "Where are you from, girl?"

Night had fallen hard, but even in the darkness I could see her. With her pale skin and light hair, she practically glowed. She looked so small and scared as she stood on the cracked concrete in her bare feet, but she answered, "Nowhere. I'm from nowhere. The guys who took me had me stay in a room over their clubhouse before they brought me here."

Well, fuck. "We're sure as shit not going to drop her off at their clubhouse."

Deacon moved in closer, lowering his voice to almost a whisper. "The Soul Suckers won her in a card game with another club, man. That's how she ended up here and why they were giving her to Pistol. She's expendable to them. And when the club realizes Pistol and his two guards are dead? They'll pin it on her. She's not a Soul Sucker, so they'll call it her fault—sound familiar?"

"They said the death of Shye's dad was her fault."

"Exactly, and she was known to those men. They have no respect for anyone outside the club. If we leave the girl here? She's dead. They'll kill her for what we did."

Yeah, they would. The Soul Suckers didn't seem to give a fuck who they hurt. The girl was the perfect example of that. Won her in a card game. That level of depravity would never not surprise me. I took a good, hard look at the girl, at the way she held herself, at the slump of her shoulders and how her eyes kept darting around as if waiting for someone to jump her. At the fear practically radiating off her slim shoulders.

The hair, the build, the haunted eyes...she looked so much like my Shye. We couldn't leave her.

"What's your name?"

Hands twisted together and voice wobbly, she murmured, "Jinx. Jinx Reid, sir."

Deacon's smirk at my being called sir by this tiny girl should have gotten him punched. I pointed a finger at him. "Don't you say anything."

He put his hands up and slowly shook his head. "I wasn't planning on it. *Sir.*"

"Fuck." I hadn't intended to take in a runaway, hadn't seen that coming at all. But Deacon was right—the Soul Suckers would likely pin Pistol's death on her. She needed to hide away until the shit blew over, but without a home to go to, that was pretty impossible. There wasn't any place safe from them right now, maybe not even Justice. But at least with us, she'd have someone watching out for her. She'd have a town to back her up.

Deacon must have been thinking the same thing. "We'll put her up at my motel. Give her a chance at a life away from these fuckers. They've been using her as a scullery maid since she was still a kid—she has no shot at any sort of life around here. Just like your woman."

I hated him using my Shye as an example, though he wasn't wrong. "And if she's on their side in all this?"

"She won't be." He blanched when I stared him down. "She's not, but if she is—if I'm wrong—I'll take care of that myself."

A lie. Deacon would never be able to *take care of that*. He had a heart bigger than the horizon and a soft spot for damsels in distress. Unless this Jinx turned out to be a danger to Justice, there would be no *taking care* of anything. "She's your responsibility."

"Done." He grinned and looked past me. "Load up, Jinx. You're coming with us."

Jinx's face lit up with a smile so bright, it actually made my heart hurt. "Thank you. Oh, thank you so much. Hey...you know you've got a little something on your forehead?"

Deacon looked ready to kill me as I grinned. "Yeah. I know. Thanks."

"Yeah, sure. I just...I want to help. I'll do anything to get away from here. And I'm not lazy—I know how to earn my keep."

That phrase punched me square in the chest and reverberated through my mind. Shye had said it a time or two—after she'd moved in with me, when I would come home to her having worked all day cleaning up after me. She'd always say how she felt the need to *earn her keep*.

Because she'd always had to.

She'd learned to cook, to take care of the men in her family, before her mom had died when she was just nine years old. She'd earned her keep all the way up until the Soul Suckers had burned down her trailer and threatened her life. This Jinx more than just looked like my Shye.

And Christ, did I want to go home.

"Make sure we've got everything and the house is clear," I said to Deacon. "Once we're locked and loaded, we'll set the fire in the garage. I want to be the fuck out of town before it really starts to blaze."

"You got it." He grinned, and I knew what was coming before he even said the word. "Sir."

———

Fires were relatively easy to set. Houses and garages tended to be dry and filled with things that flames liked to eat. Wood, paper, books, fabric, petroleum-based products—all food for the beast. You needed to be patient, though. When disposing of evidence, you wanted that fire to burn long and hot, which meant a slow buildup until it spread deep enough into the structure and far enough along the perimeter to be almost unstoppable. A little accelerant, a spark, and a slow burn through all that fuel. The fire did the work for you.

Like the one set at Camden's house a few months ago. We'd come almost full circle.

Deacon handled the setting of the fires. Yes, plural. He started two— one in the garage and one in the house—making sure the bodies were doused in gasoline so they'd burn nice and hot. So the heat and the flames would destroy as much evidence as possible. And when we were sure the fires were solidly in place and sure to burn unhindered, we got the hell out of Dodge.

"She asleep?" Deacon asked from the driver's seat. I glanced into the back where, indeed, Jinx slept.

"Looks like it."

"You see the scars on her arms?"

Her arms, her wrists, her back, her hips, her ankles. The girl was a walking billboard for abuse—both inflicted *on* her and *by* her. "Yeah."

Deacon drove on, quiet for a long time, staring out at the road as it passed. Finally, he asked, "Shye got scars like those?"

Every muscle in my body locked down at the very thought.

"Not like those, no." Similar enough...at least, some of them. But the rest? I couldn't even imagine. I'd mapped every inch of my girl's body, had touched and tasted every part of her. I'd seen the results of what Pistol had done to her with my own eyes. But she wasn't like Jinx. "No restraint marks. And, uh...she doesn't—" I swallowed hard, my throat tight at the image of my girl hurting herself. "She's not a cutter."

"Good. That's good."

Was it? Because Shye's back was covered in scars—the same ones Pistol had added to Jinx's skin—and she bore the marks from that to this day. Always would. I'd kissed that mottled flesh a thousand times, and still, she pulled away from me whenever I tried to touch her back. Hid herself under shirts and behind towels when I might be able to see them. Those marks may not hurt her skin anymore, but the burn of them—the searing pain—was embedded in her mind.

Jinx would likely be the same way, but she dealt with her hurt externally while Shye turned inside her own head. So fucking alike, and yet opposite. But Shye had me, and I wouldn't let her go too deep. Jinx? She didn't seem to have anyone.

Except us. "What are we going to do with her?"

Deacon shrugged, still focused on the road ahead. "Give her a place to stay and some work to do. See if she can adjust to life outside the club."

"And if she can't?"

"We'll cross that bridge when we come to it."

Yeah, I guessed we would. And really, there was no other answer. We couldn't have left her to her fate with the Soul Suckers, and leaving her on the street somewhere wouldn't have been much better. Deacon and I might have been the bad guys in the story of Pistol's life, but we weren't villains. We only did bad things for good reasons. Protecting Shye was a good reason, albeit a selfish one. Helping Jinx seemed truly altruistic.

Deacon drove us all the way back to Justice, only stopping for gas and coffee once. Jinx woke up as we rolled into town, looking suddenly nervous. I could understand that—new town, new people, new life. That had to be overwhelming. Sadly, I didn't have it in me to soothe her. I wanted to go home—to see my Shye girl and make sure she was safe. To curl up in her arms and forget all the bad things I'd done, while simply being grateful to have such an amazing woman in my life. To be lost in her for a few hours.

Deacon had other plans. "I need you for a quick job," he said as soon as he parked my truck. "The room for Jinx isn't set up yet, and I can use a little help moving the furniture around."

"You've got me for five." I stepped out of the truck, looking over the parking lot of the Jury Room. My blood going cold when I saw a motorcycle by the front door. "Deac."

He followed my gaze, zeroing in on the bike the same way I had. But he didn't seem as pissed off or worried as I did.

"That's our friend's bike. Fucker must be inside." The look he gave me had weight to it, and it didn't take me long to work out what he meant. The bike could only belong to one person. Parris, the former Marine who'd helped us gain information on the Soul Suckers over the past few months. Who had no reason to be in Justice. And though I'd trusted him to be an asset and an informant, he still wore club colors. Not Soul Suckers' colors, but motorcycle club nonetheless. I couldn't put my full faith in him because of that.

"Let's go see what he wants." I tucked a pistol into the holster under my arm and slipped my leather jacket on over it. No sense in upsetting anyone who happened by. Not yet, at least. "And kick his ass out of town if we need to."

"What about me?" Jinx stood next to the truck, looking so damn small and scared. "I don't want to be left alone out here."

Deacon shrugged. "Come on, then. I'll show you the bar."

"Deac—"

"It'll be fine." He shot me a grin. "And if it's not, I'm pretty sure she's seen worse."

"Probably," Jinx said, her tone completely casual. As if threats and men with guns were completely normal.

Hell, they probably *were* completely normal to her.

"You're going to be trouble, aren't you?" I asked.

Jinx shrugged. "Not intentionally, but I do tend to live up to my name."

Wonderful.

The three of us headed inside, a sad, raggedy little troupe walking into a situation that could turn dangerous or even deadly. Deacon lead the way, and I followed behind Jinx. Making sure she had protection at both ends in case this was some sort of setup.

The man in question sat at the bar wearing club colors and drinking a beer. As if he owned the damn place. He turned when we walked in, his eyes lingering on Jinx a second too long. "Been waiting for you two."

His perusal of the girl with us didn't go unnoticed by me or her. Shoulders stiff and head up, Jinx crept closer to Deacon, looking both fierce and scared at the same time. Our weakest link exuding bravery. Smart girl.

"I won't bother asking how you got in here. Doesn't really matter." I shrugged out of my jacket, making sure our supposed friend got a good, long look at the fact that I was carrying. "Something you need?"

"Not anymore, but I might have something *you* need."

"And what's that?"

He leaned back against the bar, spreading his arms wide. "Me."

"And why the fuck would I need you?"

Parris grinned. "Because I know you took out the county sheriff."

Technically, Gage took out Sheriff Baker. Not that I needed to tell him that. "Have no clue what you're talking about."

"Yeah, I figured that's what you'd say. But see, a man in my position hears things. He also gets random text messages from your men. Or, rather, their women."

I shot a glance at Deacon, who seemed as taken off guard as I was. "I don't follow."

Parris pulled out his phone, swiping a few times before reading, "'Gage shot and there was an explosion. Hurry.' That last part was in all caps. She really meant it."

Motherfucker. Katie'd sent that the night Sheriff Baker had attacked Gage's place. The night Gage had killed the lying bastard. That text wasn't detailed, but it could certainly lead to questions about things we didn't want brought up.

Time to bluff. "You remember any explosions, Deacon?"

My brother-in-arms huffed. "Yeah. At the restaurant. Some sort of pressure cooker exploded."

"And what?" Parris said, sitting back and looking far too smug. "Gage got shot with cutlery?"

I shrugged. "Couldn't tell you. Wasn't there."

"Maybe not." Parris flicked his thumb against his phone screen before reading aloud again. "'Baker gone. Justice at fault. Time to take them out. Bringing in the big prez.'"

"The big prez? Like pretzel?" Deacon bumped Jinx with his elbow, nearly knocking the girl over. "I could go for one right about now. You hungry, kid?"

"President," Parris said, glaring at Deacon. "As in the president of the local Soul Suckers club is headed this way. And he'll bring his entire crew with him. We're not talking four or five guys—we're talking a hundred bikers rolling into town at once."

That sounded like really bad news to me. "Why are you telling us this?"

"I was just going to provide you information, but I've changed my mind." He looked right at Jinx, cocking his head. "I've got a deal for you."

Something in the way he stared at the girl, at the expression on his face, brought out my protective side. I stepped in front of her, knowing I'd made the right decision when Deacon joined me in blocking Jinx from him. "I'm not taking a deal from a biker. Let them come."

"You can't win against them."

"You come here to threaten me?"

"No, I came here to save your ass. You *can't* win against them. But I can." He rose to his feet and tossed a bill he'd pulled out of his pocket on the bar. "You sticking around for this shit, Jinx?"

The world slowed down, and I turned to look down at the possible viper in our midst. "You know him?"

She didn't look too thrilled. "Unfortunately."

"Something we need to know?"

Jinx lifted a shoulder, shooting an almost worried glance at Parris. "He used to be my jailer."

"I was your bodyguard."

"Didn't do too well at that, did you?"

Parris flinched, her words causing a physical reaction impossible to miss. "Yeah, well...I'm here now. And I'm staying."

"Staying?" I asked. "As in moving to Justice?"

"Looks like it. Better change those Welcome to Justice signs, son. The population's going up by one."

"Two," Jinx said, her arms crossed over her chest and her eyes hard. "And unlike these guys, I know exactly what sort of men come from the clubs. Don't you dare think of double-crossing them."

"Wouldn't dream of it." He strolled across the room, keeping his eyes on hers even as he softened his tone. "I was on my way to Boulder."

I caught Deacon's eye, seeing the same shock I felt reflected there, before checking out Jinx's reaction. She looked...pissed.

"Yeah, well...you were late." She nodded toward Deacon and then me. "Don't let them down."

"As you wish." Parris nodded once before frowning at Deacon. "You've got a little something on your forehead."

Deacon could only glare as I chuckled. "Yeah, I know."

Parris shrugged, meeting my gaze and offering a hand. "I owe you."

I wasn't positive what for, but I had a good idea it had something to do with the woman at my side. And though I didn't trust Parris as much as

I did my men, I needed the help. Camden had left, Bishop was pretty much living in Vegas, and we still had Soul Suckers to deal with. Parris showing up in town might have been a lucky stroke. Maybe Jinx wouldn't be living up to her name, after all.

"Welcome to Justice," I said, shaking the hand he offered. "Try not to fuck anything up."

He coughed a laugh. "I'll do my best. Deacon—I'm going to need a room."

"I can handle that." Deacon raised his eyebrows and lifted his chin at me. "I've got help now. You can head on home to your woman."

My Shye. "You sure?" I asked even though I was already headed for the door.

"You've been a cranky bastard since we left. I'm glad to be rid of you."

I took one last look back before I left. Deacon, Parris, and Jinx stood together, looking like some sort of ragtag protection detail. Or a really shoddy criminal operation. Maybe both.

"I have a feeling we're going to have a lot more trouble at the Jury Room," I said.

Deacon grinned. "You bet your ass, we will."

Wonderful.

But that was stuff I could deal with at a later date. Right then, there was only one thing I wanted.

And she was likely waiting for me.

Speed limits could fuck off—I had a woman to get home to.

And a promise to keep.

Chapter 8

ALDER

Even after three days away, three murders, two fires, a biker moving in to town, and a refugee of sorts under Deacon's watch, the last stretch of road home seemed to take forever. I just wanted my girl. Wanted to see her face and smell her hair and feel her arms around me.

I also had a promise to keep, one that would finally put the rings my father had left me to some use.

I'd texted my brother that I was on my way, so it was no surprise that Finn was on the front porch when I pulled up. He looked ready to leave with his backpack slung over his shoulder, ready to give me space so I could be alone with Shye. Smart man.

I gave him as much of a smile as I could when I stepped out of the truck. "How's things, brother?"

"Good. Have fun in Vegas?"

The lie had to run deep to be believed. "The Strip was crowded, but we had a good time."

He stared me down, likely knowing those words were bullshit. Also knowing I'd never admit that to him. With the potential blowback of the mission we'd just completed and the potential legal ramifications if someone knew and didn't alert the authorities, everyone in my circle was on a need to know basis. And Finn didn't need to know shit.

My brother finally relented. "She missed you."

Those words might as well have been a stab to the heart, yet they also soothed something inside of me. Shye and I were a matched set, not wanting to be apart. Too in love to handle separations for long. I had known she'd missed me because I'd felt empty without her beside me. "I missed her more."

"Good." He helped me drag my bags out of the back and drop them on the porch, the two of us working in tandem until the bed was unloaded. When we were finished, he gave me a fist bump. "Glad you're back. If you don't need me anymore, then I'm going to head out. I want to roll over to Deacon's to see if he needs anything before going home."

"Sounds good." It took me a second to pull my head out of my ass and remember that Deacon's now meant Parris and Jinx. I wasn't sure what my brother's type was when it came to women, but Jinx was cute...and pure trouble. "Hey, Finn."

He turned, his eyebrows up. "Yeah?"

"There's a couple of new people in town. Deacon can tell you what's up, but just so you know. One's a woman. Her name's Jinx."

"Jinx? Like curse?"

"Yeah. I guess so. Said she lives up to her name, too."

He grinned. "I'll be sure to say hi and give her a Justice welcome when I see her."

"You do that. Then stay away from her."

Silence. His brows came down, furrowing deep, and he cocked his head a little to the side. In that moment, with that look on his face, he reminded me so much of a younger Finn. Of a kid.

He wasn't a kid anymore, though. "Why do I need to stay away?"

Because you're fragile. Because your sobriety is important to all of us. Because a woman can be your greatest strength or your biggest weakness. Because I can't deal with more trouble.

All things I could never say. "She was mixed up in some shit that might come back one day. Best to keep your distance."

"Distance. Got it." He slowly smiled as the front door opened and Shye stepped out onto the porch. "Looks like our time ran out. You two have a good night now."

But I couldn't answer him, couldn't even make sense of his words. My girl was there, standing in a beam of light that bathed her in an ethereal sort of glow. My angel looking absolutely radiant. And so damned happy to see me.

"You're home."

Two words. That was all it took to break my heart wide open. The emptiness inside of me disappeared, filling with the warmth that being loved by this woman always gave me. The house, the land, the whole damned town—none of it anchored me the way she did. I wasn't home until I was with her. So, yeah, I was coming home.

"I missed you, honey."

Her lips quirked into a smile that stole my breath. "I missed you too, my dragon."

Her dragon at the gates. She'd told me that once—how I was her protector. Not a prince but a dragon ready to burn down the world for her. Fitting—I'd just burned down Pistol's world for her. For us. For our forever.

And I didn't want to waste another second before we started it.

I bounded up the stairs, stopping only when I stood right before her. Practically shaking with my need to touch and taste and feel. To have. But after the past three days—after seeing firsthand the damage that fucker had done to Jinx—I couldn't just *take*. Shye deserved better than to have me overpower her, even if she wanted me to. Right then, in that moment, I needed her to give to me. To truly, utterly surrender without any coercion on my part. I needed her consent, and I'd wait for it. I'd wait forever if I had to. So long as she was happy and safe and still mine.

That pouty bottom lip I loved to bite practically called to me as I asked, "Are you okay?"

"I am now that you're home." She wrapped her arms around my waist and pulled me in close. Taking from me. Burying her head against my chest as I shook with my need for her. "I really did miss you."

"So much." Her body felt so small against mine, so fragile, even though I knew she was one of the strongest people I'd ever met.

And suddenly, I didn't want to let her go. Not then, not ever. I had her exactly where she belonged, had her giving her touch and her heart to me just as I'd wanted, and I needed to keep her there. Keep her in my arms, safe and protected but also loved. Supported. Happy.

I wanted her to be mine in ways I'd never wanted anything else.

"You remember what I said before I left? About what I'd do the second I got home?"

"You've been home for more than just a second."

Spitfire, my girl. "Marry me, Shye."

She went stiff in my arms, so I inched back, giving her room. Ready to give her my heart. She already had it, but this would make it official. I just needed to get the question right, because demanding she marry me wasn't the way I should have gone.

"I'm sorry—that was all wrong. Not the question but the delivery because marrying you is all I want to do right now. I really thought I'd plan this moment out and get all the words right in my head to ask you the way you deserve to be asked something like this, but instead, I blurted that out. You just looked so pretty and I've been dying to ask you for so long and the moment seemed perfect so I said the words instead making them all flowery and shit—"

"I don't need flowery and shit," she said, sounding breathless. Looking ready to cry. "I just need you."

"You have me. Christ, woman, do you have me. Just... Wait a second."

I raced into the house, pounding across the wood floors into the entertainment room. On the bookshelf, where I kept things like the Kennard family bible and the history books of the region, sat a small wooden bowl with a lid that my dad had made. He'd given it to my mother for her to keep her jewelry in, and after his death, he'd given it to me to hold on to. He'd told me then to use the rings if I ever found someone I loved as much as he'd loved his wife. Well, I had. And I was ready to make sure the whole damn world knew it.

After retrieving the ring I needed, I hurried back outside to my Shye. Before she could even ask what I was doing, I dropped down to one knee, my hand shaking as I held the ring so she could see it. See the gold band and the diamond. Know what was coming.

"I've been thinking about giving you this for weeks, trying to figure out how to ask you so you wouldn't laugh in my face. I know it's fast—it's so fast—but you're it for me. You've been it for me for three years, honey. Since the first time I saw you. And having you here, being allowed to love you—it's such a gift. One I don't take for granted. And I just want—"

"Alder."

"Hang on. I have something to ask you, but I need to find the words because there are so many, and you're just...you're mine. I want you to be mine. Forever, Shye. I want that so badly."

"Ask me," she whispered, staring down at me with tears in her eyes and the biggest smile I'd ever seen on her face. "Just ask me, you big lug."

Ask her. Yeah, I could do that. I could do that all goddamned day. "Will you marry me, Shye Anderson?"

"Yes," she said, nodding. So sure and strong and true in her declaration. Stealing my heart and my breath in one go. And then she was there, dropping down to her knees to wrap herself around me. To give herself to me. Planting one hell of a kiss on my lips as I dragged her against me. As I held my future wife—my fucking fiancée—against me.

"My god, you feel good." I slipped the ring on her finger, something weighty and heavy between us. A moment unlike any other as I got the first look at my physical claim to her. Mine. All mine. It'd be official soon enough, and that ring would be joined by another. Letting everyone know someone loved her, that she had someone at home who cared for her. That she belonged to someone and they belonged to her, because this marriage would be a two-way street. I put my claim on her finger, and sometime in the near future, she'd put hers on mine. And that thought? It destroyed me and rebuilt me as someone solely devoted to the woman in my arms. Fuck, I would need something more permanent than a simple band. I'd need something that couldn't be taken off, couldn't be damaged or lost. I'd need a true statement of forever.

But first, I needed her.

I tilted her head and attacked her neck, wanting to taste every inch. To savor it. To relearn her body all over again. To give myself to her and gratefully accept that which she gave to me. To worship her. She was mine in an ancient way now. She'd be mine officially in the modern way soon enough.

It needed to be soon, at least. "I don't want to wait."

She sighed and gripped my shoulders, holding on to me as I moved to run my lips along her collarbone. "Wait for what?"

"This. Us." I pulled back, needing to look into those dark eyes I loved so much. Needing to make sure she understood me. "I'm sure you have ideas and plans for what you want your wedding to be, but I don't want to wait too long. I want—"

"I want to have the ceremony here in Justice," she said, interrupting me in the best fucking way. "That's it. Marry me in the place that means so much to both of us. Give me that, and I'll be the happiest girl on earth."

"I'll give you that. I'll give you anything."

"October," she said. "Let's get married in October before your birthday."

"Are you sure? That would be less than a month." Which sounded too long to me, but I could be patient if I had to be. I could wait to give her the day she wanted.

"A month sounds so far away," she practically whined, verbalizing my thoughts. "But it will give us time to pull things together. Something small and intimate. Something truly for us."

I loved the sound of that, but still. "I can give you a big wedding if you want it. I'd give you anything."

"I told you. I don't need a big wedding. I'd marry you today, but I'd really like your family there. And I want Katie to make the food, but her hands are still bothering her, so she needs a little healing time. And everyone else—this will be enough time to get everything ready and make sure we have the people we want around us."

Yeah, it would be. "You're amazing. And so fucking mine."

Her sweet grin lit up her face before she leaned in to steal a kiss from me. "And you're mine."

"I totally am. Always have been."

That grin turned a little devilish, and she slipped a hand down my stomach to tug at the waistband of my jeans. To make me hard as stone as she whispered, "How about you take me inside so I can show you how much I'm yours?"

Consent...truly, purely, and uncompromisingly given. I couldn't ask for anything more.

I picked her up, carrying her over the threshold as if we'd already said the words that would tie us together for life. Already been through the ceremony that would make things official. Not yet. October, she'd said. Sometime in the next four weeks, basically.

I had a feeling those were going to be the longest four weeks of my life.

Epilogue

ALDER

You ready for this?" Deacon slapped me on the back, a beer in his hand and a sarcastic grin on his face.

"You're already drinking? The ceremony hasn't started."

He looked down at the beer and shrugged. "Needed it to settle my nerves."

"Why are you nervous? It's my wedding day." Thank fuck for that. Four weeks had passed since I'd asked Shye to be mine—demanded, really. I hadn't been wrong that day. They had been the longest four weeks of my life.

They'd also been some of the happiest. Every time I'd caught a glimpse of that ring on her finger, every time she'd told someone I was her fiancé or that we were getting married, my heart had swelled and I'd felt like a fucking king.

But thank god the wait would be over in a few hours.

Deacon took a drink of his beer before looking out over the crowd. "I know damn well it's your wedding day, and you appear solid as a rock. But I wouldn't be your best friend if I didn't ask the question. So, yeah, I'm nervous because there's only one right answer here."

Ah fuck. What the hell could he want at a time like this? "Ask it."

"Are you ready for this?"

I looked him square in the eye, seeing so much there that my friend was trying to hold back. Knowing he was giving me an out in case I needed one. I didn't.

"I'm more ready for this than anything I've ever done in my life."

The tension left his shoulders, and his smile grew. "Good. Because if you backed out, I was totally going to take your place."

"You'd steal my girl?"

"It wouldn't be stealing if you gave her up."

"I'd never give her up."

"I was ready, though. I'm the best man—I figure it's like those Miss America pageants. If the winner can't fulfill his duties, the best man has to step up. I'm like...Shye's backup husband."

Christ, this guy. "I really don't ever want to hear you, husband, and Shye in the same sentence again. Ever."

"Use it as inspiration to always do right by her. If you slip up—" he grinned and slapped me on the arm "—she gets me."

"I'd never do that to her."

My deadpan response earned me a laugh and a fist bump. I left Deacon to his backup husband plans, greeting our guests and making sure everything looked the way I thought it should. Shye had planned the event with Mercy Bell and Katie Baker, the three women taking over our dining room to plot out everything from what we'd wear to what we'd eat to what we'd say. I hadn't been too involved so I wasn't positive what to expect, but Mercy was walking around with a clipboard in her hand and a confidence in her gait that told me everything was fine.

Which meant I could sneak away for a few to see my girl.

———

"Everything good?"

Parris—looking like some sort of bouncer as he blocked the door into the back of the hardware store—nodded. "There a problem?"

"Nope. Just needed to see my girl."

"I thought it was bad luck to see the bride on the wedding day."

"I don't believe in luck."

His laugh followed me inside and up the back stairs, finally cutting off when the door slammed closed between us. Luck could kiss off—I'd spent the night at Deacon's motel after my bachelor party, while Shye had been at our house with Katie, Anabeth, and Mercy. I'd missed her. I didn't want to wait until the actual ceremony to get my eyes on her.

Deacon called me whipped—I was proud as fuck to agree with him.

"Shye," I called out when I opened the door to the apartment.

She appeared at the end of the hallway, smiling brightly as she tightened the tie of her robe around her waist. "What are you doing here?"

"I needed to see my girl." I nodded as Jinx—looking strong and healthy and altogether like a different person than the one we'd dragged to Justice all those weeks ago—came around the corner behind Shye. "Can you give us a few minutes?"

Jinx looked as if she knew exactly why I'd shown up. "Sure. I'll be downstairs. Just holler when you're ready for me to finish."

Shye nodded at the girl—someone she'd become good friends with—and watched her walk away. My girl's cheeks darkened with that blush I loved so much as her hand moved up to her hair. "I'm a mess right now."

Lies. "You're beautiful."

"I'm not even dressed."

As soon as I heard the front door shut behind Jinx, I closed the distance between us, sliding my hands over the curve of her waist and tugging her close. "I see that as a positive, honey."

Her lips quirked into a shy sort of smile. "Charmer."

"I try."

"You succeed." She rose on to the balls of her feet, stretching to brush her lips against mine. "You always succeed."

Christ, she was warm. Warm and soft and wrapped around me and smelling so damn good. I couldn't resist. Why the fuck would I want to?

I walked her backward, moving us into what was likely the bedroom and shutting the door behind me.

"What are you doing?" she asked with a laugh and an expression on her face that told me she knew exactly what I was doing.

"I didn't get to touch you last night."

"No, you didn't."

"Didn't get to taste you, either." I pushed her back against the wall then dropped to my knees. She was already pulling up her robe when I lifted her leg onto my shoulder. "Anxious, beautiful?"

She grabbed my hair and tugged, forcing me to look all the way up at her pretty face. "I missed you last night."

"I missed you too." I slid my hands over her hips, lifting up enough to run my lips all the way up her thighs. "Missed you so fucking much."

And I had. Too much. I didn't dive into her pussy, though. This moment—this day—meant something to me. I wanted to enjoy it, to savor, so I started slow. Licking, kissing, teasing as she sighed and rocked her hips. As she held on to my hair and moaned my name. As she coated my lips and tongue with her wetness and came on my mouth.

As she tugged me away from her pussy.

"Now. I need you."

How could I say no to the woman I loved more than anything? I rose to my feet and unfastened my pants, letting them slide to my ankles as I picked Shye right up off the floor. One kiss, two tugs on my shoulders, and a little maneuvering was all it took to be nudging my way into her sweet heat. I couldn't go fast, though. Not yet. Her pussy gripped me like a vise, so it took a little time to go deep. To bury myself inside her. Time I spent struggling not to come.

"Fuck, honey. You feel so good."

She moaned and leaned closer, her lips brushing my ear as she whispered, "Yes. So good. And all mine. Forever. You're going to be my husband today, Alder Kennard. And I'm going to be your wife."

Control...gone.

I thrust hard, pumping her full of me and pounding hard as I fucked her against the wall. As the thought of her as my wife made my balls tighten up and my heart pound. And when I came, when I growled through the biggest, strongest orgasm of my life, my future wife giggled at me.

"You did that on purpose."

"I did." She kissed my forehead. "I like knowing I can make you lose control."

I had to taste that mouth one more time, had to enjoy those seconds still wrapped in her heat with her body pliant against mine. So I did—I kissed my girl with long, measured strokes of my tongue. Fucked her mouth the way I had planned to fuck her pussy. The way I would want to when the ceremony was done and the preacher announced us as husband and wife.

"You are my world," I whispered when I finally broke the kiss. "I'll do everything I can to make you happy."

"You already do."

Hearing that, seeing the joy on her face and knowing I'd destroyed the biggest threat to her—there was nothing better. Well, there was one thing better.

"As soon as that preacher says husband and wife, I'm bringing you back here to get up under your wedding dress."

"We'll have guests to greet."

"And I'll have a wife to satisfy. Besides, I've been dreaming of this day for three long years. I want to start our marriage off right—with my face between these thighs and your hands in my hair."

"Sounds perfect," she said with a laugh. And it would be. I'd make sure of it.

Every day for the rest of my life.

Acknowledgments

As an author, sometimes a book or a character speaks to you.

Alder Kennard screamed.

Writing can be solitary, so I will always be thankful for the crew supporting me through this job.

To Brighton, who held my hand and pushed me through one of the hardest years of my life. She's got a great rack—you should read her books.

To Lisa Hollett with Silently Correcting Your Grammar. She's been my editor from the start, and I don't like publishing my words without her approval first. She called me an asshole for killing Leah—she's probably right.

To Franci Neill, who caught those final mistakes and made sure this book was as polished as could be. She also made a couple of teasers for me—how cool is that?

To my bitches—Jen, Helen, Elizabeth, Esher, Ann, Melly, Laura, and Suz. You ladies keep me sane while making me laugh. I wish for nothing but good things for all of you. Bitches forever.

A huge thank you to my husband and daughters. They take the brunt of my stress when deadlines loom or words don't flow, and they do it with smiles and hugs and more support than I could ever have thought possible.

Kristin Harte started off as a chemistry major in college but somehow ended up writing romances featuring ex-military heroes and the women who knock them to their knees...literally and figuratively. She likes drinking in the shade, snuggling under a warm blanket on a cold evening, and researching how to blow things up. Her children know nothing of what she writes, and her husband just hopes he's not at their Chicago-ish home the day the government shows up to confront Kristin about her Google search history.

When not writing good men doing bad things, Kristin can be found writing paranormal romance as Ellis Leigh, co-writing naughty novellas as London Hale, or taking her signature style into the mystery realm as Mille Thorne.

www.kristinharte.com
Kristin@KristinHarte.com